EARTHSHIPS

2030

Growing up in the Climate Shift

Book I

Bonnie Jane Hall

ISBN: 0692859969
ISBN 13: 9780692859964

DEDICATION

This book is dedicated to my husband, Raymond Gerson,
and my three children, Deborah Jane Morgan,
Darin James Douma, Davin James Douma
and
David Adwokat.

INTRODUCTION

Earthships is a fictional novel based on scientific research.
Literary fiction is not predictive, but descriptive.
Prediction is the business of prophets, not novelists.
Character personalities are based on people I have known.

ACKNOWLEDGMENTS

I thank the following people for their encouragement and talent in helping me with Earthships:
My husband Raymond Gerson, a teacher, writer and great talent.
Rebecca Maizel, Yellow Bird Editors Manuscript Critique.
David Aretha, Yellow Bird Editors. and Danielle H. Acee with The Authors' Assistant.
Thank you for your copyediting and helpful comments.

CONTENTS

CHAPTER 1

STARTING OVER

"The profound implications of climate change are only beginning to be appreciated."

–James Hansen

During the furnace—like heat in the late afternoon of a June day, our family leaves Arizona by train for Rigby, Idaho, to start a new life where our old life began. The year is 2030 and America is late in leading the race to stop the relentless destruction from climate change. As the world waits, our President, Frank Anderson, warns the nation and the world about the consequences we face by continually subsidizing the coal-burning industry. Leading scientists have written a moratorium on closing all coal-fired power plants. In these scientists' views, this would be the most effective goal for emissions reduction and give the U.S. and the world time to go totally clean and green. It is very foolish and dangerous to allow carbon dioxide to reach 460 PPM. Ignoring the warnings, state and federal governments have continued to allow corporations to sell our planet to the coal, oil, gas and lumber industries, failing to realize the sensitivity of our climate. This is the first-time Earth has been ice-free in human history, and the ice will not return in the lifetime of humankind. Once, our massive ice fields were Earth's air-conditioning. Only a few scientists have understood how sensitive our climate is to man-made climate forcing which began when man first started burning coal. Now, in the space of three generations, one third of the natural animal life has been wiped out forever.

When I think of our last few years in Arizona, silent summers and winters without rain comes to mind. The never-ending heat waves were devoid of all the wild desert sounds we came to love. Voices of the wildlife that kept us company in our desert home dissipated over time, leaving us only with the sound of the constant sandstorms. After ten years, I am now a desert person at heart and will pine for the big sky, the cacti blossoming after a shower and the dry heat. Most of all, I will miss one of the most beautiful sights in the world, the desert sunsets. But I haven't forgotten the spectacular beauty of the Idaho of my youth and delight in returning to the house where I was born.

My name is Laurel Campbell, I have curly, flaming-red hair, blue eyes, freckles and a slender athletic body. I'm a shy, eighteen-year-old girl with high-functioning Asperger's. When I was six, my parents had me tested because I was a handful. People with Asperger's, victims of a genetic syndrome, usually have poor social skills and lack verbal and or nonverbal communication skills. I remember some of how I behaved growing up in Rigby, Idaho, in an extended Mormon family of grandparents, uncles, aunts and lots of cousins. I was a little like a wild animal that wanted to live outdoors in the summer. I was too shy for eye contact and not much of a talker except when it came to storytelling. I loved to lay in fields of clover watching the clouds change shapes, to read books, draw and collect small animals like kitten's, rabbits, frogs and water snakes. I climbed the highest trees, and explored the deepest caves. Everyone around me was too busy to pay much attention, so I'm lucky to be alive. I had so little fear. I cut up people's clothes to make costumes and doll clothing because I didn't understand the words "personal property." I probably would have received some harsh punishment, except I could run faster and hide better than anyone else.

In Rigby, Idaho, we only had three or four months of warm weather and we tried to spend every moment we could outside. Our little white-frame house sat in the middle of lilac bushes and irises on two acres—a fairy tale world filled with huge vegetable and berry gardens, apple and plumb orchards and a crab apple tree near my bedroom window, my escape ladder to the world at night. There was also an old log cabin, our clubhouse and an old barn where I kept all my temporarily caged wild animals.

My parents were happiest outdoors in the summer, where we camped and fished along the Snake River. We would live in tents, going out to explore, frying trout and baking potatoes in ashes. Breakfast was bacon, eggs and pancakes—all over a ring of stones and fire. The old growth wilderness areas were so thick with majestic pine trees that one could easily get lost, and the water and air were clean and fresh. At night, we'd remove the rocks from the fire and place them in the foot of our sleeping bags, and we fell asleep watching the stars glitter overhead with the warmth from the rocks on our toes.

I felt so content and comfortable being one with the natural world, observing the grace and beauty of such an incredible fantastic and fascinating life. My curiosity grew. I would ask how it all came about, and a desire grew to protect it for future generations when I learned that it could all end. Taking part in saving lives and surviving would become a driving force in my life. I wanted the earth to survive, along with its conscious splendor and magnificent variety of species. It is The Garden of Eden in our solar system and the only earth we will ever know as home.

CHAPTER 2
THE TRAIN

"Imperfect knowledge dosen't imply uncertainties about the direction the global climate is headed."

– Bill Mc Kibben

I mostly worry about helping my family survive because I believe that this terrible nightmare humanity has created, now with unpredictable weather and above-average temperatures worldwide, could worsen and become our death sentence. My family and I are on the move. We leave Scottsdale, Arizona late in the afternoon today to avoid the worst heat. Everything we own is packed up and placed on an AI truck, programed to offload at my grandparents' farm in Rigby, Idaho, where I was born eighteen years ago.

We are seated in a fancy, first-class, air-conditioned train car in comfortable, reclining faux leather chairs. The chairs face each other, with four chairs in a group, each with a folding tabletop that can be pulled up and over one's lap. The large windows are controlled by voice to lighten or darken the glass. We can travel in style, because my father, Forester, is in the Army and a soldier's family is at the top of the list for first-class travel. We decide not to take the bullet train that travels at 500 miles an hour and doesn't stop in Idaho Falls. We chose the slower, less expensive, and more classic train.

Camellia, with dark brown wavy hair, brown eyes and dimples is my best friend and sixteen-year-old sister. She sits in a chair facing mine. She smiles at me and winks, removing her tablet from her shoulder bag and opening it on her lap.

My grandmother, Rose Mallow Morgan, sits looking out the window at the Camelback Mountains. She has pushed her hood back and exposed her long, silver, braided hair, twisted to form a hive on her crown. Looking at her beautiful sculptured features, one would never guess that she grew up in a very poor farming family. Across the narrow aisle sits Senna, our mother, and my two brothers. Fourteen-year-old Rain has dark hair and eyes and is athletic and slender with square shoulders. My brother, Prairie, is five years-old with curly blond hair and blue eyes. His pockets are full of miniature winged toy creatures. With the remote, he moves the creature slowly along the arm of his chair while muttering to himself. We sit waiting as everyone boards the train. I wonder if strangers will take our two empty seats.

I listen to Jo, my AI companion on my tablet. She is showing me a map of Colorado and Utah, the land we will travel through. I wonder how people ever lived without personal companions, as they assist us with everything in this complex world. They learn everything about each person they serve and are sensitive to all of our needs, including tastes and psychological and medical issues. Everyone in my family has personal assistant software on their tablets.

Then the train's computer voice tells us that boarding is complete and that we will leave the station in ten minutes. As the train slowly leaves the station, I feel a sensation of excitement, like butterflies inside of me. Maybe getting away and doing something different causes the fluttering. After a few hours, we have all removed our tunics and draped them over the back of our chairs as it's getting warm on the train.

A striking young man in a uniform with dark brown hair and light eyes takes the seat next to Grandma Rose. Before he sits down, he introduces himself as Sage Halley, a Marine on leave going home to Idaho Falls. He has such a natural smile and demeanor. Grams welcomes him and introduces us. I feel a spark like an electric shock when we make eye contact for a second and I think that is strange, but I mostly ignore him. He is very attractive and self-confident, but somewhat aggressive. He talks about the heat in Libya, where he is stationed. Everyone has to wear special uniforms made of fabric that, when wet, will not dry out in the heat. I think that is interesting, and ask how it works. Sage says it was copied after reptile skin with interior pockets that stay cool and wet.

Sage, with a glass of lemon tea, sits down next to grandma in the empty chair across from me. I look up and watch him, but mostly keep my eyes on the landscape moving along on the other side of the glass. He asks me what my plans are. I answer that I'm riding this train until it reaches Boise, then I'm taking the bus to Rigby. He chuckles. Is it my answer or because I keep looking out the window?

"I meant what are your plans for the future."

I turn away from the window and look at his chin saying that I plan to keep surviving and help others survive the climate shift. Grams takes over the conversation with Sage about my dad.

"Laurel's dad, Forester Campbell, is a captain in the Army training troops in Libya now, but he will be home on leave in a couple of months. He is a robotics engineer. What are your interests, Sage?"

"I am studying to be a geologist. The Marines needs geologists and have offered to pay for my master's degree if I give them two years of service, ma'am."

"Would you like me to be your Face-on friend, Laurel?"

"I don't even know you, Sage, and I'm not a Face-on fan." I finally look at his gray-green eyes for a second. "I think if you knew me you wouldn't like me. Most people don't understand me." He eats some chips and studies me.

"I already like your honesty, Laurel. I like people who are wired a little differently."

"I don't like small talk, can't dance or sing and like spending time alone studying or reading. Plus, I'm absentminded and single-focused." I glance at my mother, who raises her eyebrows.

"I like a challenge, and we are both from Idaho. Your grandma said you grew up in Rigby, so we grew up near each other," he smiles and takes a sip of tea.

With my eyes lowered, I reply, "I don't think you realize how boring I am."

Sage bursts out laughing and his spoon falls on the floor. After he reaches down and picks it up, he looks at me and says, "I'll keep you from being bored. Think about it, Laurel." He stands up and moves away. My sister, Camellia, who has obviously overheard our conversation, looks at me and cracks up as she adds, "I could use some help with boredom." I finally get to eat my snack, and between bites I tell her, "I never get bored."

Our train is moving at 130 miles an hour. The windows on the sunny side are dark but on the east side I can see an occasional rock outcropping whiz by and, in the distance, the sky is growing dark. It looks like a sandstorm is heading our way. The trains are equipped with blowers and vacuums that can suck up the sand on the tracks and blow it out and away from the sides of the train.

Prairie is playing on the floor with his virtual headset on. Grandma is sleeping in her chair and mom is talking to someone on her tablet. I am curious, so I walk up behind her and look at her tablet. She is talking to dad, and I want to talk to him also. I walk on to the bathroom.

Back in our car, I start to talk to mom when the train's voice speaks up and says that we are slowing down. There is a bridge over the Grand Canyon to be crossed and the drones will need to check out the bridge before we can cross over. However, they can't send out the drones until the dust storm slows down. The wind is blowing at 150 miles per hour, more than the drones can handle and still stay on course.

The melancholia for our family seems infectious. We are all feeling some fear due to the terrible loss of a more predictable life on Earth as we head to the dining room.

After several hours, the train stops moving outside of Paige. The avatar of the train, a flimsy projection, catches our attention as it moves among us saying, "The sandstorm is still moving too fast to release the drones and we are approaching the bridge so we will need to wait it out. The weather satellite is telling us that the storm is sitting right over us. A front is approaching from the north that will move the storm eastward, but it will take several hours to reach us. For now, we are to relax.

"Dinner will be served in the dining cars now." The avatar vanishes.

Our family sits around one of many tables covered in white tablecloths, napkins and fresh floral arrangements. There are stacks of wipes to clean our hands. We take our seats. Prairie seems worn out after playing. I place a riser under him so he can reach everything. Camellia sits next to me, keeping an eye on Mom because she looks so sad. I am feeling the fabric of the tablecloth, noticing the unusual texture and that it's stain proof. There is little conversation until Camellia looks at me saying, "I'm so worn out just getting ready for this trip. I'm exhausted—aren't you, Laurel?"

"Yes, I feel very tired, but mostly sad. I remember the first time I saw Earth from space in an IMAX movie theater. I cried, it was so beautiful, floating in the black velvet of space. It made me think of God's eye. If he has an eye, it would look like the earth.

"But what can we do, Laurel?" Rain asks.

"Remind everyone about the tragic losses we will face if we don't each try to make smaller footprints. Love and respect everyone, animals included, and treat everyone as we want to be treated. Build fortresses inside the earth to protect animals and humans from the heat and fires. We can stop the waste of food, water and energy, and make it a priority to use the sun, wind and water for our energy. We can all do our small part."

I talk too much about my obsessions. Others find these subjects depressing, so I don't help the mood at the table. After dinner, we are more than ready to sleep. I write in my diary on my tablet and talk with Jo until everyone finishes in the bathroom and I take my turn.

The lights in the car are dimmed, so I find my way to my recliner with the use of my medical wristband's light. The steward placed a small pillow and lightweight blanket on my chair. After I am tucked in for the night, I think about the look of the drones as I drift off to sleep. In my dream, the drones look like hundreds of beautiful fireflies inspecting parts of the bridge in the dark of night.

I wake before dawn and the train's not moving. I can hear the sand hit the window glass. The sound startles me as I remember last night's vision, like previous premonitions. There are three men in bodysuits with their faces and heads covered, like Arabs. They are working on the tracks on the other side of the bridge. They seem to be digging up the sand between the tracks and dropping a machine in the hole, covering it with sand and laying a slender cable over each track. They can't see me as I watch everything they do. I listen to their speech but can't understand the words. One man turns and looks right through me; he senses me. They turn and run slowly against and through the blowing sand. I'm wide awake, alarmed, thinking I must warn the train's engineer. I'm running through the cars toward the front of the train. People are asleep, and I wonder if this is part of my premonition. It feels so strange, but my heart is beating so hard in my chest. I see someone in a uniform ahead—he turns toward me with his arms out ready to stop me.

"Please listen!" I say as I crash into him. "I saw some men ahead on the train tracks working to blow up the train."

The man grabs me and pulls me into a room and shuts the door. He sits me down.

"I don't want you waking everyone on the train. Now what's the problem?"

"Like I said, something bad is going to happen to the train. I'm feeling very nervous."

"No, your words were that you saw some men working on the tracks to blow up the train."

"I did, I did!"

"How were you able to see that far away? The train is on lockdown."

"Please understand, I have premonitions, I always have. Maybe it's part of my Asperger's."

"Your what?"

"Asperger's. I'm different, my brain is wired differently, and I see things sometimes before they happen."

"Who are you?" the man asks, removing his cap and running his fingers through his black hair.

"I'm Laurel Campbell, my family is sleeping in 308."

He is getting in my face. I like my territory and move back against the chair.

"Please just have a drone check the tracks on the other side of the canyon. A drone with a camera can pick up the black cables running across the tracks."

"You have just had a dream, young lady."

"No, my dreams are different from my premonitions."

"In what way?"

"Premonitions are crystal clear and orderly. Dreams are muddled—detailed, but non-sequenced."

"I will have to talk to your parents and wake my captain," he says. "Don't leave."

I feel like I haven't slept at all, but I'm wide awake and feeling shaky and nauseated. I have the urge to run back to our car and get my family off the train, but what about the rest of the people? I have to wait. The captain is a tall woman in her forties and very grumpy. I go through everything again. She asks me a lot of questions, like whether I have been treated for any of the common mental problems, and what prescriptions I'm taking…and on and on.

Finally, I say to her straight, "Talk to my mother and grandma. Because if you don't check the tracks on the other side of the bridge before you start the train, I want my family off and if we have to, we will walk to Paige and find another way to cross the desert. I am recording my conversation with you on my tablet." I remove it from my bag and hold it up.

"We'll check it out, give me your mother's number—then go back to bed. The winds are still too strong for the drones." I give her the number.

I don't believe them, but walk back to our car wondering, which car Sage is in. With the flashlight on my medical wristband, I check out every recliner and find him in the car next to ours. I stand over him, waiting, wondering if he will believe me. Why would he when he doesn't even know me? I wouldn't want him to die, anyway.

"Sage!" I shake him. "Sage, wake up!"

"What…. What, who…. Laurel, what are you doing?"

"Shush. Sage, I need your help." He is half awake with heavy eyelids as he raises his recliner.

"What's wrong?"

I sit on the floor and tell him my story very quietly. "What should I do? What if they don't believe me?" I ask him.

"Let me check the weather on my tablet. The wind is dropping fast—the drones can be sent out in a half an hour."

I like his messy hair.

"It's 3:52 AM; get your family ready to leave while I talk to the captain."

"Thank you, Sage."

I walk on to my car and wake everyone but mom, she is already awake due to the call she received from an irate captain. I help them get ready to leave. I think they believe me from past experience.

We sit waiting, so sleepy that no one talks. After thirty-five minutes, Sage comes to our car. "They are sending out the drones now to check out the other side of the bridge as well as the total structure."

Grams asks Sage to come sit and join us for coffee. Sage takes the chair next to me and runs his fingers through his short hair. When the waiter brings our coffee, my hand is shaking so much I can't pick it up. Sage holds my hand and says, "We will be all right now." Another hour has passed.

We feel the slight vibration of the train as it moves. I jump up for a look out the window. The glass is dark so I press a plate in the center below the window and say, "Lighter." The glass starts letting in the light of dawn. When I can see outside, I say, "Stop," and push on the panel again. We must be moving toward the bridge. I want off the train. Sage looks at me and can tell what I'm feeling.

"Sage, we won't be able to get off the train once it's on the bridge."

Sage jumps up and I follow him to the captain's office. The train is long, and we are both out of breath as we pound on the captain's door. My anger is bubbling to the surface as she opens the door.

"Don't keep us in the dark!" I yell, "We want off the train!"

She glares at me and tells Sage that the drones have returned and found nothing unusual on or past the bridge.

"Stop the train and let us off!" I demand again. Sage looks at me.

"Are you sure, Laurel?"

"I know what I saw, Sage, and I'm not willing to take the chance that I might be wrong when it could mean our deaths and the deaths of everyone on the train! At least let your passengers vote on this. The cables could be covered in sand by now and the drones couldn't see them."

The captain yells with anger and has the train stopped. "I can have some men ride the rails ahead but it will take them some time to get there and back and we will be late for our connection," she grumbles.

The engineer enters the room to see what is going on. The captain explains everything.

"Maybe we should just throw her family off the train—she might just be crazy," he tells her.

"Better late and crazy than dead," I answer.

Sage with a quickness of mind says, "are you willing to put all these people's lives on the line when you can check it out? And, by the way, has this situation ever happened before?"

"Not on this train."

"You can use your cart with two men to ride the rails across the bridge and travel a mile over to the other side," Sage is aggressive and self-confident when he speaks.

"We'll use our electric carts," the captain tells us, "Two men will go and call if it's safe and we can meet them on the other side of the canyon."

"That may be very dangerous if the bomb is pressure-sensitive," Sage explains.

"Better to lose two than two hundred," the captain answers, not believing anything will happen. "Contact Central, explain the situation, and let them know why we will arrive late," the captain says to the engineer. He leaves the room.

Sage and I return to my waiting family. I explain what is happening. We just have to wait. We are served a breakfast selection of sweet rolls, fruit, coffee, tea and juice. The train's computer tells the passengers that the crew is checking the tracks ahead.

After lunch, we hear and feel a powerful explosion shaking the train and I burst into tears. Later, we are told that two men have been killed on an electric handcart while checking out the tracks. The cables of a bomb, covered in sand, were so sensitive that removing the sand triggered the bomb. We will spend another day on the train going nowhere until the tracks are repaired. We pray and I continue to cry for the brave men who died and in gratitude for our lives. The helicopters will arrive soon with the people to repair the damage and remove fragments from the bomb for testing. We should be able to continue our trip tomorrow morning; the train's avatar says.

Within hours, the news of our ill-fated trip catches up with the Internet and Sage and I are getting hundreds of messages on our tablets. I won't talk to anyone. Then, the captain comes to thank Sage and me, telling the people in our car our story. I am feeling so embarrassed and frozen from everyone trying to hug me and flatter us; I just want to crawl into a hole. Sage, understanding my distress right away, grabs my hand and pulls me away. We go to the bar and sit. Sage orders a beer, and I, a ginger ale.

Dad calls mom; he heard what happened to our train. When I return, mom announces a call from dad so we all grab our tablets. It is so good to see his smile on Face-on. Prairie is sitting on mom's lap so he can see dad with his sparkling warm brown eyes. He is so handsome in his brown and gold-toned Army uniform, with a serious expression on his face as he speaks.

"Hello, Rose Mallow, travel seems to agree with you. You are lovelier than ever."

"You look fine, Forester. I can see they are at least feeding you well."

"Yes, the food is plenty, but not very tasty, I really miss the wonderful flavors of Senna's creations. She is an excellent chef. Thank you for teaching her your skills, and thank you for coming to live with us. We can really use your knowledge, mother."

"I feel fortunate to have been asked to join you, living alone is not something I've ever looked forward to."

"There will always be a home for you with us, mother Rose. You have blessed me with the love of my life, my beautiful wife."

Dad next looks at mom.

"Senna, darling, I miss you. I miss my family and I'm so glad that you are all alive and well." I see the tears in his warm brown eyes as he looks at Prairie.

"Hi, Daddy."

"Son, you are growing so fast and I miss spending time with you and your brother." Prairie tries to hug the tablet. Dad then looks at Rain.

"Hello, Rain. Have you been looking out for your sisters?"

"Yes, Dad, I'm doing my best."

"Well, I'm proud of you son, such a fine young man. I wish I could give each of you a big hug." He then winks at Camellia and she gives him her sweet, dimpled smile before saying, "I love you, Daddy."

He asks, "How goes the online studies?"

"Good. I'm learning a lot about the body for my nursing and vet degrees, but someday I'll need the practical experience. Come home soon, Daddy." Next, he looks me in the eyes. I drop mine and he laughs.

"Sunshine, what's going on in your life besides saving a train full of people?"

"It was a premonition, Dad. My life revolves around chores, studies and Earthships. I miss you so much, Daddy. Why don't you ever call me?"

"I have been trying to call you all morning. You don't answer."

"Oh, I'm sorry, I've been getting so many calls and texts from the media that I dumped everything."

"Thank you for warning everyone about the bomb, I know how hard it is when people don't believe you."

"Dad, it's very hard to convince someone without evidence. I met Sage on the train. He's a Marine who believed me and helped convince the captain of the train. Without him, your family would be walking in the desert."

"Is he nearby?"

"Yes. Do you want to say hello?"

"Yes, dear."

I found him with Rain. I put Sage on.

"Yes, sir, this is Sage… It was rough, sir… Thank you. I'm just glad Laurel trusted me with the information. We all owe her our lives." Sage hands me my tablet and we say goodbye to Dad.

Dad's last request is to make certain the supply boxes marked "pharmaceuticals" have all been placed in the underground cellar at the Halls' house in Rigby. Everything else should have been carefully stashed in the big barn behind the house on the acreage.

We all spend another night on the train and I keep thinking about the beauty and mystery of the Grand Canyon, a great reminder of the age of the Earth and how many tribes may have set their eyes on its depth who are now extinct.

CHAPTER 3

SENNA

"A new study in 2017 suggested insect populations had declined by 70% over three decades."

– by Euan Mc Kindy, CNN

Mother has thrown back the hood of her delicate, pale peach tunic and unzipped the front, exposing her cream-colored bodysuit. Bodysuits are in fashion and necessary everywhere in the world if you can afford them because they keep your body cooler in the heat and warmer in the cold; everybody wears them to protect the skin and keep it from losing moisture. The new bodysuit fabric is created from cloned caterpillars' silk, combined with spiders' webs. The textiles are amazing: as light as a feather, flexible as thin rubber, and strong as leather. They are designed by the fashion industry, woven and created by robots that we call "bots."

Mother looks great in bodysuits. She has a lovely slim figure, high cheekbones, and large blue eyes. She's always in fashion, an enigma, looking like she just stepped out of a magazine, yet she works so hard every day, constantly on the move with four children and no maid. Now, she will have gram's help. When I think about mom, I realize how confused I have been about her, because she is quiet and very reserved, seldom offering a word about her thoughts and not always showing an interest in our thoughts and feelings now that we are older. She is kind and gentle, but aloof.

I wonder if the reason I don't remember my mom ever hugging me as a child is because I didn't let her. I feel ashamed for a kind of detachment I feel for everybody. Yet, I love my family. I guess it's part of having Asperger's syndrome. I was never good with hugging or making eye contact except with my grandma, Della Campbell, who helped deliver me into the world. Over time, I've learned how I'm expected to act in my family, so I should be a great actress by now, but don't feel I am, but then I can be cynical.

I think about Sage saying my mom is beautiful and I realize she is also vain and fragile. Nevertheless, she loves my father and he trusts her enough to let her lead the way. He seems highest on her list, her sons are second, Camellia and her mom next and me last. She always has her favorites and I'm not one of them. My father shows his love for me and its possible mom feels a little irritated that he likes and understands me. I wish she understood me, but she doesn't. I don't know how to fix that. She always worries about her looks and her work. Nowadays, she is more nervous, and yet I can't help but feel a deep and tender love for my mother, for no one will ever pronounce my name the way she does. I want to understand and share her sense of loss, her separation from husband and home, and a familiar life gone forever. But I just can't imagine being anyone but myself. In the past, I haven't put down roots and had to force myself to be disciplined. That, and my curiosity and questioning everything and refusing to assume anything gets me in trouble with mom.

We arrive at the train station in Idaho Falls and wait for an hour for passengers arriving and leaving. We continue by shuttle with tickets connecting us to an AI bus line that will take us to Rigby. Sage catches up with me after we leave the shuttle for the bus station. He comes up behind me and touches me on the shoulder. Startled, I turn and face him. "I tried to catch you at the train station, but lost you in the crowd.

"Sorry, if I frighten you, want to get your address so we can text each other. I get so lonesome in Libya."

"Thanks, Sage. Without you we would still be walking across the desert or at the bottom of the Canyon."

"Oh, I think you had things under control before I arrived in the picture."

"You're kind, Sage, but seldom does anyone believe a crazy girl. I know from experience." I reach out my hand, he smiles and gives me his small tablet. I add my name and text-dress.

He says, "You should give me yours in case you need someone to believe in you again."

He voices the information, and hands my tablet back. We both laugh, I'm still looking at his chin, I glance at his eyes and realize that they are sage green.

"He asks, can I take your picture?"

"I guess…." He snaps the button on his tablet." Then, before I can stop him, he hugs me and I just stand there not knowing what to do next. When I catch up with Camellia, she says, "That's no way to treat such a handsome guy—hang on a little longer," and lets out a hearty laugh."

"What's so funny?" Rain asks Camellia.

"Laurel is."

Rain looks puzzled, out of the loop, and that just increases the fun for Camellia, a great teaser.

When we get to our bus, a uniformed man with a name tag helps us with our many bags. Camellia and I are last in and I sit next to Rain.

After everyone is seated, and the bus leaves the station, Rain asks, "What were guys laughing about?"

I look at him and say, "Sage gave me an unexpected hug and Camellia thought I should have hugged him back."

Rain always wants to be on the inside with Camellia and me, but feels on the outside and that hurts and makes him mad. Sometimes I'm angry that he always wants to hang around us girls. But then I get mad at myself, who else does he have?

"Whats funny about that, Laurel?" Rain asks.

"I don't see the humor, but she does. You might find it funny if you wanted to hug a girl," I say, while removing my tunic and placing it on the back of my seat.

"You should hug Sage. He helped and believed you, Sis."

"I know, Rain. It's just hard for me to hug people I don't love."

"I wish I had a girlfriend to hug."

"I can tell you will be the guy girls go crazy over, you will probably become a missionary to keep them away from you." I finally get him to laugh.

"I worry about living in an Earthship," he tells me.

"An Earthship is just a different kind of home, living inside the earth will give us even more protection. The home will have a special glass and silicon-insulated roof that will change colors with the weather and collect rainwater, storing it in huge cisterns underground, so we will always have fresh water if it rains."

"Will it be dark inside, like a cave?"

"No, Rain. It will face south and have big windows on that side to let in lots of light, enough to grow fruit trees and vegetables along the front hall. Also, as much light as we want will come through the roof. All the energy to keep the lights and everything working will come from solar cells embedded in the roof and from the wind turbines on the property, so we will be fine. Plus, living inside the earth will keep us warm in winter and cool in summer. The ships are not something new just made better over time. People all over the world and in fifty states in America live in Earthships."

"You know a lot about Earthships, but won't they be too expensive for us?"

"No, they cost about the same per square foot as a home above the earth. Having a glass dome for the roof will add to the expense, but then we will save a lot by living off the grid. No bills for gas, water and electricity."

"That makes sense."

"Well, you know I study architecture, and I helped dad design our Earthship. I think you will love this home. Rigby is small, but bigger than when I lived there. About 10,000 people live in town and another 10,000 outside of town. But we have a lot of family nearby so you will find friends your age."

"Thanks, sis, you make it sound great. Better than my imagination."

I feel a tap on my shoulder, turn around and see mom.

She says, "I overheard you talking to Rain and you make me feel better about the move, but we still have so much to do."

"I think you will be surprised, people will show up to help us. You know how close-knit Mormons are, Mom."

As we ride the bus, my mind wanders and I think about my mom, again feeling guilty that I love her, but don't feel the same way about her that I did Grandma Campbell. Mom is a brilliant woman—a botanist with good intuition that she acts upon. She told dad in 2017 that they should sell our home and get ready to move north. She knew if they waited that they would never sell the house and they had a lot of equity tied up in it. Dad agreed, so they put the house on the market, and in 2017, mom sold the house and their stock in oil and gas and put the money in green energy. She has always been able to do anything she sets her mind to and is always busy with a project, yet she knows when to stop. On top of that, she makes delicious and healthy meals for us. Her home is very important to her, and it is always clean and beautiful.

I remember as a child that she loved to read and kept a library of books in the house; that enticed me to start reading at a young age. The books were mostly stories about living in the wilderness with dogs, horses and wildlife. She was drawn to the history of the American Indians and books written about some of the famous old Indian chiefs. She collected books on native and medicinal plants. Some of her favorites are winning at cards, holding babies, discovering a new plant, shopping, having dogs, fishing and creating a beautiful life for us. She and my Grandma Della gave me such a good start in life. She is a good mother.

When we arrive at the Campbell house in the morning, after spending the night in a hotel on the edge of town, I'm reminded of Della Campbell, dad's mother and a second mother to me. She was the kindest, most lovable person I have ever known. She taught me how to be a kind human before she died from diabetic complications when she was too young. I was ten at the time. Two years later, Grandpa Warren Campbell died from a broken heart. He couldn't live without Grandma.

CHAPTER 4
RIGBY

"The latest science shows that this wave is already breaking over our heads."

– Bill Mc Kibben

Online, Dad took care of getting us moved and settled in Rigby and even had a friend he could trust show up the day the AI truck delivered our stuff. Also, a couple of men met us at the house. Dad hired them to help us move things into the house.

The cottage hasn't been lived in for several months. Before that, dad rented it out to a couple of schoolteachers. The white cottage was built in the '50s with a thirty-foot-wide porch that has been closed in. It is a single-story with a basement. The windows are boarded up and everything needs paint. The grass is dead, but beautiful trees line the sidewalk and property lines. Behind the house is an old, weathered red barn and a small building for chickens.

I hear the moans of everyone when we pull up in front of the small house. We left a big beautiful home in Arizona, but I feel excited thinking of all the possibilities to improve the cottage and it's only a temporary home. A beautiful park of huge, old oak trees and flowering lilac hedges are across the street and take up four blocks, with swings and merry-go-rounds for kids nearby.

Dad's sisters and their families, who live in Rigby, came over today to help us get the house ready so we can move in. Our two uncles pull the plywood away from the windows to let in the light, but that would also let in the heat. Then they hose the house down and get rid of all the spiders, then work on the hornet's nests. The two aunts help us vacuum and clean up all the dust and scrub everything. We then move some of our stuff from the barn into the cottage and put things away, then make the beds. We have a simple meal of vegetable stew and sourdough bread together, enjoying our visit and then they leave for the day.

We put away our clothes, and even though it's getting late and we are very tired, Camellia and I decide we could use a walk. Rain tags along. We take our tablets in our shoulder bags. They are light and we can talk to our AIs. So, we head out and down the sidewalk and across the street to a sidewalk going toward town. The air is dry and smells of wood fires. A warm breeze tussles the leaves on the trees, a pleasant evening for a walk before the sun goes down. We cross the street at an intersection and head toward my old gray brick elementary school.

Wow, it looks exactly as I remember it. Camellia also remembers this school. Six long concrete steps lead you to the locked front door. I remember when I wrote with a crayon on the columns that hold up the overhang, and I was punished in front of all the kids. They watched me spend most of the day with a bucket and a brush scrubbing over the marks. I was terribly embarrassed. The school is very rectangular. We walk around and through a gate to the back and the playground seems the same. Camellia says that she remembers playing here. We sit rocking in the swings while Rain climbs the monkey bars. Playing in the yard brings back memories. I was so limber, strong and athletic in my childhood. I could climb the pole supporting the swings by swinging back and forth one hand above the other until I reached the top. I could never do that now.

Next, we walk several long blocks on Second Street to our old, white-painted, wood-paneled home with a fireplace in the living room. The property is approximately two acres and the house sits back a long way from the road. We sit in the lumpy grass, the underground homes of big Angle worms. We used to catch them by flashlight before a fishing trip. Rain remembers dad mowing the grass, not the mouse that ran up his leg, or how hard it was for us to get his pants off because he was going crazy. Camellia remembers that we shared a room with one bathroom for everyone, and that Pal, our German Shepherd, always slept at the foot of my bed.

I tell them about mother's elaborately decorated Christmas trees that were covered in beautiful ornaments and angel hair and of the candy ribbons, divinity, chocolate-covered cherries, fudge and dozens of wrapped gifts every Christmas. I tell them about Easter holidays and dipping eggs in colors and putting decal designs on them. If the weather was good, we'd go to the woods for an Easter Sunday picnic with the excitement of an Easter egg hunt. The house looks so small now. It felt big to me back then when I read books on the floor in front of the heat from the fireplace. That house, in my mind, is like a treasure chest containing some of my fondest childhood memories.

I ask my siblings if they remember all the snow. Camellia remembers the huge dinosaur we built with snow one winter. Rain can't remember snow. I tell them my best memory of winter was all the castles and forts we built and our snowball wars.

As we all walk home, I tell them about a few of the amazing things I remember about life in that house, like the night the giant from *Jack and the Beanstalk* pulled up the roof on the corner over my room and looked at me. Dad had to sleep with me that night, I was so scared. Then, there was the Christmas Eve that I stayed awake to see Santa come. I saw him and his reindeer pulling his red sled up into the sky while Santa waved at me watching him from my window. I was so excited that I woke everyone in the house.

Now that we are settled in the cottage, all day every day is work, work, work, as there is so much to do to get ready for winter. Mom and Aunt Essie take turns tilling the garden area to the left of the house near the irrigation canal for a fall and winter crop. Then Mom, Essie and Camellia start planting while I put together the greenhouses we ordered. Each greenhouse will be eight feet wide by thirty feet long. The ribs are PVC pipe that I will bend into arches by hammering metal stakes into the ground every two feet. Then I will fit one end of the pipe over the stake and the other end over the spike eight feet away and parallel with the first end of the pipe until I have fifteen arches over the first rows of plants. Next, I have Aunt Edna help me attach them together along each side and the closed end with PVC clamps to make it very sturdy. We work all day building the frames for two greenhouses. Tomorrow the contractors are coming to start working on the Earthship. And mom will help me cover the greenhouse frames with two huge rolls of fabric for each house. The first layer is a fabric screen and the second a heavy-duty, clear, vented plastic cover. Once installed, battery-assisted remotes can raise and lower each covering. Grams made us lunch and we thanked our aunts together for all their help before they left for the day.

Grams makes three meals a day for us and keeps an eye on Prairie, who is trying to help Rain clean and get the chicken coop ready. When I check, Rain has him sorting out all the same nuts, bolts and screws into plastic containers so they can put up shelves and boxes for nesting.

At the end of the second month in Rigby, we have accomplished a lot and are able to report a long list of completions to Dad, including having a new metal roof installed with a special paint that takes the place of solar cells, and wood blinds to keep the heat outside of the windows. Ceiling fans are installed in every room of the cottage. Mom walks around with her tablet in hand, showing Dad pictures of everything we have done, and he is impressed. Dad is really eager to get home and get to work. Camellia tells him not to worry, we will leave plenty of work for him. He has a good laugh over her remark. She is very outgoing and good with people, just the opposite of me, and yet we have a great relationship. She understands me, better than I do her.

I am feeling so happy about the greenhouses. With heaters and grow lights, we can grow some fresh food and share it with others even in winter. This will really help us survive.

The building of the Earthship awaits us and we are all eager to see its progress. From a distance, we see all the heavy equipment and hear the noise of machines digging up the earth. A row of towering trees and shrubs along the sides and front of the next-door property keeps things a little concealed from everyone. Even though we own the land, we have not ventured over since our arrival until today, when we all walk to the construction site. The afternoon is overcast, but in the nineties, so we take water with us to dri

The trees overhead are changing to their autumn colors and patterns, a feast for our eyes after the Arizona drought, but we miss the songbirds we thought would have remained in Idaho. Where are the larks, finches and bluebirds? Where are the squirrels and the butterflies, ladybugs, daddy longlegs and bees? We haven't seen them, and that scares me because I remember the Rigby of just ten years ago, with all the larks that used to wake me in the morning.

Rain picks up on my thoughts and asks, "Mom, have you heard any songbirds?"

"No, honey, I guess they have moved to Canada."

I look over at her, dressed like me in a light cotton, brown and peach shirt and dark brown casual pants. Rain and Prairie wear shorts with cotton t-shirts. It is quiet at the building site; the men must have taken the day off. In the distance, we can see ten-foot piles of soil and long worms and the giant shovels that have been digging up the earth. We can see the rectangular hole in the earth; it is about six feet deep and sixty by forty feet in size. Behind that is a big boxcar in the ground, and at each end is buried huge plastic cisterns to hold water. A rubber liner covers the bottom and sides of the pit, and on top stands corner pillars on a concrete foundation and temporary wood steps to descend into the pit. Later, an elevator shaft will be installed. I understand everything I see and try to explain how it will end up. It's hard.

"When we get back to the cottage I will show you the blueprints," I say. "I hope it doesn't rain before they get the roof on, and I don't see a tarp large enough to cover the hole or piles of dirt." I speak more to myself than anyone.

"You sound worried," mom says.

"I am, because it would be a big mess and have to be pumped out and delay the project. I have the phone number of the contractor on my tablet—I'll call when we get back."

"Let's go," Camellia says, "so we can see the blueprints. I can't make heads or tails of the pit."

We all agree and we're heading out, but soon realize that we are missing Prairie. Returning, we call his name…nothing. I start running around, then everyone is looking for him. Is he in the pile of tires? Rain grabs a dead tree limb and starts poking in the tires and at the bases of the mounds, and Camellia tries removing the large caps on the cisterns to see if he has fallen in.

I yell, "If the cap is on he couldn't have fallen in."

"Sorry, I don't know where my brain is right now," she answers, looking up to see where else she could look.

"The trucks." Mom and I say it at the same time, but it's hard to believe he has made it to the trucks in so little time.

We take off running toward the heavy equipment at the back of the property. We try the doors to the cabs, but he could never open them since the doors are so heavy. Mother is crying when we find him asleep in the bed of a pickup truck. Rain crawls in, helps him out and gives him a piggyback ride home.

At the cottage, I call Peter, the contractor working for dad, and get his voicemail. I leave a message about the roof for the Earthship and that I need the names of contractors who can add insulation to the cottage. It is hot inside the small house. The interior of the cottage contains two bedrooms, one large bath, an eat-in kitchen, a living room, a front porch, a back porch for the laundry and a stairwell leading to an unfinished basement. We four kids sleep on the front porch using clothesline rope and sheets as walls for privacy. We each have room for a twin bed, a small chest of drawers, and a bookcase across from the foot of our beds.

Camellia tells our afternoon story about the loss of Prairie to Grams. She looks at Prairie for a moment and then gets down beside him and just holds him for some time. Rain breaks the moment by telling us the chickens we had ordered would arrive tomorrow.

"I haven't checked out your work on their cages. I should do that before they make it to their home."

"Go look, look now, Laurel."

"I think I will, brother," I answer as I walk to the back door.

Before dinner, I kiss Rain and Prairie, telling them the chicken coop looks great.

"You guys did a great job, and tomorrow you can put a layer of hay in each chicken box on the shelves so they will have soft beds to roost."

"Camellia, I guess you will be the goat girl," I tease.

"What are you talking about, Laurel?"

"Someone has to be responsible for the goats when they arrive."

"Do I look like a goat girl? I am not building a goat barn."

"You don't have to build a barn because their little barn will arrive with them. I just have to tie down the corners by hammering some stakes in the ground. Your job will be to feed them, give them fresh hay for their beds and milk them."

"Did daddy say I had to be a goat girl?"

We all crack up, and her eyes are on fire she is so mad.

The next day, Botswana is in the news. The country in Africa is like the Great Plains in America where farmers grow wheat and raise cattle. Three million people have been supporting themselves on subsistence farming and raising goats and chickens, but for some time now, life has become more difficult for the people of Botswana. Soaring temperatures, howling winds, and costal storms are causing a catastrophe and millions of people are without food or water and left drowning in sand. These people have no place to go because no country will take them in Africa. Food has become so expensive and water scarce that many people cannot be helped. Supply lines are very long even though countries are trying to help them. Because there are so many places and people needing help all over the world, the people of Botswana know they will die. I feel so angry that the heat rises in my body. My mind just can't accept letting them die. I know they can be helped if everyone tries to move them to a better place. "Why can't we all come together and help them?" I put down my tablet and wipe the tears from my eyes thinking, *I will not let my family die like that.*

Camellia has read about Botswana on her tablet and comes to me crying. I am sitting on my twin bed on the closed in-porch of the cottage. There is a fire in my solar plexus because of my rage over all that is happening in the world. The deaths of so many has hardened me some, more than my little sister. I have to believe that only the body dies. I hold her and suggest she try to remember that we do not die. And I hold her feeling powerless to make a difference. We could send money—a drop in the bucket—but would they even receive it?

The summer in Rigby passes without rain but the days are growing cooler. We never know what can happen next when it comes to the weather; we might have another heat spell. There is still plenty of water in the big irrigation canal to give a healthy start to our newly planted Washington apple, Bosc pear, and winter black plumb orchard near the canal at the side of our property. Planting an orchard is more of a gamble now than at any time in our history, but it would be great to be able to depend on some fresh winter fruit if we succeed.

Our dad instilled in us the idea that it is ideal to prepare for the worst and hope for the best. We will can a lot of food and dehydrate the rest. We are storing enough supplies to last us, as well as animals that we find that managed to survive and extra people, for several years. That is why we have a shipping crate in the ground near the Earthship with an entrance to it through the back of the house near the laundry. The steel crate will be insulated, covered with earth and vented.

Mom is sitting at the kitchen table, and Grams is making bread with a heavy-duty mixer and bread attachment. She has four bread pans lined up and ready to fill on the counter. I sit down by mom and greet everyone.

Mom says, "Good morning, Laurel." Grams comes over and gives me a kiss on the cheek.

"Love you," She smiles and returns to the bread.

"What are you up to, Mom?"

"Ordering heirloom seeds for the gardens as well as more "Thrive" foods from the Internet. They have vacuum-packed number 10 cans of whole grains for bread, beans and pasta plus dehydrated food like potatoes, onions and root vegetables. Everything is edible. The foods will keep for twenty-five years if unopened and kept cool underground."

"What about seeds for the chickens?"

"I've ordered lots of feed for all the animals. Your dad thinks we should get a couple of horses because they can get to places a vehicle can't sometimes." Still in her robe, she looks at me with her sparkling blue eyes. "So, I'm ordering bushels of oats." Her shoulder-length, wavy, blonde pillow hair has not been brushed yet.

"That means saddles and all the things horses need…and they need a lot of care," I answer, still looking at her hair.

"Well, I guess horses will come in handy if the roads and cities are torn up by storms, ice, snow and bombs. We never know what will happen next."

"Camellia doesn't want to be the goat girl. Who will be the horse girl? Rain and Prairie have the chickens and goats covered except milking."

Mom laughs, running her fingers through her hair.

"Camellia might like being the horse girl, she will be a vet and it sounds better."

"The problem is we don't know anything about horses, Mom."

"Well, I guess Camellia knows a little, and it will give us another thing we need to learn to survive." Mom replies.

"Dad will have to buy the horses when he comes home 'cause I know nothing about horses."

"I agree," she says, getting back to her tablet.

"Now I can't remember what I came in the kitchen for."

"Laurel, would you check on Prairie for me?"

After losing Prairie a week ago, I decided to have Camellia put a small implant just under the flesh in the back of his shoulder so our AIs can track him.

"Wow, my first operation. My studies, are already coming in handy," Camellia said.

I suggested she go ahead and put an implant under everyone's skin; dad would approve. Mine is today. Camellia deadens the spot so I feel just a little pressure. I remind Mom that she can track Prairie on her tablet. She has forgotten about the chip.

We find him with the goats, trying to get one to let him go for a ride, but the goat doesn't like the idea.

I say, "Prairie, wait for the horses."

"Real horses?"

"Yes, dad wants horses. I guess he'll get them when he comes home on leave."

"Great!" At first, his face lights up, and then I guess he starts thinking about how big they are and a frown develops. I return to the house. I haven't read the text I received from Sage. I lie on my bed with several pillows stacked under my chest and open my tablet.

"Jo, please find me the text from Sage." Before I can read it Rain says "Knock, knock."

"Come in, Rain."

CHAPTER 5
SHIP BUILDING

"Removing a mountain top to get coal is barbaric."

–James Hansen

That evening, Rain comes to my room and knocks on the wall. We sit on the bed and he talks about how worthless he feels not doing anything to make things better in the world. I tell him I know exactly how he feels.

"In reality, though, we are doing more than most, Rain, because one-third of the people and animals in many countries are running for their lives, one-third still do not believe in science and are asleep and one-third actually know what is going on with the world. The third asleep don't pay any attention unless something terrible is happening to them. Then, they think it's just a fluke of nature. Rain, we are awake and more animals and people will have a chance because of what people like us will do." Then I give him a little more information.

"Early on, I was reading scientific papers and books by scientists and watching documentaries on what was going on with the shift in the climate. Once humans began burning coal on a large scale, the geo-engineering of forced climate change began. Many farmers kept detailed journals regarding the times the sun rose and set, the date and details about the weather. Records go back to the turn of the century and beyond, and include detailed information on any changes in the earth, sky or gardens. Scientists used information from the past and started getting better data about the condition of our planet. By 1957, we had satellites that followed changes in the earth, now, highly advanced smart computers analyze our planet. Scientists once took ice core samples that showed us what happened to Earth's climate over the last 600,000 years. Human pollution continues to poison all life in our world and the poor countries that have caused the least damage will suffer the most. Still, many people who can, are making preparations for whatever future they and their children have left. I keep notes on climate change in my diary and try to keep up-to-date on the latest scientific information. We are helping by growing food and sharing it with others, and we will do much more. Don't worry, it looks bad, but we will survive."

We say goodnight and both go to bed.

I checked my tablet and have a text from Sage.

> Laurel, Hi.
>
> Are you enjoying living in Rigby again? It would be interesting to know how you see it now that you are nineteen. I imagine you are quite occupied with preparing for the worst to come like my family is doing.
>
> I have been moved from Camp Pendleton to Fort Hood in Texas, too many weather problems in southern California

right now. I'm sure you know about all the fires. Please take note of my new address. This Fort is a big city, easy to get lost in. I hope I don't have to be here long. I have made a couple of new friends, both good guys. One is from Seattle and tells me about fish die-offs from heat waves and flooding. The other guy is from New Orleans and says that the city is a goner with constant flooding. A house needs to be on stilts now to keep dry. I hear so much that I could share, but it's depressing as hell! I'm glad, on the other hand, to be learning so much in my studies about the earth and human nature.

I just wish we could have had more time together before separating. Please write soon. I will be looking forward to your letter.

I'm thinking about you.

Love,

Sage

Tonight, I couldn't keep my eyes open, I will answer Sage in the morning.

The following day, after answering Sage, I am daydreaming when I hear Mom call my name.

"Laurel, would you like to go for a walk with me to the Earthship?"

I close my tablet and stick it in my shoulder bag. "Sure, Mom. Just need to change my shoes."

When I return wearing my comfortable, lightweight athletic shoes, I ask Mom, "Where are the kids?"

"Camellia and Rain are playing with the goats, and Prairie is helping Grams make cookies."

It feels like a typical October day in Idaho, but it isn't. The deciduous trees are completely bare, and the few leaves are curled up and swirling in the breeze. It's a little early for everything to have turned brown. The former colors of rust, brown and gold that covered the ground are now brown, and the air smells like burning piles of leaves. Mom and I cut a path through the trees along the border between the lots. In the distance, we can see that the walls of the Earthship are in place, and as we close in on the site, we see how they are constructed. Between the concrete block walls and soil is a layer of rubber and thick foam insulation. I suddenly feel so happy and excited seeing this house take shape and knowing it will help us survive.

Half of the walls are below earth and half above earth. Above the soil line, the concrete blocks are covered with gray-green-streaked slate. The wall facing south is open above the earth for the windows.

"So, what do you think, Mom?"

"It's hard to visualize yet, but it looks like the blueprints."

"Exactly, Mom, and once the roof goes on and the tires and soil is filled in against the three walls, you will really recognize the house." We walk down the stairs into the house.

"How will the walls inside be finished?" she asks.

"With textured and painted drywall. You know that the blocks are glued together with a special glue? The bond makes them stronger than putting them together with concrete."

"I guess the thing I'm concerned about is earth floors, Laurel."

"The idea is hard to get used to, but you'll have to see how beautiful they look and how wonderful they feel. When installed over a liner, they are more like leather when finished. You can try it in one room and see what you think. They are healthier due to negative ions, Mom. I would recommend bamboo for the kitchen, laundry and bathrooms, and maybe for the dining room because of water use."

She looks at me and smiles. "Well, I guess they are more than dirt. I can always cover them with cork or bamboo."

"Yes, I'll show you some pictures."

"Well, let's walk back, honey. I was curious about the progress."

At the cottage, we are met with a platter of chocolate chip cookies and little Prairie smiling and saying, "Look at the cookies Grams and I made."

"Wow, they look delicious, little brother, can I have one?"

Mom and I kiss him, take a cookie, and walk to the kitchen. I bite into the cookie as Prairie watches me.

"Good, huh? The goats love them."

"You gave these delicious cookies to the goats?"

"Yeah."

"Oh, no, honey," I say, laying my cookie on the dining room table so I can remove my shoes.

"I just gave them each one, sis."

"Well, just one is good."

He returns to the kitchen and Camellia comes in, eating a warm cookie.

"I hope you washed your goat fingers," I say, and she laughs. "Have you learned how to milk yet?" I ask.

"Oh, you are so funny, Laurel, I bet you don't know that Grams knows and will milk the goats."

"Don't think you are giving that job to Grams. She has so much to do," I say, teasing.

She doesn't know what to say—just looks at me, "I don't want to be a goat girl, Laurel."

"Okay, Camellia." She is near tears and I have gone too far. I give her a hug and say, "Sorry for teasing you." I go to the kitchen to see if Grams needs help.

"Mom, will dad be home for Christmas?"

We keep asking and she replies, "He hasn't told me yet, let's plan on him coming home, anyway."

The vegetable gardens are covered with the fabric screen to give the plants plenty of light. The winter squash, greens, lettuce and radishes are growing beautifully. We are already picking some lettuce leaves, chives and radishes for salads. I am learning so much about growing food. Learning new things that can help us and others survive is great.

We are ordering some Christmas gifts online. I am looking for warm thermal sleepwear for my family's gifts. So far, December has been in the seventies by early afternoon and the fifties at night, but I have a feeling it will get a lot colder. It's also possible we have lost winters now without ice. We had hoped to be in our new home this month, but it doesn't look like it is going to happen. Even though the insulated, tornado-proof roof is installed, and the soil is piled up along three walls, making the house look like it is part of a hill topped with a glass dome, the interior in unfinished.

We also decided to have a second insulated barn built over a basement with a commercial elevator so we could put the animals underground if needed and we could store their food below. The construction crew is also working on the barn.

In the evening, I send another note to Sage telling him I have been away from Rigby so long, living in Arizona, that my birthplace seems like a dream remembered, but then, both the past and future are dream-like to me. After all we have allowed to happen to our planet and all the suffering caused by generations of neglect, only the present seems real to me.

Dear Sage,

I've been doing everything I can to help my family survive, yet trying not to get attached to the results. It keeps me sane so I can handle our daily rituals and meet each new obstacle head-on. We are trying to be ready for winter, if we have a winter. We thought our new home would be finished so we could move in and be better protected, but the construction is running behind because it's hard to find products for this kind of home. I guess many other people are building Earthships.

Do you get a leave for Christmas? How is your family? Tell me a little about them.

Your Friend,
Laurel

CHAPTER 6
FORESTER

"In 2008 20 million people were displaced by climate change."

– (UN estimate)

"Dad's been hurt!" Rain yells. I'm cleaning the bathroom. I drop everything and run to his voice.

"Rain, did you say Daddy's been hurt?"

We are all in the kitchen watching the shadow of fear and sorrow move across his face.

"How do you know, Rain?" Grams asks, drying her hands.

"It's on the news, on my tablet." He hands his tablet to Mom, and she reads out loud:

News Alert! Bomb blast kills and injures soldiers at the American Technical Training Installation Center near Al Jubail, Libya. Terrorists penetrated the barriers and detonated two bombs. An investigation is underway. A list of injured soldiers is provided below. More to follow.

I watch Rain's expression; his face is drained and tears run down his cheeks. I feel like my heartbeat has slowed as I hug him. We are all in shock.

Mom reads through the list and finds Dad's name among the injured. Everyone starts sobbing as we sit down. Mom sends him a text, hoping he might reply. Next, she calls Uncle Lesley, dad's best friend. He will know how to find more details about dad. I know dad will get the information to us if he's conscious. We all sit.

After reading the news from Libya, Uncle Lesley says that he will let us know as soon as he gets some information. Lesley married Dad's baby sister, Essie. He and dad are like brothers, hunting, fishing and they worked together in Alaska years ago. Our families are also very close. Malachite, their oldest son, is a few years younger than me, and Nolina is a couple of years younger than Camellia. Lesley is a hardworking, quiet, kind and a humble man. Essie, like her mother, Della, is the sweetest, kindest and most honest woman around. She is also an excellent cook.

Their whole family comes over to support us. There are lots of hugs and good food while we wait. Essie takes over the kitchen while Grams milks the goat, gathers eggs and feeds the animals. We are so stunned that we just wander around in shock.

After lunch, Camellia suggests a game of hearts to take Mom's mind off the time. Mom loves card games and she usually wins. With two decks, six can play. Begging Mom again and again to play, Camellia finally wins and gets Mom to the dining room table. Lesley waits for a call from a major in the Army that he knew. The adults and Camellia, Rain and I sit around the table. Mom is handed the cards to shuffle and deal. Prairie runs off to play. It is a quiet game.

Later in the day, when the call comes through for Lesley, he moves away to find a private place to talk. We wait at the table while Grams freshens up our glasses of water.

Lesley returns with a story to tell. "Try to let go of the fear you're all feeling."

I feel myself relax a little.

"In Libya, the soldiers were seated in the chow hall when two bombs exploded. Your dad sensed something was about to happen, and he jumped to his feet, yelling, 'Take cover!' He pushed the table over on its side to save the guys by giving them some protection, which left him and some of the men sitting near him exposed. They were hit with flying junk from a dirty bomb. Two terrorists were able to get on to the base by killing two guards with paralyzing injections and then changing clothes with them. They blew themselves up with the bombs in their backpacks."

"Your dad was rushed to medical for a diagnosis and surgery to remove imbedded objects in his back and to stop the bleeding. His spinal injuries consisted of two small fractures, some nerve damage and tiny fragments of bone and metal objects. He is being injected with Nanos programmed to remove the fragments. A special cellular cement will seal the fractures. He will be moved to the VA hospital in Boise for observation for a week. Then the continuing weekly injections of the T cell treatment can be given to regrow nerves, bone and tissue in his own home. The medical staff are sure Forester will completely recover."

I now realize Dad also has premonitions.

"How soon before I can see him Lesley?" Mom asks, holding on to his arm.

"In a few days, he will be in Boise and all of you can visit him there."

"Can I talk to him?" Mom continues.

"The nurse will call you when he is conscious. Right now, he's sedated."

Mom is shaking and sobbing with fear mixed with relief. We are all shaken and Lesley and Essie sit a moment and drink some water, the glasses in their hands shake. I hug Rain, who had been so worried about Dad that he has kept a daily track of his movements on the news feeds. Rain has tears in his eyes. Prairie is also crying as he holds Mom's hand.

Before Essie can start on the kitchen cleanup, we take over, so Essie and Lesley leave for home. We hug and thank them and ask them to stay for a while, but they want to get home. Their kids are tired, and Essie is very upset knowing her brother is hurt. After we clean up, everyone starts getting dressed for bed. I ask Mom if she wants someone to sleep with her. She says Prairie is upset so she will keep him with her for the night. Then I ask Grams if she needs someone to sleep with her.

"After all the trauma, I have faced in life, it doesn't get easier," she says. "I've just become harder. I'll be fine, honey." I hug her.

The rest of us stay up late talking under the dim light of the front porch as we lay in our beds. Camellia is explaining what Dad is going through medically. We ask a bunch of questions about the time needed to heal. She says everyone is different, and that makes it hard to know how long it will take for him. During the night, I am restless, waking up from dreams of trying to get to my dad.

Two more days pass before Dad calls us. First, he talks with Mom. Then she tells us to get our tablets so we can see and talk to him. Her eyes are red and puffy. Dad looks good sitting up in bed, and he wears his great smile.

"It is great to see all of you! When I first woke, I thought I might be dead and that I might never see you again," he says. "I felt so terrible, then the nurse came into my room and asked, 'Why are you crying?' I said I was blown up in a bomb and now I'm dead and will never see my beautiful, loving family. She said, 'You are alive and you are going to be fine,' and she laughed. I cried again I was so happy, and here you are."

He knows just how to make us laugh. The rest of our conversations are upbeat. He will be flown to Boise in the morning and that day will be full of seeing doctors and filling out paperwork, so it will be best to wait until the following day for him to have visitors.

He ends by saying, "You probably already know the people around me are treating me like some kind of hero just 'cause I knocked over a table. I'm wondering if you will do me the favor of treating me like 'your old dad' when you come to visit me?"

I feel better after seeing Dad, and I know so much is possible now that advanced Nano, cell and cloning technologies are being used to treat people. I am eager to visit him, but mom, Camellia and Essie will leave for Boise in two days. Mom wants sis to go because of her background in nursing.

The day they leave for Boise mom rents an AI car to transport them. The car arrives at our house. I stand at the window in the greenhouse hall watching the car leave. Rain, Grams and I will go in a couple of days if someone can take over the goat milking.

While the three of them are in Boise, I spend some time at the Earthship, selecting interior colors and measuring for furniture arrangements. Rammed earth tires are used to hold the earth in place and away from the front. From the front, there is a view of a flat area where there are triple panes of glass windows with louvers inside the glass, framed in stainless steel, which rise tapering back toward the roof. The elevator entrance is on the right side near the front. The house now looks like it is rising between two hills. Stepping stones lead the way to a pebbled concrete deck in front of the elevator door.

At the right side of the house through a hall, is a small garage with stacked batteries along one wall. After opening the wide side door, you enter a large elevator, push a button and drop to the first floor. Containers on the window side of the long hall are twenty-four inches wide. This is the greenhouse entry, where fruit trees and both fruit and vegetables will be planted using the gray water, filtered from the sinks, showers and washers. The water will drip through hoses into the plant containers filled with peat moss compost and bales of straw to contain and grow the plants. The greenhouse also serves as a long hall connecting several rooms across from the windows.

Arched passages lead into a large dining room with an unusual kitchen. A special forty-two-inch-wide stainless gas and wood pellet range is along one wall of the kitchen, and a larger-than-average stainless sink is followed by two drying drawers to replace a dishwasher. The kitchen also contains a special low-energy, heavy-duty, insulated, stainless refrigerator and freezer. Then to the left of the dining room is the family room.

The house also has four bedrooms, two and a half baths, an office, a laundry room and a safe room. A wide back hall leads to the garage and storage container. Looking at the house from outside, one can see oval-shaped vents at the tops of the glass dome, used for ventilation and survival in excessively high drifts of snow.

Jo, my AI, is helpful in providing measurements and taking pictures of each room to help me select the fixtures that will add enough lighting to darker rooms. Light, pale, slightly shiny surface colors will be used in all rooms except the bedrooms where people prefer darker colors. On my tablet, Jo makes lists of all hardware and fixtures to be installed. After the cabinets arrive, she can add the door and drawer hardware. I leave the house and walk toward the gatehouse to see how it has turned out before going home to start ordering hardware and fixtures.

On our property line near the roadway and gravel driveway that leads to the Earthship, are two slate-covered concrete block columns with an area sheltered by a pitched roof between the columns, shelter for mail, packages and a call button to notify anyone in the house who wants to visit. Rain helped the men dad sent to install the electrical system, so he knows how it works.

The Boise VA Hospital has beautiful gardens and lovely terraces. Grams, Rain and I take the elevator to the fourth floor and it opens on to a great view of the city in a large window that faces east. The walls are painted a soft gray blue-green and the corridor is covered in cork flooring. We find room 412. The door is open, and as soon as I see my dad's face my tears come.

"My sunshine, come give me a hug." I wrap my arms around his neck as he leans forward and I kiss his cheek. I can't really hug him the way he sits. He places my face between his palms and kisses me on the forehead.

Then he turns to Rain. "I have missed you, my son," he says.

"I worried about you and missed you so much while you were in Libya, Dad," Rain says.

"You shouldn't worry; I was fine then and now. Do you know that by using retroviruses in a controlled way to spread modified genes like T cells, people are healed? The copy divides and replicates to become nerves, or whatever tissue or bone it needs to become. This treatment works. I'm healing and will be as good as new. I can walk with a cane, but soon I'll be running."

"Come, Rain, and sit by me." Dad pats the bed near his lap. Rain sits. "I don't know if seeing me like this will make you feel smaller, like you have a lot of growing up to do just to help your dad. You don't need to feel that way because I am healing and will have full use of my body." Rain starts sobbing; Dad touched the right button. He holds his son and says, "I love you, too."

Then he holds Gram's hand, kisses her on the cheek and says, "Dear Rose, I'm so glad you're here. Senna seems to be distraught over my injury. I can walk, but the doctors want me to keep the pressure off my spine for a few more days so it can heal. I will be my old self and home by next week. As soon as I know my release date, I'll let you know. Please help me cheer Senna up."

We spend the afternoon with Dad talking about Rigby and his parents. I tell him how the cottage affects me. The feelings of love have returned for my grandma and grandpa. So many memories now fill my brain, and I miss them all over again. Dad says the house will have the same effect on him.

We tell Dad the glass silica solar cell roof has been installed on the Earthship.

"Great news, now all we need is a lot of sunshine. Like you, my daughter." I laugh. Then Rain changes the conversation, turning to chickens and goats and asking if we are really going to get horses. Dad says 'yes' about horses and has some good laughs over Prairie trying to ride the mother goat and Camellia's insistence that she will not milk goats. We talk so much, we seem to wear Dad out. It is just so good to be with him again. He gives us more hugs and kisses before we leave him for the long drive back home. During the trip home, I feel so happy again knowing my dad will be fine. I appreciate him even more, feeling so fortunate in having him for my father.

On the way home, Rain and I talk about America being ready for the shift.

"It seems like our politicians have plans only for a future of geo-engineering and wars," Rain says. "We have plenty of terrorists due to climate change because drought throughout the Middle East have taken away a sustainable lifestyle. Starving people can't grow food without rain. No food, no infrastructure and no jobs leaves no hope. At least soldiers get some money to feed their families."

"If you have money you leave for the camps in other countries. If not, you fight and die," I add.

"These wars have been going on for as far back as I can remember.

"Soon they will run out of people to kill," Rain says.

"As you know, there was plenty of time and early warnings that climate change represented a far greater danger to our future than terrorism," I go on, "But the military industrial complex pays our congressmen to vote for wars. Our money is spent on guns, ammunition, ships and planes instead of helping to eliminate the reasons people have to fight."

"In a rich country like America, most states haven't even stockpiled food and water, so they now fear a great famine will soon be upon them," Rain adds, looking at his tablet. "American prairies, where grain was grown, are going through a seven-year drought. And with seven inches of topsoil over a lake of sand, rain is desperately needed."

"A lake of sand?"

"Yes, millions of years ago, the Great Plains was a lake that eventually dried up," Rain answers.

"The private sector is doing the most to help us out of this mess by reducing our dependency on gas, coal and oil, but now they are getting rid of coal because of the cost. I just hope other governments around the world will move fast in following us, or we could have a war like the one in the Middle East," I tell Rain. I turn up the car's heater. It is turning colder outside.

"Are you hungry, Rain?"

"Yeah, I'm kinda hungry."

"How about you, Grams?" I look back and notice she is asleep. "We will stop and get something soon."

Rain then talks to me about Dad being an expert with guns. He saw the arsenal Dad keeps locked up. We pull up to a small soup and sandwich cafe. While we eat, Rain tells us that Dad is ordering sentinel drones and stationary bots to keep cameras on everything around our property.

"Mom told me we just received the county permits to install a large wind turbine at the back of our property and wireless sensors all around our homes and barns that would send out a debilitating shock and notify us through our tablets if we have intruders," I tell Rain.

"The sensors will only recognize the people they are shown as safe," he says.

Grams adds, "We need to have some warning signs made to let people know they are in danger if they move on to our property before the system is turned on.

I found some protein bars in my purse, passed them out and we drove on.

Days after our return from Boise, happiness returns to the cottage. Dad is home now, and able to walk with a cane. I write this in my diary in big letters because I missed him so much. His doctors want him to nap for two hours after lunch and be in bed by ten o'clock. He is still healing and never complains. Mom is so full of joy now that he is home and will never be sent into a war zone again.

Our first Christmas at the cottage and we didn't put up a Christmas tree—no room and no trees—so we string wires of hanging multicolored lights throughout the main rooms. Fire has destroyed so many trees including pine trees. I believe the Christmas tree tradition is about to end. Another warm front comes through, and in a few days Christmas will be celebrated. It is still in the seventies and overcast in the afternoons. Summers are longer now. Fall and spring lasts just three or four weeks, and that is wiping out fruit trees. The wild bees, ladybugs and butterflies are almost extinct, so in the spring we will have to buy a hive for our trees. Our trees are too young to bear fruit yet. My question is, will they stand a chance?

CHAPTER 7
CHRISTMAS

"What will it take for people to wake up to human-induced climate change?"

– Neil de Grasse Tyson

The Earthship is almost ready for us, but we will wait until after the holidays to move in. We kids are wrapping gifts in our porch bedrooms. I am finishing up with wrapping when Prairie peeks in and asks for help.

"Bring your gifts here. Look at my mess. Let's not mess up your bed." We stand for a moment looking at all the colored ribbons and paper, scissors, name-tags and tape on the floor.

"Okay, Laurel, I'll bring 'em."

Once they're wrapped, we all pile the gifts in the corner of the dining room. The house smells so delicious with Gram's use of pumpkin, cloves, coriander and other spices. The apple and pumpkin pies make my mouth water. She and mom are making the pies and rolls for Christmas dinner. Tonight, is Christmas Eve. We invited some of mom and dad's family that live near us, Uncle Lesley and his family, Aunt Edna and Earl and mom's youngest sister, Aunt Willow and her husband, Keith. Their four children live in Idaho Falls, not far. We also invited mom's brother Bruce's wife and daughters—he passed away in a terrible fire. The house will be packed.

"It's easy to forget those struggling to survive when you look at our abundance," dad says, looking at all the gifts in the corner. He's thinking way beyond those gifts.

"Having you safe at home with us has made us the happiest and most fortunate of families," Mom says, while holding his hand. Their eyes meet and he pulls her close, leans over and kisses her lips.

I am happy they seem deeply in love, I wish life could be like this forever for them.

Once I no longer enjoyed the belief in Santa, the lie made me angry. I stopped enjoying Christmas. I think when I was little and really believed in Santa, I had him mixed up with God or Jesus. I believed in Jesus and talked to him about all the problems in life, especially why God made humans. He must have known they would ruin his beautiful world.

Before bed, I put my diary in the drawer and am about to fall asleep when my tablet buzzes. I reach over, turn on my bed lamp and pick up my tablet.

"I have a message from Sage," Jo says. "He is home on leave, Laurel, and wants to meet you tomorrow at your house."

"I'll talk to him, Jo."

"Hi, Sage. Tomorrow isn't the best time, we are having a house full of company. I have to spend some time with them."

We argue online until I agree to a later time of 8:00 p.m.

"Yes, then we can go to the dance hall in your car."

On Christmas morning, the family is up early. Too bad that it's a day without snow. We eat a breakfast of buckwheat pancakes, maple syrup, strawberries, goat yogurt and coffee or tea. We don't buy food from other countries anymore except coffee, because the cost of shipping is excessive now that oil and gas are heavily taxed. That's why it's necessary to grow our own food whenever possible. But we have food in storage purchased before the tax. That food consists of items that can last for several years if kept cool or dehydrated.

As we open our gifts, Dad suggests, "You might want to take turns playing and singing some beautiful Christmas carols now." The tablets are out. Rain finds a Spanish carol and plays his guitar and sings along with it in Spanish. He has such a wonderful voice. They know the English version and join in with, "I want to wish you a Merry Christmas."

Prairie finds "Jingle Bells," and they sing along with him. I don't sing because I like being in the same room with my family. Camellia finds "White Christmas" and they all sing more, and so the morning goes as the paper piles up and we unwrap our gifts. I have this thing about trying to save everything because I'm not sure how long before we will have to furnish our own. I jump up and start pressing out the folds and stacking the wrapping paper in sheets. Then slide it into paper bags. Next is the ribbons and bows in bags to be stored. I'm thinking our homemade gifts will become the norm over time. I made some fabric-covered boxes that turned out nicely this year and everyone seems to like them.

After I dress for the day, I put on an apron and help in the kitchen. Camellia is washing dishes and I start drying. Mom is working around our feet, sweeping the bamboo floor, and Rain and Prairie go outside to feed the animals.

"Camellia, who did you get to milk the goat when we went to visit dad in Boise?" She hits me with the dishcloth and it's wet.

Scrunching up her face, she says, "Mom knows how to milk, she used to milk cows when her parents had a farm."

"It's good that she remembered how," I say, teasing her. "What's it like, giving dad his shots?"

"Because they have to be inserted between the vertebra in four places it's a little more stressful for me, I'm just glad they were able to mark, each insertion spot like a tattoo."

"How much longer will he need them?"

"I'll know as soon as they read the last blood sample I sent to the lab."

As we hang up our aprons I tell Camellia that Sage is coming over later today to take me for a drive.

"Why did you agree to be alone with him? Oh, I get it," she says, as she smiles and winks. "You want to be alone with him."

"We are going to a dance hall, I'm not afraid of him, I'm a big girl and I didn't know where else we could go that's public."

"Go bowling or ice skating," Camellia replies.

Later, people start arriving. It is good to see my Aunt Willow and her husband, Keith. I used to help her with her children. That's when I started babysitting.

After a late Christmas dinner and a happy time visiting, the doorbell rings and Rain comes to tell me Sage is at the door. After I left for the door he must have told everyone it was my boyfriend because everyone followed me. I ask Sage in and introduce him to my extended family. Sage looks even more attractive than I remembered him in his uniform. I tell Mom and Dad we are going out for a while to dance.

"I can tell you, Sage, that you won't be able to resist Laurel's out-of-the-box personality and charming ways, but you may already know that," Dad says. "You could find yourself with a broken heart, so take it slow, because she is more than you bargained for."

"Thank you for your advice, sir. I will be careful and take it slow."

"Oh, Dad, you know I have no charming ways, you must be thinking about Camellia." Dad just smiles at me. Everyone who overhears the remarks laughs because they probably don't find me charming.

"We won't be late," I say, and we leave, walking to Sage's car. He opens the door for me, and I am so surprised.

"Sage, you have a driving car! Wow, I haven't seen one in years."

"Yes, I like to drive and work on cars. It is electric, of course."

"Can I drive it?"

"Sure, you can, sweetheart, but I have to teach you first."

"Dad had an old truck he drove in Arizona and he taught me how to drive when I was sixteen."

He starts the engine. We take off toward downtown and I'm thinking about him calling me "sweetheart." *Does that mean he's sweet on me?* As he drives he asks me about my education and what I want to do with my life.

"I'm studying landscaping and green architecture. I want to design and build inexpensive bio-shelter homes for people."

"That sounds like an interesting career."

"What do you want to do?" I ask him.

"Terraform planets."

"Wow, do you suffer from megalomania?"

"I don't think I suffer from a mental problem," he laughs. "I like huge, complicated projects. Of course, we start with smaller areas depleted of everything from misuse."

"Then you must believe humans can survive?"

"We are very adaptable and that gives me hope even though, yes, I know the methane is bubbling up through the oceans as we speak. We should be capturing and burning it; then it would be less toxic. Then again, if things get really bad our descendants may build cities on the shores of the Arctic Sea."

"Well, we should do the best we can, enjoying every moment as though it may be our last. We don't know everything," I add.

We park in front of the dance hall and go inside. The band is country and western, not my kind of music. There are decorations and colored Christmas lights over the bar and candles on some of the tables. We walk up to the wood-paneled bar and I order a ginger ale and Sage orders a German beer. We find a corner booth where it is slightly quieter. The place isn't packed, but has several customers on the dance floor. Most look like retired people whose children forgot about them on Christmas. A few stragglers sit at the bar alone, trying to cheer themselves up with a few drinks. It really is a depressing place to spend a holiday. The waitress brings our drinks, a candle in glass and some popcorn.

"Sage, I'm not a good dance partner because I can't seem to follow and I've never dated. Boys were never interested in me. I warned you, I'm boring."

"Oh, boys were interested, just afraid of being turned down. You are presenting me with a challenge," he says, placing his beer bottle on the table and getting to his feet.

He pulls me to my feet and we walk to the dance floor waiting for the band's new song. Sage is very forceful as he pulls me into him, and after a few of my stumbles, he starts to lead me! Sage is so strong, I have to follow his moves, and after a while I catch on and enjoy dancing with him. We drink, eat and dance until twelve. When I tell him to take me home he agrees, and when he opens the door we are in shock. The temperature outside has dropped by thirty degrees in three hours. We rush, shivering, to the car. Sage starts the car and turns on the heater. Then, my tablet buzzes.

"Hi, Rain, it's really cold outside."

"I know, sis, that's why I'm calling. I'm sorry, I'm so distracted with company I forgot about watching for changes in the weather. A severe cold front blew in from Montana an hour ago, it's going to drop to fifteen degrees before morning."

"Rain, can you guys turn off the underground sensors now? There will be animals ahead of the front trying to find food and shelter and we don't want to hurt them. Cover up the chicken coop and goat barn with the insulated covers. Ask dad about putting out extra food and water if you see any deer or other animals. We could give some young animals shelter in the barns."

"We have been talking about the same things, Laurel."

"We are on our way home, Rain."

Sage drives me home as it starts to snow, he asks to stay and help us, but I want him home before the freeze. Plus, we are both cold outside of the car, where he pulls me into me in a tight hug.

I tell him, "Get home before the roads are covered in ice, I'll talk to you later."

As he turns to drive out onto the road, I see several deer in his headlights. I run to the house. Inside, I hurry to my room and find my coat, slip it on, then cut up a few apples and go out back to open the new barn and call to the deer. Two youngsters are curious enough to come close, I throw a few apple slices on the ground for them and drop a trail of apples into the barn. I walk over to the goat barn, slip in, and open a bag of goat pellets for the deer and fill a bucket with water. I go back to the barn and watch the deer. When they have all gone into the barn, I shut the doors so the building will stay warm inside. The goat barn and chicken coop are covered, so they should be okay. I go back into the house and make myself a cup of tea in the microwave. I guess everyone is in bed.

The next morning the house is chilly and I hate to get out of my warm bed where it's cozy. I lie for a while thinking about last night with Sage and decide I like him. I should check on him. I grab my tablet and send him a message.

Are you ok? Thanks for last night it was fun.

After, I take time to fill in my diary. Eventually, hunger gets me up, and I pull boxes out from under my bed, opening them until I find my body suit and a robe.

Dad, wrapped in a flannel robe, has made himself a cup of coffee and is sitting in the kitchen looking out the window at the falling snow when I walk up to him.

"Good morning." I look at the snow.

Then, I recall a memory of waking up after it had snowed all night. The morning was so quiet and everything was covered in a blanket of soft, downy snow unmarked by any print, like a soft white blanket. That was until I jumped from the steps backwards onto the snow and made angel wings. I was six years old.

"What did you say, Dad?"

"You don't have to settle for the first guy you meet."

Looking at his serious expression, I chuckle and say, "I'm not going to settle for anyone, Dad, I'm young and have a lot I want to accomplish in life, but I do like Sage."

"I'm glad to hear you say that, because you have lived a very sheltered life and haven't met many young men."

"That's right, Dad, and the way the world looks, I may continue to live a sheltered life."

Mom and Grams come in to say they have started breakfast. Grams asks, "Did you have fun with Sage?"

"Yes, he's a good dancer and can actually lead me. He seems nice, and I like him, but time will tell. By the way, the barn is full of deer. I didn't want them to freeze, so I talked them into spending the night." Grams chuckles.

"Have you heard anything about the weather for the next few days?" I ask, cutting up an orange in the kitchen.

"No, I haven't checked," dad says. Mom and Grams shake their heads.

Rain, with messy hair and PJs, walks in asking, "Do you want to know about the cold front?"

"Yes," I mumble, my mouth full of oranges.

CHAPTER 8
WINTER FREEZE

"Climate change over the past century can be simulated with the most unerring accuracy."

– Mark Lynas

"Give us a weather report on Idaho and surrounding states." Rain opens his tablet and asks his AI, Zak, and it replies that a balmy afternoon the day before Christmas turned into a massive freak snowstorm and cold front that is now bearing down on the northwestern states from Canada. Eastern Montana was hit with baseball-sized hail when tornados created powerful updrafts that kept sucking up the falling hail. It collected more and more ice until it was heavy enough to fall in large chunks. When the cold updrafts moved into Wyoming, thousands of birds caught in the updrafts froze and fell to the earth like hail. The storm is bringing snow to Idaho, which will turn into freezing sleet by late afternoon. This is a very dangerous front with the expected temperature to become as low as thirty below. On farms and ranches, we will need to place hay or straw piled up along fences, buildings or trees and bushes to give animals shelter. The weather report says to stay in and bring animals inside if possible. The insurance companies say the damage to people and property from this storm will be in the multimillions. Rain turns off Zak.

Everyone in the kitchen leaves looking for warm clothes and coats while I drink my first cup of coffee, then run to catch up. We all work together in the frost and blowing snow all morning to get the bales of hay off the truck and dropped in mounds along the tree lines and against and between the greenhouses. Then, we surround the chicken coop and goat barn. We also feed the animals and pick some greens and other delicate foods from the greenhouses and turn on the heaters. We cover the fruit trees that are each surrounded with a chicken-wire cage with large canvas tarps. Before going inside, I check on the deer and Camellia gathers eggs. The deer look fine.

We are all freezing, exhausted and hungry and miss Arizona's heat. Grams scrambles a big pan of eggs, adding some greens, mushrooms and small red peppers. Camellia toasts a loaf of bread in the oven. Rain sets the table and adds butter and homemade preserves. I make a pot of coffee and get out the blueberry and honey goat yogurt. At the table, everyone is wearing their body suits because they also keep the heat in when it is cold, and on top of them we wear our warmest sweaters and scarves. The cottage was never insulated for thirty below temperatures, and we moved most of our wool blankets and down comforters to the Earthship.

After breakfast, which turns out to be lunch, most of the family takes a nap. I write in my journal and read my incoming texts. I have a reply from Sage.

On the drive home, the snow started coming down fast so I had to slow down. It looks like the ice will hit this afternoon. Dara, my sister, is making sugar cookies and my brother, Ash, is playing with his new computer game. My parents left to visit friends. I already miss you and hope to see you before I return to Fort Hood on Jan 2 at 8 AM. I like you, Laurel. When can I see you?

I'll let you know, Sage.

As the day draws to an end, the house gets colder, and I realize I haven't asked Rain how long this cold front will be hovering over us. I grab my tablet and ask Jo. It takes a few moments for her to complete her research. The current front will be with us for five days and it will be followed by a stronger and colder front with wind gusts up to sixty miles an hour that will move southeast at twenty miles an hour.

I know it is time for a family meeting so I buzz everyone's tablets and ask to meet in the kitchen, which is the warmest room in the house. I put on a pot of coffee and warm some soy milk for hot chocolate for Rain and Prairie.

"You don't have to tell me what you're thinking, Laurel," Dad says with a twinkle in his eye.

"It's going to get even colder and windier with the next front, Dad."

"But it's so cold to be moving," Mom replies.

Camellia, half asleep, drags her body in the room and plops down in a chair. It seems I woke her from a wonderful nap. "What's going on, Laurel?"

"We need to move to the Earthship tomorrow morning."

"You've got to be kidding! I've already experienced freeze and thaw once today."

"Camellia, sooner or later we have to move to the Earthship, and once we do we will be a lot more comfortable," Dad remarks while looking at each one of us. "It is going to get a lot colder than it is now. I'm wondering if you'll feel better about the move if I have the new house nice and warm for you? I can go over now and start the pellet fireplace and heaters for you."

"We don't need to because the house won't be below sixty-eight degrees, Dad," I say. "That's a lot warmer than this house is now. I'll drive the truck over and have everything heating up in a few minutes if you need it warmer than that." I offered.

"Laurel, I will go check it out. I think it will feel good to our cold bodies if it is warmer," Dad insists.

"Then take Rain with you and we can start packing," Mom answers.

"You know you don't have to treat me like an invalid, Senna!" Dad bellows. "I'm fine to drive. I need a little exercise and I want to see the house. I am going to get dressed and go."

Later, we hear the back-door slam and Dad drives the truck out of the old barn behind the cottage.

We find several flat packages of good-sized boxes in the cellar that have to be put together. Camellia and I start making boxes and Mom and Grams start filling them. We start in the kitchen filling boxes with linens, pots and pans, bowls, dishes and small appliances. Soon, all the boxes are full. We will need to dump this stuff in the Earthship before we can fill anymore boxes. We look at each other and laugh, all thinking we have way too much stuff. Next, we fill laundry baskets and hampers with bathroom items. I stop to look out the window, but it is covered in ice. I know it has stopped snowing as Dad drives the truck back behind the cottage. The back door blows open and we yell, "Too cold!"

Suddenly, there is a dog in the house just sitting in front of the door looking scared. The door opens again and Rain and Dad stomp in.

"I wonder if we have anything to feed a mutt?" Dad asks.

Prairie asks, "Where did it come from, Dad?"

"The dog was waiting in the cold at the door of the Earthship."

"Why would a dog wait where there are no people?" Mom wonders aloud.

"Could be the workers were feeding him at the house and he kept coming back, waiting," Dad says.

"Here!" Mom throws Rain a towel, "Wipe him down, he will have to stay on the back porch until he gets a bath."

"The dog reminds me of the German shepherd you had in Scottsdale, the one that died. What was his name?" Grams asks.

"Kazan," I reply.

"Yes, that was the one."

"Is it a male, Rain?"

"Yes, Sis. Then let's name him Kazan."

"He is a little rustier than Kazan was," Camellia says, feeling his fur. "I think he has some Chow DNA."

"That's why he is missing his tail," Grams concludes.

"The dog just seems to be smiling," I add. After each of us stroke him and he licks all of us, we get back to work and Kazan follows Rain. They are both looking for food in the cellar. Later Kazan is happy eating goat pellets, drinking out of his own bowl and slopping water all over the floor in the enclosed back porch. He has a heavy coat, so he won't get very cold.

I ask Dad, "What did you think of the Earthship?"

"I can tell you that it will do the job in keeping us comfortable, safe and alive, but I would rather let you discover that for yourself."

"What did you think of the earth floors, Forester?" Mom asks.

"They look fine, but I wasn't able to test them out, darling."

"Should we start moving in the morning, Dad?"

"You might not have noticed, but it isn't going to get any warmer for weeks. It's too late now, but in the morning after breakfast will work."

"As you can see by the kitchen crowded with boxes, we have a load to go and we can take turns dropping stuff off," I say. "And if there is room, we can add a couple of beds for the boys with bedding. We need these boxes; bring them back empty. Camellia and I can take this load first thing."

"Rain, can you help by taking your beds apart tomorrow?" Before he can answer, Prairie says, "I will help you." Rain gives him such a loving smile. "Good, I will need your help, little brother." They take off to look for some tools.

The next day, after several agonizing trips back and forth, we decide to stop for lunch and a nap. Then, we continue freezing trough the move. We give up at 4:00 even though we haven't finished. We will finish tomorrow. We lay around the rest of the day and spend the night in the Earthship. While Mom and Grams make grilled cheese sandwiches and hot lentil soup for dinner, Camellia and I put stuff away in drawers and closets and Dad drives back to check on the animals and make sure they have enough to eat and drink. Later he says, "The deer are getting very familiar."

After the boys' beds are put together and made up in the bedroom off the short hall at the back of the dining room, they go to bed. Dad puts the rest of the beds together. Our twin beds are in the room across from the boys' room. Camellia and I will share the room. Grams takes the second guest room with a queen-size bed. Mom and Dad have the master bedroom off the family room hall with a king-size bed. One bedroom has no furniture. All the beds are made, and since the house is a constant seventy-four degrees, we are comfortable and very tired when Dad pulls in. He parks in the garage at the far-right side of the long hall through the greenhouse hall. We don't hear him since we are enclosed in earth, but we hear his voice as he passes us saying goodnight.

"I'll probably have nightmares in this house," Camellia says as she lays on her side facing me in the twin bed.

"Why would you have nightmares?"

"Buried under tons of earth, an early grave," she answers.

"Earth is on each side of us and a structural, fire retardant, solar-controlled, glass and steel roof is on top of us. I guess Dad never told you about the importance of an Earthship?" I ask.

"Every one of you have told me about what we've done to the planet and about the CO2 and methane problem. But an Earthship seems a bit extreme."

I turn on my side to face her. "Can you imagine how many people and animals are running for their lives at this moment?"

"Well, not really."

"I wish I could forget sometimes. In the world right now there is either war, floods, droughts or starvation and dehydration going on around us, not to mention freezing weather like ours. We live in our own little isolated world and that makes everything else seem unreal. Our seemingly safe and comfortable world may not stay like this forever. Our civilization is already dying. Dad has been making plans for a long time, he and mom saw this coming." Camellia yawns and turns on her back. "I can tell you what dad told me, but only if you can stay awake." I say.

"Tell me."

"When dad was a boy, he started studying scientific journals regarding research about what CO2 was doing to the planet. It was discovered that humans were adding more CO2 than had been in our atmosphere for millions of years when the earth was a greenhouse—too hot for human habitation. The Amazon rain forest is known as the lungs of the earth because they take in so much carbon and convert it into oxygen, so you can imagine how scared he was when in 2005 the Amazon was going through its worst drought in decades. Fresh water had to be flown in to the villages. Fires were burning in areas that in the past had never burned, and huge rivers had dried up and were becoming mud. Scientists were afraid the entire ecosystem might collapse. We lucked out that time, because before the end of the year the rains came and put out the fires."

"The rain forests are still doomed. Stupid people are burning them down to grow palm oil and feed cattle and governments haven't stopped illegal logging. The fewer trees there are, the less rain; and more drought leads to more fires and more CO_2. We lose enough old forests to cover Rhode Island every day on the planet. The Earthship gives us a better chance of surviving for generations. Are you still awake?"

"Yeah. I'll wait for the second chapter."

"What is that?"

"How this house helps us survive."

In the following two days we are able to finish moving into the Earthship, but we wonder what to do with the cottage. Dad suggests making it better so it can be lived in. I like that idea, because I know we will soon be overrun with people coming north to make a new life for themselves, and there are swarms of people migrating all over the globe.

We notice Dad is walking better, he no longer needs shots and we are relieved. He spends his morning hours at his desk on his tablet doing research and making plans to get more involved in local government. He is already well-known in the state for his help in finally getting the incremental tax passed on oil coal and gas. He gave speeches all over the country in the 2020s, reminding people that they have to have their trash picked up, and that CO_2 is the trash left after burning fossil fuels. "Let's start getting it picked up," were his words. He is great at giving the kind of speeches people can relate to and he has a real fire in the belly when it comes to his stand on climate change. He is also in touch with his old unit in Libya, and is busy getting the military bots in place on the property to protect us. Dad built a special takeoff ramp for the drones in the peak of the new barn. The deer don't seem to mind his working and making a lot of noise. He did have to clean up a few piles of manure and cart it off to the compost bin before he could work among them. It is still freezing outside so we will have to hang on to the deer for a while. Camellia gave Kazan a bath in the shower with her so he is now allowed in the house. He favors the boys' room at night.

At the breakfast table the next day, Dad says, "Some people believed James Hansen, and others, about the effects of climate change and many Republicans didn't. James, a NASA scientist, was right when he testified to the Senate back in the hot summer of 1988. "He begged to differ with the consensus on how fast the ice sheets would melt due to global warming." The common belief was that it would take hundreds of years for all of the ice to disappear. The ice became thinner and thinner and kept retreating every year during the summer months. In 2020, the last sheets of ice slipped into the sea."

There are tears in Dad's warm brown eyes as he sits looking at us. I think the sixth extinction is well underway, as well as a new-age that scientists call the Anthropocene, meaning the time humans totally take over the forces of nature. The human forcing began during the industrial age and that was the beginning of a new age when we started forcing the climate to change to suit our civilization.

"Why were we chosen for these years, Dad?" I ask.

He says, "Can you think of a more exciting time in history to be born? On one hand, we are on the threshold of the greatest advancements in medicine and technology and on the other we are coming to an end of an age unlike any ever lived in modern history. We get to be the observers of the singularity. Witnesses to a brave new world where anything can happen and so many opportunities exist for humans to become *humankind*."

I could think of nothing to say, but Dad gave me a lot to think about. I guess we are lucky because we haven't kept our heads in the sand. We are as prepared as we can be. Maybe now that our government has banned the use of coal, we can start to listen to the scientists that have ideas on how to correct some of this mess, but can they when the problem is as big as the planet?

The dark, freezing, overcast days are now covering us and add to my depression as my mind hovers like a bee over the word *extinction.* I understand something few scientists like to talk about, the dimming of sunlight reaching the earth because of all the particulates in the atmosphere that act like a blanket in the upper troposphere. This will not make our planet cooler. Actually, the opposite is happening. We will still be able to use our solar roof, but it will not be as efficient. Due to the tilt of our planet, we should naturally be entering another ice age. Without enough sunlight, we can't grow grains. My heart beats like a drum and my brain cries out for all the children, humans and animals suffering around the world. There is always a lag time, because our world is so big that it takes some time for our actions to catch up with us. All of these things are on my mind. I am scared and shaky as I spend my days helping sort through our things and putting them away in our new home. I've forgotten about Sage's request. I send him a reply.

> Hi Sage, we moved into our new home and it took several days in the freezing weather. I have been so busy I forgot about getting back with you, I am so absent-minded. Sorry. Let's meet this weekend, if that works for you
> Laurel

CHAPTER 9
SAGE

"El Niño is not just stronger, it may be permanent."

– Mark Lynas

On Saturday, Sage, dressed in a dark down-filled jacket, gloves and a fur cap that covers his ears, arrives along with his young brother, Ash, for lunch at 12:30. Ash has shoulder-length hazelnut-colored hair tied back on the sides in braids. He has freckles with unusual ash-colored eyes. French braids in both men's and women's hair is in style now. He is Rain's age but a little stockier, shorter and shyer. I meet them at the elevator door and apologize for the mess in the greenhouse hall. The small fruit trees and grape vines have arrived and mom is working on getting their roots in the peat moss mulch and straw, but some are still in boxes.

I offer to take their outer wardrobe and hang up the jackets. Ash hesitates, then takes off his down covering and hat and I place them in a nearby closet, then I have them follow me to the dining room.

Sage says, "This place is both warm and amazing."

Sage and Ash follow me into the kitchen where Camellia, mom and Grams are finishing the lunch preparations. Everyone says hello to Sage and I introduce Ash. Camellia gives them a hug and shows off her dimples. The guys smile, returning the hug.

Several trays are on top of the island cabinets that separate the kitchen from the dining room. We each pick up a tray of food and place it on the dining room table that sis has set. Mom pushes a buzzer on her tablet and tells her AI to notify everyone that lunch is ready.

Rain is followed by Prairie and Kazan, they say hi to Sage and Ash. I mention that I asked Sage to bring Ash so Rain could get to know him. Sage nuzzles Kazan and tells the boys his family has a big dog, Butter, a Great Dane. "Ash mostly takes care of him and they are best friends," Sage says.

"Ash, do you go to a school?" Prairie asks.

"Do you mean school in a building with other kids?"

"Yes."

"In Idaho Falls and Rigby, like most small cities and towns, everyone is educated online now. I bet you miss playing with other kids like I do."

"I do. My old school in Arizona was mixed—two days a week in school and two days of online classes from home."

"The only classroom schooling I've known is kindergarten grade," Ash said.

Dad arrives and Mom says, "Let's sit and start eating before the food is cold."

"People don't have to wait for me," Dad grumbles. "Hello, Sage, welcome.

"Thank you, sir, this is my brother Ash," Sage says, putting his hand on his brother's wrist.

"Happy to have you with us, Ash." He nods. The food is passed along and we eat.

"This stew is delicious and the dumplings are incredible," Sage says.

"I'm glad you like the stew," Dad replies, "having Grams around is equivalent to accessing the finest chef, and it's all done out of love." Grams just smiles, then to change the subject because she is embarrassed by the attention, she asks Sage about his family.

"My dad died when I was very young. He was in an accident and lost a foot and a hand, he couldn't get a job, so my mom, in her twenties, worked to support us. Dad grew very depressed about his condition and started drinking. One day my mom came home and found his body, he had killed himself. Many years later, Mom married Jay Hawking, a good man who became like a father, but mom wanted me to keep my dad's name. Jay gave me my sister Dara and brother Ash Hawking. We have a happy family."

"Oh, Sage, that is a sad story, I'm so glad it has a happy ending," Grams says as I find his hand and squeeze it.

"Will you come back to Idaho Falls after you leave the military, Sage?" Dad asks.

"Sir, I am studying geology, engineering and computer hardware online and will continue until I have a master, then I will go through all the written and lab tests and field work before I can earn my diploma." Sage sips some water and then continues. "I doubt Idaho Falls will be able to give me the work I want to pursue."

"What work do you want to pursue?"

Sage swallows the last bite of his dumpling and takes a little water.

"Terraforming, sir."

"Sage, what is terraforming?" Prairie asks.

"Prairie, terraforming is when people and or machines change the atmosphere, temperature and landscape on purpose to make a place more livable."

Sage starts on his salad. Dad looks at him as if he admires him, and then he eats some stew.

"That sounds like very interesting work, Sage," dad says as he lays his soup spoon in his bowl and picks up his fork.

"Terraforming must be a very complex project, and needed all over the world, but it would seem beyond our capabilities," Camellia says, looking at Sage as she fills his water glass and then sits down. "Is it anything like geo-engineering?"

"No, we started doing that when we started burning coal. The climate is engineered by humans now, not nature," Sage answers.

Dad adds, "Sage is right about that. Some scientists had that figured out before 2000."

Sage continues, "With the help of our deep-thinking computers and latest tools, we can accomplish terraforming now."

"From what I have been reading about the Luna Project, we will need to terraform under the dome and a lot of soil will have to be made for the job," Rain adds.

"Yes, but when the new base on the moon is up and running, it won't be so bad, and that would be an incredible experience," Sage adds. "A lot of minerals for enriching the soil will be hauled up to the moon one day on a space elevator, an invention mentioned by the writer Arthur Clarke. We had to wait for the right technology to build it. Someday over time, we will build the elevator and I hope I get to play a part in the Lunar Project. Elon Musk proposed building a space elevator that will run from the earth to a space platform and base. But I can't explain how it will work."

"I can't imagine anyone wanting to work on the Moon unless the earth becomes as bleak as the moon" I reply. "I would rather just die on Earth than live on the moon." Everyone just looks at me and I wonder why I always have to give my opinion.

Sage and Ash are ready to tour the Earthship, and Camellia and Prairie ask if they can tag along. They have never received the tour. First, I show them the greenhouse hall. I tell them the water collected on the roof ends up here after being used and filtered many times. That gray water feeds the fruit trees and gardens being planted in front of the bulletproof windows. The walls are painted a shiny pale yellow to reflect the light. The floor in this area is slate, used for its non-slip natural look and easy-to-clean texture. Then, we walk to the end of the long greenhouse hall.

"All main rooms on your right are connected to this hall," I tell them. "Notice all the passages into rooms have doors, but above the doors are tall, arched, louvered openings to let in heat and light. Also, one end of the hall has a door leading to mechanics, easy access to plumbing, wiring computer systems and security. On the other end is the entrance to the elevator. You have seen the main rooms. Most rooms have ceiling fans. This room is open to the dining room, and between them is a concrete fireplace with a covered exterior in slate like the hall floor. This column helps support the roof, and when necessary warms the house by burning hard, recycled fiber pellets, more for atmosphere and looks than heat, because the house stays warm enough.

"You have seen the dining room and kitchen. The water used here comes from the roof and is then filtered and collected in cisterns. Water leaving here is filtered and used for cooking, drinking, showers and washing clothing and linens. Then, the filtered gray water is used to feed plants, and after that it is used for flushing toilets."

Then they learned that many floors are made from earth, a mixture of clay sand and oil six inches thick. They are leather-like and healthy when walked on in bare feet. The bathrooms, laundry, kitchen and dining room have bamboo floors. The temperature stays at around sixty-eight degrees without added heat in the summer and winter. The short hall behind the family room contains the master bedroom and bathroom, and the hall behind the dining room contains two small bedrooms that share a bath. The hall behind the kitchen has a laundry, pantry, office, storage and a hall to an underground storage cellar.

"Let's walk to the end of the greenhouse hall. On your left is a guest room and half-bath suite. The hall at the end of the laundry leads to a garage. So, what do you think? You have all been so quiet."

"It's amazing," Sage says.

"I live here and even I think it's pretty awesome," Prairie says.

"What are those four things in the ceiling, Laurel?" Ash asks as he points up to the filtered vents.

"They are vents that open and close automatically if it gets too hot or damp in the greenhouse. If you look up when you're outside, you will also see some tall pipes of glass that adds light and ventilation and is a lifesaver if we have a big snowstorm."

They also learned that the Earthship is a bio shelter, completely self-sustaining. Like a tree, it draws from the earth everything it needs without harming the planet.

"Our energy is off the grid and is drawn from the wind, a wind tower, sun, solar cells, earth in which we grow our organic food, and sky, the water filtered from rain and collected in gutters and cisterns. Also, the house is hard to destroy, built from material like the lifetime roof. No lead contaminates. The material in the construction of the house won't pollute or burn."

"What about flooding?" asks Ash.

"That's a good question. We might get wet, but the house wouldn't be seriously harmed. Let's go outside for a moment." I open the big metal doors and we go up in the elevator. "You see how the earth covers the house on three sides? At the top, the roof hangs over the soil. At the bottom are trenches covered in rocks. The trenches will collect excess water and carry it away from the house to a collection point near the outside greenhouses where there is a canal."

"Won't the soil on the sides of the house be washed away?" Sage asks.

"No, because of the wide overhangs, and also, under the soil are rammed earth tires filled with a clay soil, and a mesh and sandy soil and peat moss that is planted. The mesh and the roots of plants will keep the soil in place."

"I think I'm cold enough. Let's go inside," Camellia says, and we follow her into the Earthship.

After we finish the tour, we separate. Rain is waiting for Ash and they take off to the play area. Camellia takes Prairie with her to feed the animals and Sage and I sit in some comfortable patio chairs in the greenhouse and talk.

"Do you think you will be staying here after you graduate, Laurel?"

"I will start my online business here; this house will be my base. But I will have to travel a lot to design and oversee the building of Earthships. If you are around, I will use your services sometimes. I can't build without soil tests and digging big holes in the ground."

"I may be around sometimes. I am amazed at what you have done here and I can see now that this house is a fortress that can save lives. I would like my family to live in one."

"When your family has the land, I will help them build an Earthship of their own."

"How much do they cost to build?"

"About the same as any well-built, above-ground home."

"Will you build some entirely under the earth?" Sage asks.

"Without question," I reply. "In many places that's how people will survive."

"You really think it will get that bad, Laurel?"

"Worse than even I can imagine, and I have a great imagination. But I don't know how long it will take to get very bad. We know for sure it's getting hotter every year, and very little has been done to stop CO2 until now. I think we will be lucky to even survive. Many scientists don't believe we can survive. Evolution doesn't mean adaption. We can adapt to temperatures a few degrees higher or lower than what we are used to, but climate shift includes less light, food, water and oxygen. Nature creates some animals with mutations in their DNA that allows them to be different enough to survive. Maybe there will be people who can live on fungi, mushrooms and grub like insects. Some people survived the black plague through genetic differences. We cannot escape our fate, but we must confront extinction. If we have a future after the death of our civilization, we can't deny what is happening, or panic over it, but we need patience and love to help others survive. One never knows; we just might find an undiscovered nearby planet we can screw up all over again."

"We are trying to get to Mars," Sage says.

"Yes, and we would have light, but not enough oxygen, and I don't think we have time to move so many people to another planet.

"Mars will have to be terraformed which will take thousands of years and more." Sage added.

"You are right, Mars would only work in the far future."

"You and I and our families are powerless against the future. We can make the best preparations for what lies ahead and do our best individually by trying to be good human beings. The rest is not in our hands."

"Do you see a future for yourself, like being married with children?" Sage asks.

"I'm not really focused on me now, but with the right person, yes. I like family life; it's the best for me. Right now, I'm focused on helping people and animals survive. If not to survive, then to experience less suffering. As soon as the freeze has passed, I will start looking for animals and people to help. Right now, I have a barn full of deer eating the goat pellets." Sage chuckles.

I continue, "My sister is the real humanitarian. She is going to be a fine nurse and a veterinarian. Rain will be a meteorologist and I don't know about Prairie yet. Mom is a botanist and Grams is our teacher. She knows how to do almost everything." Sage smiles and nods.

"Dad says we will need horses. We listen to him because he knows all about survival. He has known for a long time that we would face this. No one would listen to men like my dad when there was time to reverse the effects of climate change. If you or your family needs survival information, talk to my dad."

"Sounds good, Laurel."

"Do you feel like going for a walk, Sage? I could show you the rest of our place."

"It is cold, but a walk would be good and I have a warm coat in your closet." We head out to get his coat.

"Let me run and change into warmer clothes, then we can go. You might find Ash and let him know." From my closet in my room I put on my down coat with a hood and my down-wrapped boots and wool gloves.

I find Sage, Ash and Rain at the elevator door. "I guess you boys were in the mood for a walk, also," I say.

"Yes, if it's okay with you," Ash says.

"Of course, Ash."

I open the big doors and we take off, walking around the back of the Earthship. I point out the French drain that moves the drained water into pipes underground. Then we walk to the new barn, where horses will be kept. Inside it is light and airy with its clear fiberglass roof. Rain is eager to show Ash the goats. The baby is so cute. Rain opens the door to the goat barn and they play while Sage and I laugh. Rain brings them some carrots, but not enough, it seems. The goats want more and are mouthing them everywhere. We check on the deer in the old barn. They hide toward the back as I fill up their water bucket with the hose. The deer have become quite tame, but they notice a couple of strangers among us. Then I show everyone the chicken coop. Next, we walk to the cottage and I show them the greenhouses. We go inside one to check the indoor temperature, and with the lights and heaters on, it is forty-eight degrees inside from front to back.

We walk past the empty cottage on the way back to the Earthship and Sage asks, "What will happen to the cottage now?"

"It will be used for guests or people who need a place to stay for a while. We will insulate it better and give it a metal roof, try to make it more fireproof."

Ash and Rain race each other back to the house.

Once inside Ash asks, "Why did you call your house an Earthship?"

"That name came up in the sixties or seventies by a guy that started experimenting with what he thought would be an inexpensive, self-contained way for people who wanted to own an off-the-grid home and live away from cities. Over the years, they worked out all the problems and perfected these homes. They believed Earthships could save humanity from world disasters. Also, the houses were originally mostly earth and tires and not very attractive. The name probably stuck because of the Noah's Ark story, but I don't know for sure."

"Ash, I think it's time we leave for home and help Mom out," Sage says after checking his watch.

"Okay. I'm glad we met, Rain," Ash says. "Text me if you want to spend some time together."

"I will, Ash, you do the same."

Sage reaches out for a hug. I hesitate, and he asks me why. "As long as I can remember I've had what they call the fight or flight response, an acute stress response that can be part of Asperger's symptoms." I answer, then relent and hug him. He holds on, whispering in my ear, "Text me. I may not see you again for a long time. I will keep in touch."

"Take care," I whisper.

Sage leaves and I walk back to the kitchen after redressing for indoors.

"You might want to check out your tablet for the BBC online news." Dad says.

I sit at the table and open my tablet, then tap the BBC icon. I see the headline, "Food Riots in America."

> *States in the Midwest that have been in drought conditions for six years have run out of food, except for what is held by the black market and the rich land owners who hold the rights to any water left. People are angry and fighting to survive, as they break into warehouses looking for food. The National Guard has been called in to protect property. Charity organizations are bringing food and water.*

I am angry. It is the poor that always seem to suffer. Those states are governed by very conservative governments who preach trickle-down economics. The food and water are not trickling down to the poor people. It is usually the more compassionate people who support the food banks and try to help the poor. At least that is my experience. Now even more people will be heading north if they can even afford to travel.

"Mom, I think as soon as it warms up I should install two more greenhouses where we can grow food to supply a once-a-week farmers' market in town. What do you think?"

"It's a good idea, Laurel, if we can find some help in planting, picking, boxing and delivering," Mom says, looking up at me.

"Maybe you haven't thought about how we're going to protect all this food yet?" Dad asks. "After all, what happens when outlaws decide to take it from you?"

"You're right, Dad. I haven't thought that far ahead. I guess that will be your job. Maybe we could find a family who would work for food and shelter. We have the cottage. How about asking some of your Army friends to help protect the food?"

"I don't have any Army friends who live in this area. But I'll contact those I know and find out if they know someone who would like to move here and help us. You probably already know not to take the problem or its solution online. We might attract the wrong people."

"Yes, Dad, but as far as helping with planting and boxing, some of our relatives might do it for food. Sage's sister and brother might like a job. I don't think their family is doing that well. I will call Sage's mother. Also, since Uncle Darwin died, their family seems to be having problems earning enough to feed themselves."

"Laurel, you are right. They could use some help. I will call Meadow and feel her out," Mom said.

"Okay, Mom. Right now, I need to check on the animals."

The next day I call Sage about asking his mom if the kids would like helping. He says both kids have a lot of extra time. His dad has a job in the building trades and his mom works for Idaho Potato. Lily calls me in the evening and asks if I will meet her for coffee at the Main Street Cafe in the Falls at 2:00 tomorrow and I agree.

Mom tells me that Meadow and her kids would love to help for food. I ask Dad how to figure out how much to pay them in food.

"You could ask them what they think is fair for the number of hours they work," Dad replies, looking up from his tablet. "Better yet, ask your AI to figure something out for us. They are better at that sort of thing than we are." I order two more greenhouses to put up as soon as the freeze has passed.

I meet Lily at the Main Street Cafe. She is a medium-large Swedish woman with long, golden blonde hair tied up. She is dressed in a skirt and blouse with a warm wool sweater on top and a Camel hair coat is swung over the back of her chair. She is the only woman sitting alone so I assume it must be her.

I walk over and say, "Hello, I'm Laurel." As she looks me over, I give her my hand and she lightly squeezes it.

"Sit," she says. "Sage has told me so much about you." *He does not know that much about me,* I think.

"He is a nice young man," I say. Her blue eyes widen when she replies, "*Nice* is not the right word for Sage. He is perfect in every way."

"Sorry, but we have just met and spent very little time together, so I don't really know him yet." The waitress takes our orders for coffee.

"We will be text pals and learn more about each other over time," I say. "You must be a little worried about him being so far away." She motions to the waitress.

"Yes, I am. I never wanted him to join up and wish he had just let me pay for his education."

"I'm looking forward to meeting Dara. Ash is a delightful boy."

"Yes, Ash is a sweetheart with a great sense of humor when you get to know him, and you will like Dara. She is like a second mother to my boys."

"My sister Camellia is about Dara's age, and my brother Rain enjoys the company of Ash. They should all get along just fine."

"So, what work would Dara and Ash actually be doing?" she asks. The waitress brings our coffee.

"Lily, we will grow food for a farmers' market in town. I will find a good place for the market. We grow organic vegetables. My mom is a botanist. I have talked to the food bank and people around town and there is a shortage of food in the markets because of the drought in some states and flooding in others, due to climate change and higher food prices. Helpers will learn how to use tools for tilling, planting, weeding and harvesting then help fill the truck and deliver the food to the market. I'm sure many people around town grow their own food and might want to sell some, and if they want, and the food they grow is organic, they can join our farmers' market."

"That sounds like a good idea, Laurel. More and more people can't find jobs because of AI implementation. With smart electric cars, trucks, buses and all other forms of transportation, all drivers are out of work. All cashier and bank clerk jobs have been taken over by robots, and that's just a part of the job loss because of AI, leaving millions without jobs. People are having a hard time just surviving, and now the cost of food has gone through the roof."

"We won't charge for the food, but will take donations from those who want to give just to help pay expenses. At least we will experiment with this plan and see if we can take in enough donations from people and businesses to cover costs."

"The workers will get the best education and training in growing vegetables. While learning how to grow food for you and your family, they will be paid by the hour with a variety of food. My AI is figuring out a fair way to pay workers with food."

I explain how it would all be done and she seems to think it's fair. Then I finish a great cup of coffee and set my white porcelain cup down. Lily is concerned about how the kids would travel back and forth and I remind her it's only twenty miles. She will talk to her children about how many days a week they want to work and let me know.

"This is my card, Lily. Just call or text me and we will see what we can do."

"You can't start until the weather warms up a little," she says.

"Right."

"Thanks for meeting me, Laurel."

"Sure. I'm glad I got to meet you, Lily. Goodbye for now. I'll see you later." I walk out, get in the truck and stop at the feed lot before I drive home.

Twenty-six days pass before the sun peeks through the overcast sky and the earth starts to warm a little. The deer in the barn are set free. But they hang around. Rain is letting the goats outside, Prairie opens the chicken coop and Kazan is trying to coral all the animals. He must be part sheepdog.

The second order of greenhouses arrives, and I start putting them together. Mom and Dad take off in the truck to look at horses at a nearby ranch. Grams helps the boys pick the winter squash, kale and leeks. Before Rain finishes, he pulls a few carrots for the goats and deer.

When Mom and Dad return later in the afternoon, they seem pleased because they found two young Morgan's and two Anglo Arabians they like. They took several pictures; the horses look beautiful to us. They are going to think about it overnight and let the owner know tomorrow.

After all the chores are done and the dinner dishes washed and put away, Camellia and I listen to the latest news on the climate from her AI, Cas. Some scientists have figured out a way to use our trash that can't be recycled to create coastal islands by blending and encasing trash in a fibrous concrete product that will last forever. Coastal islands will cut down on erosion and protect vulnerable areas from storm surges and rising oceans.

By 2050, the sea level rise is expected to be six feet higher at low tide and the geography of the world's coastlines will look radically different. Much of humanity will have to move to higher ground, leaving everything central to what they knew as a civilization for thousands of years to the seas. In spite of this, the greed never ends as the Arctic Ocean nations, Canada, Denmark, the United States, Norway and Russia, are battling over mineral rights. But the most terrible story is that of Earth, where living species that have evolved toward perfection over millions of years could be destroyed forever in the space a few human generations.

"It is hard for the human mind to accept that life can be erased so quickly and with such leaden finality," wrote Mark Lynas in *Six Degrees.*

That night Camellia and I talk about surviving in the Earthship and all the beauty and wisdom life has created for the earth that will be gone. We hold one another and talk until exhaustion overcomes us.

Throughout the spring, the farmers' market we start becomes very popular. In Rigby, our first is across the highway from the railroad tracks and on the corner of Second Street under some big old trees that I once climbed in my youth. May is warming up with many days over 110 degrees, so we install a large, shady tarp over the market tied to tree limbs. I used to wake to the songs of birds and remember how thick the ladybugs and daddy longlegs were in the spring; now they are absent. I will need a beehive for the gardens. The evenings are our salvation, as it cools down into the seventies. We string up lights so we can work at both the market and greenhouses after dinner.

After we bring in the bees, we begin growing more food than one farmers' market can handle. So, we set up another market in Idaho Falls for Dara, Ash and Lily to help manage. They are all honest and hard-working people. Sage and I keep in touch, and he is happy our families are working together. The markets are only open on Saturday and Sunday mornings and evenings, so it isn't too much trouble, but it helps so many people get some fresh organic food in their bellies. It is a lot of work to grow everything, but we have more help now.

I don't have as much time to help with produce now because I've started my online business of designing Earthships, which keeping me busy on my tablet, designing, ordering and traveling. I am building one house in Twin Falls, Idaho, and another in Nampa, Idaho. I receive free advertising online through the Earthship online host, where I am listed as a designer and contractor in the Northwest for Earthships. I have to check on the progress and quality of materials I have ordered and the work by my subcontractors every two weeks. Camellia is taking online classes in nursing and veterinary medicine and physiology. She's working twenty hours a week in Rigby's hospital and ten hours a week in a large animal vet hospital outside of town.

My cousins Verbena, Marigold, Nolina and Yarrow as well as Grams and my brothers Rain and Prairie help out when they can, working the gardens for the farmers' market and food bank, now that Ash and Dara are working in the Falls gardens. Rain and Prairie feed the animals and gather eggs. Mom and Grams can and dehydrate food. Dad is busy installing security systems and defense bots in case we are attacked, and he looks after the horses, bees, the truck and the machinery. I help with anything whenever I have time

In August I turn twenty years old. The last year has flown by. The large canvas tarps over our markets help for some shelter, but the rain comes and the downpour feels like a waterfall, so the tarp won't hold and people don't come. After getting permission, we tell people they can pick up produce at the high school auditorium until the rains pass, and Dara does the same thing in Idaho Falls. Dara is a smart and a very lovely young woman. She and Ash handle most of the market in Idaho Falls. So far, we don't have a problem with people trying to steal from us—maybe because the food is free. But donations are accepted, and so far, the donations are enough to pay for the cost of the operation.

My job sites in Twin Falls and Nampa are far enough along that I don't have to worry about big holes in the ground filling with water from the rain. But the owner in Twin Falls has decided to put up a temp shelter so they can keep working on his house.

Dad decides he wants to add another above-ground tank to hold extra water near the new horse barn. The men have to work in the rain.

September comes and passes with continuous rain coming down in sheets and flooding low areas. The dark, overcast days have an effect on our emotions, making us feel the hopelessness of our situation at times. We must use less energy, because there is less wind and sunlight for our solar cells. Even though we have energy stored in batteries, we are frugal. We mostly stay indoors, except for going outside to feed the animals, milk the goats and gathering eggs and produce.

Then, one day in October there is a sudden change in the weather. The sky looks like crinkled foil, strange and otherworldly. Then electrical storms come with the sound of rippling aluminum, brilliant flares of flashing white light and explosive, crackling booms, frightening everyone with thoughts of the end of the world. The animals go crazy, trying to get away and hitting the walls. All of our buildings are grounded as well as most of the trees, so we should be safe from fire. In the house, the earth muffles the sound, but the animals are terrified, and we decide the horses could hurt themselves, so we take them to their underground basement in the horse barn. We put the goats and chickens in the cellar under the cottage. That seems to work. All of the animals are much calmer. We don't know what happened to the beautiful deer. They never came back.

I keep in touch with my clients and subcontractors on my tablet for the next couple of weeks. I also start the plans for another Earthship. So, I feel no pressure. Camellia is eager to get back to her work at the hospital and vet clinic, but the roads are too dangerous; they are covered in mud and streams of water.

Rain brings me his tablet to show me the weather patterns around the world. The weather is not normal anywhere. Temperatures in Antarctica are almost seven degrees warmer than usual compared to historical figures. There is so much moisture in the atmosphere, due to high temperatures at the poles and the warmer Atlantic Ocean currents, that many countries are experiencing flooding, mudslides and torrential rains. Northern China, Siberia, northern Russia and northern Europe are being drenched. It is snowing on the East Coast of North America. There are no signs yet of it stopping. Another news item catches my eye and I ask Zak, on Rain's tablet, "What's the latest news?"

I find out the people of Central America are fleeing what's left of their nation after an 8.4 earthquake and a Tsunami struck the Pacific side of El Salvador, Nicaragua, Costa Rica and Panama on October 23. The land mass that used to form a connection between Mexico and South America is sinking from all the quake and water, leaving behind two islands, one half the size of Nicaragua, and another one-third the size of Honduras. Fifteen million people are losing everything and are scrambling to survive as their homes fall into the ocean.

CHAPTER 10
DEATH IN THE OCEAN

"Human-made climate forcings are now in total dominance over natural forcing."

–James Hansen

Some, mostly women and children, have been picked up by boats and ships. Officers toss life vests to the people, but they have no room for them on the overcrowded ships. They return over and over again to pick up more people. Many survivors on those ships are taken to South America. Others are picked out of the ocean and taken to Mexico. Millions are left clinging to the islands and the wreckage. Anything that will float is being tossed into the water to help the people survive until more ships arrive for their rescue.

America's Navy and Coast Guard have been sent to help, and Mexico is sending more boats and ships to save people. Military helicopters are also on their way, loaded with food and bottled water for the people who have survived the devastation.

The previous three years of constant drought has left Mexicans starving and suffering from dehydration and disease. This year Mexico received a lot of rain, but it's doubtful they will be able to help the refugees. They are taking them to northern Mexico, and dropping them off to be held in camps where they can be registered. Then the ships return to what's left of Central America to pick up more people. In the meantime, a scientific study is underway to find out if the climate shift has anything to do with this earthquake.

A telepresence conference is being held at the White House with the leaders of Mexico, Canada, Russia, Cuba, and South American countries. They are meeting this afternoon with the President Anderson to discuss solutions to this terrible calamity.

Mexicans, Guatemalans and Hondurans have been crossing the borders into America for many years, and there has been a huge increase in the numbers. Some have fled for their lives due to the water wars and others have fled to survive a terrible economy. Now they must all flee, for they have no country.

New Mexico's Governor Santos, Texas' Governor Miller and California's Governor Larkin are demanding that the federal government take charge of the borders to make sure that all Central American refugees coming across be processed and treated with respect and kindness. These people need to be held temporarily until a permanent home can be arranged for them. Larkin, Santos, and Miller are asking President Anderson and the federal government for help with food and medical supplies. Private donations will be coming in from religious and humanitarian organizations for clothing, bedding, tents, baby formula, diapers, etc.

Workers are setting up places that will receive shipments of needed items in Mexico, California, Texas and other states and border towns that are accepting refugees.

Larkin is planning to meet and negotiate with Nevada, Montana, Nebraska, Idaho, Wyoming, Utah and Alaska to take refuges. He says it is our duty and obligation; we are our brothers' keepers. California and other northwestern states have received a lot of rain this winter. Their lakes and rivers are overflowing and their aquifers are finally full. He goes on to say, "The refuges will help us later. Now we will help the people of Central America and Mexico. We have one condition. They must make new lives for themselves in our least populated states. Within a few weeks, once agreements are made with the states involved, the good people of Central America who travel to North America will work to build a new life with homes, towns and businesses. The states and the federal government will help them succeed."

At the dinner table this afternoon the family talks about the latest crisis in the news. After everyone is served, Grams sits down. She makes us a big bowl of steamed spinach with a slightly sweet fruity vinaigrette dressing, as well as navy bean, potato and cheddar cheese soup. We are lifted with the news from President Anderson that America will help our Central American families.

"Don't start eating too quickly," Dad cautions. "You may want to thank God for all your blessings." Everyone bows their heads and thinks about the right words to say to God. Then everyone prays internally. My family are Mormons, but don't always follow all the rituals.

"We need to get ready for another winter by insulating some of the buildings, like the cottage and barns, and fence the property with inexpensive electric wire and metal stakes. We could start to have a problem with people with tribal mentalities. We have more than our share of gangs nearby. I plan on getting involved in this immigrant crisis because there will be many people opposed to us helping these suffering people, so I will be creating some enemies and I want you to be prepared for trouble. Maybe you will take a bit of advice that could save a life. I would like all of you to learn to shoot and take care of a gun. Let me know what day and time would work for you to meet on our new shooting range."

"I didn't know we had a shooting range, Dad," Rain remarks.

"We don't now, but we will before we need it." Dad looks at him with a devilish smile.

"I think I get it, Dad."

"Do I have to?" Camellia asks. "I don't even like to touch guns, Dad."

"Give it a try and see what happens. If we are ever attacked, we will need everyone. Everything looks calm now, but things can quickly change, and you have no idea how bad it can get."

I understood Dad's worry, being a student of history. I will be on the shooting range.

One day in late November, the electrical storms stop as quickly as they started and we get back to a normal life. The air is chilly, but the sun is shining again.

Our target practice gun maintenance lessons are on Wednesdays from 10:00 am until noon. Our practice range is two miles away in an empty acreage that used to be a slaughterhouse. The old buildings have been through a fire, but some logs are left standing, and we use one to tack up our target. We also get some exercise and take Kazan with us, but we have to keep him on a leash at the firing range. We get our choice of guns, looking for one that fits our hand and feels comfortable. I choose a small eight-shot revolver. We find out how bad we are at hitting the large target after each of us takes a turn firing several rounds, except Dad, of course. He explains that learning to shoot is only for self-preservation. We will need a lot of practice. Kazan is happy that we need so much practice. He loves the walks every week.

In December everything is worked out with the states to take a number of refugees. The number, having to do with resources in each state, is worked out by AI software. Every state has some people vehemently opposed to the idea. A police force will be put together to protect the refugees in each state. That doesn't sound good. We still haven't heard how many refugees Idaho will accept. I worry about Dad. He will be in the middle of this because he has been speaking out all over the state in favor of helping the refugees.

Prairie comes in my room and asks me what refugees are. "Did you try looking the word up on your tablet?" I ask.

"I didn't know how to spell the word."

"Well, then it's hard. This is what I do. Watch now." I pull out my tablet and call on Jo.

"Yes, Laurel."

"Jo, what is a refugee?"

"A person who has been forced to leave their country to escape war, persecution or a natural disaster."

"Thank you, Jo."

"Did that help you, little brother?"

"Yes, but can I stay and talk to you for a while?"

"Of course, you can. We haven't talked in a long time."

"I miss you, Laurel."

"I have missed you, too, little brother. I guess we have all been so busy around here that we have neglected one another. Come sit by me." He scoots over on the bed. I pull him up next to me and hug him. It feels so good that we hug for a long time.

"Did that feel good, Prairie?"

"Yes, I like hugs."

"I needed one also."

"You must be feeling lonely. You have been neglected and you have no children to play with."

"I do feel sad. Sometimes Rain gets tired of me following him around and he yells at me."

"I used to do the same thing to Rain. He always wanted to play with Camellia and me. We both loved him, we just needed some private time. Thank you for telling me how you feel. We can do things to make you feel happy again. You will see, but for now, let it be a surprise. We each get to name a horse. Have you picked out a name?"

He is shy and wiggles around for a few seconds, then says, "You won't laugh, will you?"

"No, I won't laugh."

"Skywalker."

"Wow, that is a great name. I remember how much you loved those old movies about Luke Skywalker."

"Yeah, that's where I first heard the name. Laurel, have you picked out a name?"

"I haven't thought about a name. I might need your help."

"I'll think on it, sis."

"What are you learning at Khan's Academy online school?"

"Lots of great stuff, but my favorite is making things. We're learning how to use 3D printers, and to make stuff out of different elements. In chemistry, we are learning how to mix chemicals to produce different reactions. And in robotics we are creating our own drones. Mine is a grasshopper drone. We are studying ants. Did you know they are most like us? Did you know that they use chemicals to communicate with one another?"

"Why are they most like us?"

"They help each other make complex structures by working together. And they will give up their life to protect another ant."

"Do we own a 3D machine?"

"Yes, that's how I make things."

"Have you studied earth science?"

"Yes, some about how rocks are formed."

"Oh, I loved learning about rocks and clouds. You are having more fun than I did. I would love to see some of the things you are making. Will you show me sometime?"

"I would like to."

We spend time together until Mom buzzes us for dinner.

At the dinner table, I am able to get Prairie reveal the name he chose for a small chestnut Morgan colt. Everyone likes Skywalker for his name. The family is working at coming up with names for a Morgan filly and an Anglo Arabian mare and her yearling colt. We settle on mother's name, Lyra, for the Arabian mare, and Camellia names the yearling Dorado and Rain names the Morgan filly Cassiopeia. We write the information in our tablets or tell our personal companions and give them all the detailed information on ages and birthdates, shots, medical information and family lines. Mom and Dad, when he's home, have been brushing, feeding, cleaning up after, and training the horses. They have a nice clean home in the barn now that the electrical storms have subsided.

Before bedtime that evening I tell Mom about Prairie feeling sad. She says that he hasn't been getting much attention. I suggest she find a program for him to attend once a week just to be with other children. She agrees to do it for both boys.

As Camellia and I get ready for bed, she tells me she is going back to the hospital and her vet classes the first of the week. The storms have passed and the roads have been cleaned up. I think it is a good idea, and she is so eager to get back to what she loves doing. I will be checking on my construction sites next week. I plan on a round trip, taking the bus to Twin Falls, renting a car and driving to Nampa to check out everything, then returning the same way.

After we're in bed, I open my tablet and talk to Jo. Camellia is reading.

"Jo, how many refuges is Idaho taking and where will they be placed?"

"The parties in the local government are still arguing."

"How many people survived the quake and water?"

"Approximately twelve million people survived."

"So, you are telling me that over three million people have died?"

"Yes, I am."

"This must be the greatest disaster of all time."

"It is the greatest disaster in modern times."

"Have they worked out where they will live?"

"Approximately five million want to live in South America, and South America has agreed to take three million. The two islands left from two countries can handle 600,000. Cuba has agreed to take 500,000. America, Russia, North Africa, Canada and other countries will take the rest. The deadline is January 1, 2033. So, they are taking their time."

"Has any state made a decision, Jo?"

"Yes, Utah takes 47,885. They will be given some federal land in the southeast corner of the state. The second state is Montana, taking 56,612."

"Thank you, Jo. Let me know when you have more information on the refugees."

"I will."

Then I write a short text to Sage.

Sage, the last time we talked you weren't very happy over the constant movement from tent to tent that you've had to endure since your return from your holiday. Have you settled yet? At least it sounds like they keep you busy. Time should fly by and it will all be over before you realize it. I'm sorry you have to suffer with the heat.

We have four horses now and yesterday we named all of them. So, it seems the boys will learn to ride. I haven't been on a horse in a long time, but I'm looking forward to riding, it's fun.

We are grateful for an end to the lightning storms; four horses were going crazy. Thankfully, Dad put a basement in the barn for them. That made all the difference. They calmed down immediately. Next week Camellia goes back to school and I travel to my job sites, this will be good for both of us. I think I'll take everyone ice skating this weekend. The boys are suffering from cabin fever.

Sorry I do not have more to say.

Laurel

I turned the light off. Camellia falls asleep with her face on her tablet. I gently move the tablet from under her head.

We spend Saturday cleaning up the greenhouses and getting the soil in shape for a winter crop of kale, spinach, lettuce, chard and leeks. We plant only two greenhouses; the others will be started in the spring.

On Sunday afternoon, I take Camellia and the boys ice skating in town. The Ice Palace is part of a shopping mall with restaurants and a theater. The rink is open to the shops and people sit around the rink eating at metal tables, while a large audience sits on auditorium seats. The ice is filled mostly with teens. We have fun, even though we are on our butts more than our feet. The good skaters are laughing at us, but we don't care because our fat butts protect us. We just have the giggles and everything is funny. When we get home, we take the horses for a little ride and give them treats of apples and a good brushing.

We think by December we will have a better idea about the plans for the refugees, believing the numbers of refugees for Idaho will be around 50,000, but we have heard nothing. I ask Dad if he knows anything.

"Can you imagine what it will be like to be homeless, without a job and no food in the winter in any of the states chosen?"

"No, Dad, I can't, and these people are used to living in the tropics. I can't imagine places are already built to hold this many people?"

"How would it feel to move in with a strange family through the winter months? Strange food, language, habits and customs?"

"It really would be unpleasant, Dad. Is that the plan?"

"That was our government's first plan."

We receive our letter from the government asking citizens to do their part and take in a family. If we sign the letter agreeing to take a family, a representative from the family placing and planning committee would visit us and bring pictures and information about the refugee family and explain all the details of how the program works. Dad wants to know how the details work first, so he calls the city councilman's office and makes an appointment.

December, and it's still in the seventies. Yet it is overcast every day now, which won't help our solar cells receive as much light. Also, our wind turbine isn't putting out much energy because we haven't had much wind. We can store a lot of energy in our batteries in the garage, but Dad doesn't want us to become too dependent on them. We will use them in real emergencies. We always use the energy to run the refrigerator, tablets and items that give us protection. Our on-demand hot water heater is very efficient, and we can shower at least every three days. We go to bed early because of the poor lighting, and we use only warm water for cleaning up. Our stove has two burners that use pressed recycled plant chips to burn for heat. At least the house is warm enough. We wear our clothes a lot longer before we wash them; the exception is our underwear. I'm not complaining yet. At least we have warm water.

Robots, androids and artificial intelligence, or AIs, replace workers in almost every industry and many people can't find jobs. The people who can are starting small online businesses. I worry about all these refugees finding jobs or creating jobs. I hope they're not going through hell to get here only to die or watch their children die of starvation. Dad finds out from the city councilman that our government can't get most citizens to take in perfect strangers. I'm not surprised, because people have isolated themselves within their families and close friends now that they get all their entertainment and conversation on the Internet and from their tablets.

Many people hardly ever go out of their houses unless they have to now because they have lost interest in the natural world.

Over the last ten years, hundreds of thousands of Americans have been moving farther north because of flooding and heat. But few have arrived in Idaho. The Gulf Coast and southern coastlines and islands are no longer habitable unless you live in a houseboat or have a house on piers and use a boat to travel. The oil rigs are still operating even though the oil is heavily taxed with the exception of those in Houston. That part of the country, including Florida and the Gulf Coast states are under water. Yet, some commercial fishing still goes on. The water is so warm and acidic that most shellfish are gone and only the toughest life forms continue to struggle.

I'm so glad Sage will get a two-month's pass to come home again this year for Christmas. We have been talking about everything having to do with the refugees and what's happening to our planet. I really like talking with him because he keeps up with so much that is going on with science, technology, archeology, the earth and medical breakthroughs. I am looking forward to spending some time with him. He is the only person I have found to share my more complex thoughts with and he has such clarity on the subject of quantum physics. Rain and Ash have stay-overs about once a month; they have become close like brothers. I think Ash wants to be more disciplined like Rain is and Rain wants to learn how to be more emotionally detached like Ash is, so they are a good match. Mother enrolled Rain and Prairie in a classical Tai Chi class and they like it so much they talked Ash into joining.

Camellia and I enjoy riding the horses. In the winter, the irrigation canal is dry and we ride fast along its side for four or five miles looking for wild animals. We are overjoyed some days—like yesterday when we spotted an animal and slowed down. The horses were snorting nervously.

"What is that, Laurel?"

"It looks like a black bear. I wish I had field glasses. Wait..." I pull out my tablet and snap it open. "Jo, can you see that animal ahead of us?"

"It is a pregnant American Black Bear."

"Take her picture, please."

"Would you like a close-up?"

"Yes, Jo."

"I bet she is eating everything she can find to get ready for her hibernation," Camellia says. "She will give birth this spring. I wish we knew where her den was so we could look for her again."

"So, do I, Camellia."

She is watching us but keeps her ground. After a while she turns and slowly walks away out of sight. Our horses are prancing, so eager to run, and we give them some freedom and they take off like rockets.

Coming back on the opposite side of the canal, we spot a gray wolf at the three-mile mark.

"Wow, he is just a mile from home. I hope he can't hear the clucking of our hens, or the crow of Mr. Rooster," I laugh. He stands looking at us and tilting his beautiful head back and forth, listening for something. Jo takes his picture and he backs away. Our horses want to go so we take off for home.

In the barn, we give the horses a rub down with towels as they snort and prance around us. Then we check their hooves and get out the brushes and they calm down. We talk about how excited we feel over seeing healthy-looking wild animals still alive in town. We are so eager to share the pictures with family. Still in the barn, I ask Camellia, "What's going on at the vet hospital?"

"Yesterday I got to help deliver a colt. It was all messed up and the mother had been in labor a long time." She continues, "A CAT scan showed the colt coming out backwards. I was able to get my arms inside the womb and turn the poor baby until his head was in the right place. Then the mare pushed and he came into the world," Camellia says, removing a pebble from Lyra's hoof.

"That sounds really dangerous. You could have broken an arm."

"The horse was sedated, but yes, it is dangerous. Thank goodness it seldom happens in nature."

After we give the horses fresh water and food, we leave, locking the door.

"Is Sage coming home for Christmas?" Camellia asks wrapping her shawl around her shoulders.

"Yes, sis, he has a pass." I button my jacket.

"You think you'll go dancing again?"

"Maybe, why?"

"I will invite my new boyfriend over and we can double date." My mouth drops open and I look at her as she winks and chuckles. Then we run to the house to show everyone the pictures on our tablets.

CHAPTER 11
DESPERATE TIMES

"700,000 climate refugees will soon be on the move."

– Michael Kimmel, The New York Times in 2017.

Three million men, women and mostly children die in the waters off Central America. People around the world are stunned over the tragic loss of life. Now almost twelve million devastated, desperate and broken people are without everything including a country. South America has accepted three million, with financial help from Australia. Canada is taking two million with the help of foreign aid from several European countries. South Africa will take one million with help from the more affluent countries in North Africa and China will take 500,000. Russia will take one million. America will take one million. Ireland needs single women or women with up to two children. They will take one thousand. Scotland and Wales will each take one thousand.

The people of Central America will have the choice of where they want to go if that country and state is accepting refugees.

The world leaders believe it will be helpful and make it easier on the refugees if their host countries can give them a good start and feeling of belonging by giving them a small parcel of land in underpopulated areas where they can start their own villages and towns, surrounded by their own people, culture and lifestyle. This will help them to heal faster from their great loss. After they have had some years to settle in, they can spread out if they wish. There is a huge amount of government land in America, so lending the refugees land should not be a problem, except for jealousy by some people.

My family is devastated over the news, and we can see on our tablets the pictures of bodies floating on the surface of the water as they are being carried out to the sea by the giant waves. We want to help, and will send money and blankets, not knowing what more to do but wait.

I have been crying off and on for days.

We are all moping around and finally, I say, "Maybe we'll feel better if we get busy on the cottage, painting and cleaning up. A refugee family could live in the cottage and help us around here. I will make an appointment to have insulation blown in between the walls and attic. Let's make it look nice for a family." That got me going. I need to act to feel better. I want to pick out some cheerful bright paint colors for the rooms, so I go to town to the hardware store. I order a new white-coated metal roof to reflect heat.

Our new project makes me forget about Christmas, but then how can you celebrate when so many people are hurting? We all agree to save the money we would have spent on each other and buy gifts for the refugees when they come. I would rather just skip Christmas this year, but Aunt Essie invites us to have dinner on Christmas with them. So, we accept her invitation. Grams will make and take a pumpkin pie. Mom will make a fresh salad with our garden greens. Camellia and I make Christmas cut-out sugar cookies, frosting each bell, star, tree and camel in bright holiday colors. It is seventy-six degrees on Christmas Day in Rigby, Idaho. We eat outside on a large picnic table in the backyard under a big old elm tree at their small home. Aunt Essie and Uncle Lesley are in their sixties. They come with their youngest son, who is older than me. He used to babysit us. I had a crush on him back then; he was such a handsome boy.

The conversation that day is about the old days and all the fun we had together camping out along the Snake River. The men and boys would fish for freshwater trout and the women would fry the fish. The children would eat it faster than they could catch and cook it. It was so good that the flesh would melt in my mouth, the skin crispy and delicious. Talking about the good times was a way of counting our blessings at a time of hardship for so many. We never mentioned anything that would make us all feel sad, except that I was constantly reminded by Mom about my lack of eye contact.

After dinner and before the pies, we all play cards, tease and laugh until we cry over stories about tangled lines and fly fishing—about trying to get a boat in the river and ending up with the car in the river instead, about catching the smallest fish, biggest fish or ugliest fish in the river and about the time we were chased by a bear and another time by an elk.

Camellia and I help by washing and drying dishes. Then we stuff ourselves with pie and call it a day. It was a real fun-filled time.

Sage is home on leave and we plan on going dancing tomorrow. Camellia asks if she and her new boyfriend can join us. Sage says yes.

On the day following Christmas, Sage picks us up at eight. Camellia looks adorable with her wavy hair filled with a spray of fake cherry blossoms and a pink Asian-style, slim-fit long dress and matching jacket. Her boyfriend, Cannon, is a medical student she met at the hospital. He is tall and well-built, with light brown wavy hair and brown eyes, a nice smile and a great sense of humor. In his relaxed solid brown slacks and a matching V-neck tunic in shades of brown and blue-green, Cannon looks like a model. I wear my forest green jersey knit, slim-fit dress with a matching short-wasted jacket.

Mom answers the door and Kazan barks until he smells Sage, who ruffles his fur. Camellia introduces Cannon to Sage and me. I grab my jacket and we take off, but not before I see Rain's sad look and it brings tears to my eyes. I know how he feels. I go to him and give him a hug; I feel so guilty. I know he wants to share in whatever we are up to. He only wants to be more grown up.

I get in the car and sit next to Sage. He talks with Cannon for a while and I watch him. Sage is so articulate with a natural interest in others, and he's a good listener. I can't understand his interest in me. We tell Cannon about our last date and how cold it turned that night. Tonight, it is in the high sixties and we are not expecting a drastic change. I checked the weather before we left. Camellia and Cannon change the flow and talk about work at the hospital. Sage grabs my hand and squeezes it. We park in the lot in front of the Romance and Dance Hall. Inside, it looks just like it did last year. I wonder if they just leave the Christmas decorations up all the time. I lead the way to a quiet corner with a linen-covered table and four faux leather upholstered chairs. The place is dark, except for the bar area and a large chandelier in the center over the wooden dance floor.

We sit and a waitress brings us a candle in glass and a menu of drinks and snacks. Sage and Cannon order beer, Camellia orders white wine, and I order ginger ale. I've always dreamed of dancing to Latin music, and as a tango starts, I look at Sage and say, "Let's dance." Soon, we are on the floor doing our version. I tell Sage I would like to take Latin dance lessons someday, and he says we can do that as he twirls me around. Camellia and Cannon sit talking. The next dance is slow and mellow. Sage pulls me in close and I notice Camellia and Cannon join us. I put my head on Sage's shoulder, enjoying our closeness. He kisses me on the cheek. I raise my head to look at his face and he kisses me on the lips. A tingling sensation fills my body. I pull away because wanting him scares me, and I put my head back on his shoulder until the music ends. We walk back to the table.

We are joined at the table with Camellia and Cannon, and we eat some peanuts, talk and drink. Then they get up for the next dance. Sage says, "I'm sorry, I've been thinking about kissing your beautiful lips for a year and I couldn't resist."

"Sage, I pulled away because your kisses feel so good and I want it to go on forever. That scares me. My emotions scare me."

"Why, Laurel?"

"It's a new feeling for me, Sage. I don't want to lose control. In time, I'm going to understand this feeling and how to hold onto myself."

"I'm sorry it scares you. Remember, emotional feelings can be enjoyed almost as much by mentally reliving them over again and again. When we are apart, I will enjoy kissing you by imagining the kiss tonight, every night, and I hope you can, too."

Camellia and Cannon return, and he holds her hand for a while. I ask about his future plans.

"I will stay in Rigby until I receive my bachelor's in pre-med, then I'll go to a medical school to become a doctor and study advances in molecular treatments of diseases." Cannon says. He was raised in Provo, Utah, by Mormon parents and a big family of siblings. He has three sisters older than him and three younger brothers. His father is a humanities professor at Brigham Young University.

It is a cool, damp night, and as Sage drives us home, we talk about the refugees. Cannon can see danger ahead because of narrow-minded bigotry among some conservatives. Sage agrees, but we choose helping in any way we can, regardless. I tell them we plan to help a family who wants to work for food and a home.

Before Sage leaves us at our house, he asks me for another date.

"Where do you want to go?"

"I want you to meet my family. We can go out for dinner; do you like Italian?"

"Yes, I do."

"Will Tuesday the twenty-ninth at six work for you? I'll pick you up."

"Let me check." I pull my tablet out of my shoulder strap bag and ask Jo if I have anything planned for the twenty-ninth." She says I don't.

"Okay, Sage, I'll see you then." We kiss goodnight and Sage walks me to my door, then drives off. I enter the house and leave the door unlocked for Camellia, who is still talking to Cannon.

I get ready for bed, and when Camellia comes in we talk about Sage and Cannon as she gets ready for bed, and I'm surprised when she tells me she's known him for a year, but that he just asked her for a date. She asks me how I feel about Sage and I tell her the truth, that I don't have enough experience to understand my feelings. She smiles and seems relaxed and happy. Maybe it is the wine. When I turn out the light she is already asleep.

The following day, I ask dad if he can take me to Idaho Falls in the truck so I can pick up some fixtures for the cottage at Everything for the Home Shop.

"When would you like to go?"

"Whenever you're free, Dad. We need some new light fixtures, a new toilet, a pedestal sink and grab bars for the cottage bathroom."

"I can be ready in an hour."

"Okay, Dad." While I wait, I check on the horses and move them to the corral so they can be outside for a while. Then I go back to the house to tell Rain they are out and ask him to go for a ride with me. He's ready and comes running. Prairie is with him, so I put him on Cassiopeia with me and Rain gets on Skywalker and we ride along the canal, galloping along the worn trail, enjoying the cool day, until I have to get back. Rain says he will rub down both horses and Prairie will help. I tell them to keep an eye on all the horses in the corral because of wild animals.

Dad drives the truck into the driveway and we leave for the city. We talk about the time it could take just to record and process all the Central Americans. I tell him that I worry about them waiting so long.

"It's easy to think too much about the things we have no control over, and that is almost everything in life," he says, "Let it go."

"You're right, Dad, but I'm not able to control my mind yet."

We arrive at Everything for the Home Shop where the old Home Depot used to be.

Dad says, "I'll drop you off; I have an errand to run. I'll pick you up in forty-five."

"Okay, Dad, see you later."

As I walk to the storefront, it looks crowded for a Monday. I start paying attention when I see the signs people are carrying as they picket and I try to get past them. When a man tries to stop, me I smash his foot with the heel of my boot, then I turn toward another man who is also trying to stop me and I hit him with a punch he wasn't expecting. The manager opens the door for me and the men back away as I back up into the store, breathing heavily. As I walk to the bath remodeling section, I feel the gun in the back of my pants for security. I focus on the selections, and pick out a toilet and pedestal sink. I walk up and down the aisles looking for a salesperson. I ask a woman with a little girl why there are so many people picketing outside the store today.

"I think there's going to be trouble in the store," she says.

"What started this?" I ask.

"It's about an ad this store ran in the Sunday paper. A journalist wrote an article about the 50,000 refugees that will be competing with us for food and jobs in Idaho. The owners of this store are helping the refugees. They were interviewed in the media as saying the refugees would be good for Idaho. People around town didn't like their answers. I think this is the beginning of an even greater division between the ultra-conservative and the more liberal citizens in Idaho."

I ask, "Do you think the war is starting here in this store?"

She reaches down, picks up her daughter and places her on the seat in the shopping cart.

"The men tried to stop me from entering, but the manager came out and held the door open for us," the woman says. "The store owners and operators are in favor of the refugees—more business. This store may now be a target and how can they keep it all outside?" She then turns and pushes her daughter toward the robot. I follow, still looking for help.

I notice no one is smiling. People are milling around mumbling to one another. I find a young man to help me in bath remodeling, his nametag says "Todd." He types up the order for the sink, toilet, grab bars and a new faucet set for the sink and new shower. Then he walks over to the lighting department with me and adds the light fixtures with ceiling fans. Everything can be delivered on Saturday, January 17. Walking to the robot to pay for my purchase, I suddenly stop in my tracks. A fistfight is in progress between a few men, and the store's security guard has his gun pointed at the men while telling them to leave the store. A short, stocky man with a face full of whiskers drops a gun hidden in his sleeve into his right hand and points the gun at the security guard. I have my gun out fast to support the guard. When "Whiskers" realizes one of us will get him, he runs out the door along with two other men.

Everyone looks at me laying on the floor, where I dropped as soon as I thought I might have to shoot, in case someone else in the crowd had a gun. It all happened so fast. I get up and notice Dad standing at the robot, and talking with the guard. I get to my dad while hearing the sound of sirens outside the store. Suddenly, there are cops everywhere.

The police officers take my name and address and I am allowed to leave with my father. In the truck, I am finally struck by what just happened and I start shaking.

"How would it feel if you laid down, honey? You could put your head in my lap."

"I don't think it would help, Dad. I've never been so close to shooting a person before. I'll be okay."

"Think about taking your gun with you whenever you leave home, you did the right thing and may have saved a life."

"I will, Dad."

I seldom read the local news, and a change in my habits is overdue. I need to start paying more attention to what is going on around me, I'm never good at watching people and I can't read their body language, but I'm usually very visual when it comes to my environment. The first thing I notice when I stop at the drugstore later in the day are a few people wearing t-shirts that say, "No Jobs in Idaho for Refugees." I can foresee the problems, especially if the movement gets too big.

The following day, I meet Sage at 5:30. As he drives, I tell him about the incident at the shopping center and the t-shirts at the drugstore.

"I've also seen a few of those t-shirts. Sorry you had to point your gun at someone, but I'm relieved that you weren't hurt, honey."

"Dad wants me to carry a gun whenever I leave home, but I don't know if I want to go that far."

"Maybe you should listen to your dad."

"I'm surprised. I don't know why, but I would have thought you wouldn't want me to carry a gun."

"You must be trained in how to shoot and handle a gun, or your dad would never suggest it."

"I am, he has taught me very well."

"Stay safe, you know how gun-crazy people are in this country. Protect yourself."

"Do you carry a gun, Sage?"

"I never talk about it. It's best if no one knows if you do or don't. You're safer that way. Yes, I do, Laurel, but never tell anyone."

We meet Sage's parents at a small, cozy Italian restaurant named Angelo's. Through the window, I see his family seated at a big round table.

It is a cool windy day, so we hurry inside. Sage introduces me to his stepfather Jay, a big, friendly man with curly hair that is turning gray. I greet everyone else. The waiter seats us at the round table. Dara is on one side of me and Sage on the other, and then his mother, brother and father. After we order, I start a conversation with Jay about what he does in the building trade. I am impressed, because he is a decorative plasterer. It's almost a lost art, plastering walls and ceilings. I ask if he is teaching his trade, and he says he has a few students interested in following him. Most are not interested because it's hard work and you have to be strong and not afraid of heights.

Dara is eighteen, tall and brown-eyed with wavy chestnut hair and lots of freckles sprinkled over her nose. She looks like her brother, Ash. She is taking online courses in software design while going to Idaho Falls Community College a few days a week for classes in liberal arts. She seems nice to be around, she's very positive and likes to lead. Ash, with the same coloring and freckles, is quieter, more thoughtful and his eyes are the dark gray of ash. He is fourteen and wants to be a game designer. Ash is online- and home-schooled by Sage and Dara.

When the food arrives, we jump in and its delicious. Sage offers me wine.

"No thanks, I've never developed a taste for wine. I would like ginger ale if they have any, or iced tea will be fine," I say. Lily looks very pretty and I compliment her on her beautiful complexion.

"My beauty cream is Vaseline, just plain old petroleum jelly," she says.

"Well, it really works on you."

"Thanks," she replies.

Between bites, she asks me about my life and family. I find out she was born in Sweden and came to America as a young woman. She met Sage's father who he is named after, in Coeur d'Alene, Idaho where they fell in love and married. Sage was a young boy when his dad died.

A lull in the conversation follows, then Ash asks about Rain. I tell him he is fine, "He seems to really enjoy your company and the classes in Tai Chi." We talk about the immigrants, Lily is opposed to them living in Idaho.

"They won't be living near you, Mom, you may never see them," Sage says, Dara adds her endorsement of the refugees. She disagrees with her mom. I keep quiet for once. It is getting late and we are stuffed. I thank everyone for a wonderful afternoon, and I want to invite them all to my house, but I have to check with mom and Grams for a good day for a dinner party.

Sage drives me home and holds me close. "I want to spend time with you," he says, "I won't see you again for a year." We snuggle in the car when he stops.

"We can see a lot of each other while you're home, Sage. I have little planned for the next two months and I have no boyfriends."

He pulls up to the driveway and parks near the gate under the trees, he looks in my eyes and whispers, "I just want to hang on to you for a little while," and he kisses me by gently brushing his lips across mine. We are barely touching every feature on each other's face and neck with our lips. It is electrically charging, before it goes too far, I say, "Thanks for giving me the opportunity to meet your parents. Goodnight, Sage."

I walk the driveway to the house. I need the walk.

The following day the local news station mentions the fight and incident at the Everything for the Home Shop in Idaho Falls. The man who aimed his gun at the guard is being held in the local jail. I think I may have made an enemy for life. Groups are forming on each side of the issue, and those against the refugees are picketing businesses, trying to keep the public from shopping in stores that are in support of the refugees.

Sage buzzes me on my tablet's Face-on and asks if I am upset with him over last night.

"No," I reply. "I just felt like it was time to stop, things are moving pretty fast."

"I have the self-control to stop, sweetheart."

"Sorry, I don't know if I do, and I don't know you that well yet."

"I know you don't, but I want you to try and trust me. Will you see me tomorrow?"

"Yes, come over and we'll go horseback riding, the weather will be cool, but sunny. A good day for a picnic. Invite Ash, he and Rain can have some fun. Come at eleven if that works for you. If Dara is free, she should also come, Sage."

Mom hears my side of the conversation. I am in the kitchen, and as I fill a glass of water Mom looks at me, smiling

"What's Sage like?" she asks, as she cleans the sink.

"He's real, he never pretends, intelligent with a quick mind, aggressive, kind, affectionate, modest and a good listener, but those are just words. I don't know him very well."

I drink some water and continue, "We are interested in many of the same things, and I like him. I'm not sure about his mother, but I like the rest of his family." Mom is now making a couple of sandwiches and she looks up and asks, "What about his mother?"

"I'm not very good at reading people, she seems most attached to Sage, understandably, but I get the feeling no one would be good enough for him in her mind."

"Do you think she has control over him?"

"No, Mom. She's just overprotective. I'd like to have his family over to meet you and see what you think, Mom."

"Sure, we can do that before his leave is up."

"Sage returns to Libya on January 18, we'll have to make it a lunch. I think Lily works nights. I'll find out from Dara if she comes tomorrow."

"Your romance must be getting serious." Mom looks serious herself as she waits for an answer.

"I don't know how I should feel about him, this is new to me."

"It's hard for you to show affection," Mom says, "Especially with strangers."

"We can't get too serious anyway with dates a few weeks out of a year. He wants to work on the moon! I don't see how it will work out, Mom. I'm definitely not going to the moon. But I like spending time with him while he is home."

CHAPTER 12
SAGE LEAVES

"The earth we knew as home will become a lifeless desert like the planet Mars, if we continue on as we have."

– Bill McKibben

January sneaks up on us without snow. During the sunlit days, it's in the fifties, dropping down into the thirties at night, cool enough for the winter fruit trees. We keep the roots heavily mulched just in case it turns colder. Even without heat, the house is very comfortable. Our cisterns are full of water again. We have stockpiled food and we're getting a great supply of fresh greens from the garden. We are truly blessed, and I feel great knowing we have a good start for survival. I feel like I should order bolts of lightweight white cotton fabric, buying lots of sunblock for the future and be doing more for the refugees. In my free time, I work on the cottage, and the family helps. We have ordered a new white-coated metal roof and it will be installed next month.

Idaho will receive approximately 50,000 Central Americans. Meetings are arranged with members of the community, and Dad is asked to be among them. He is accepted because he is well known as an engineer, military man and community organizer in the state. He will meet with officials of the Idaho Department of Lands. They supervise endowment state lands that need to produce revenue to support schools. The meetings will be held at the capital in Boise. Members will discuss the merits of loaning some land in southeastern Idaho for the benefit of the refugees and the state.

Today, Sage brings his brother and sister along for some fun. Camellia and mom have met Dara. She has let her hair down today, and it is shoulder length. She and Ash would be twins if they were the same age. Rain and Ash run off to see something on Rain's tablet. We sit in the family room on leather recliners around a large round table in the middle of the room. We insist people take off their shoes for this room's floors of polished earth, it is cool and feels good underfoot. Sage asks me about the floor.

"As you can tell, it's as hard as clay tile, but looks and feels like leather," I reply. "The Earth is full of electrons and they flow into everything and help keep you relaxed, it's healthier and easy to keep up."

"How do you clean dirt?" He chuckles.

"Vacuum up the dust and once in a while spray with a film of water and oil then sponge mop dry. How does that sound?"

"Easy, like you said, Laurel."

Grams hears our conversation and adds, "When I was a girl we lived in a house with dirt floors, they were as hard as concrete and not as lovely as these." She looks at Sage and says, "I know what you're thinking. I wasn't living in a cave, it was a big, old farmhouse."

Sage laughs, saying, "Well, most nights I sleep in a tent on a dirt floor in Libya."

"Why are you there? We aren't at war with them, are we, son?"

"Almost, Grams, we are there to protect our embassy."

"I don't understand why we need embassies around the world," she says. "We've been involved in one war after another, embassies don't seem to help."

"Our president believes that if we pull out of these countries, the fighting and deaths will be much worse, Grams."

"I will pray for you, Sage."

"Thank you, Grams."

Mom, dressed in a pale blue cotton dress comes in and asks, "Are you hungry?" We all say yes. "Come and get some food then," she says and turns toward the dining room.

As we sit, Dara speaks up, "This house is so unusual. I just love it."

"Thank you, Dara. We also love it and thank everyone for all their hard work," Mom says as she dips the dark lentil soup into our pottery bowls. We then pass around a tray of veggie sandwiches on homemade rustic blue cornmeal and buckwheat bread. Dara comments on the great sandwiches of sliced tomatoes, goat cheese, avocados grown in the greenhouse hall, dill pickles, ranch dressing, and lettuce.

"I hope everyone likes them," Dad says as he joins us.

Everyone says hi to him as Mom fill his soup bowl.

"We have coffee, tea or hot chocolate," Grams says. "Give me your orders."

Prairie asks, "Daddy, can we ride horses today?"

"Sounds fun to me, son. Don't ride too fast after eating. Some people find it's a good way to stay slim, but you are fine the way you are."

Prairie just looks at Dad for a while, but Ash starts to chuckle and Prairie says, "I get it." Then everyone laughs and the talk turns to Libya, with Dad and Sage comparing experiences.

Then Dad looks at Sage and says, "I leave tomorrow for Boise and will be gone for a few days, so I might miss you leaving for Libya. I'll just say it now. Take care, Sage. Be safe and come home soon."

"Thank you, sir. I hope your meetings in Boise proves successful. Mom and Grams, thank you for a great lunch."

"Rain," I ask, "Take Sage and you guys get the horses ready while Camellia and I clean up."

"I would like to help," Dara says.

Camellia leaves with Rain. I wash this time and Dara dries. Everyone has left the kitchen except the two of us.

"What do you think, Dara?" I ask as she starts helping.

"I like your county life," she says, picking up a plate and smiling. She seems very softhearted and kind.

"How are your classes going?" I ask as she dries the plate.

"Great. I'm learning so much about creating and designing, using a smart computer and special 3D software." she says, removing another plate from the rinse water to dry.

"I know what you mean. I use a smart computer and 3D software to create my Earthship designs." I say, scrubbing a bowl in the soapy water.

Then she tells me a little bit about what she is doing with 3D software and how much it has helped her to have more confidence in her abilities. Especially when people praise her for her inventiveness. She dries several items to catch up.

The horses are ready, snorting and prancing with eagerness. Sage and I will sit out the first ride and go for a walk while they ride off.

Sage and I walk from the back of our property to the front and then on to the sidewalk that runs along the road in front of our house. We enjoy the chilly sunny day. The road is lined with trees that have all lost their leaves.

As we walk I tell Sage, “I used to ride my bike down the middle of this road.” I’m looking up at the arch of limbs formed by the trees. “In the summer, it’s like riding through a beautiful cool tunnel. See the park across the street? That’s where I spent many evenings after sneaking out of my bedroom window.”

“What did you do in the park at night?” he asks.

“Laid on the roots of trees and listened to their songs.” Sage laughs and squeezes me.

“It sounds like you spent a lot of time growing up right here.”

“I lived so near to and loved my Grandma Della. She always took time out for me and taught me how to embroider, crochet, knit and bake. This place was a second home for me, I feel something of my grandma remains in this place.”

“Is it because of Mormon teaching that you believe we go on?”

“No. Well that’s where I got my feet wet, but I don’t think so. I was a spiritual person at an early age. I meant more of my grandma’s consciousness is part of the total consciousness of Earth. James Lovelock, an early writer on climate change, believed Earth’s geosphere and biosphere are an integrated entity—a living consciousness he named Gaia. Human minds may be drops in that consciousness. What do you think?”

“I didn’t have a religious upbringing,” he mentions as we walk, “I’ve given little thought to the depth of life. I have thought about free will and read books on the latest findings in brain research. I no longer believe in free will.”

“I don’t either, Sage, and I don’t understand time.”

He stops and hugs me. It feels so good and he smells so good. Why have I always resisted being hugged by others but not by him? We walk on past more houses built in the 19450s.

“They are so old I’m surprised they haven’t been torn down,” Sage comments. “I guess people like their charm.” We stand for a moment to study them. “Not much demand for land like this, anyway.”

“Do people still live in them?” Sage asks, pointing at houses.

"Yes, but they have probably been updated inside."

We turn back, holding hands, and he starts talking about his life as a child alone with his mom after his dad died. His mom had such a hard time making enough money to support them after his death. He remembers times of hunger in Coeur d'Alene. Then, after they moved to Idaho Falls, there was more work for his Mom working as a barmaid and they were okay. He was going to school while his mom slept because she worked nights. She woke in the afternoon and made him a meal and they talked while eating dinner. Then, she got dressed and went to work. He was left alone many nights. She wasn't the same. Something died in her when his dad died.

We stop, and I hug him, "I'm sorry you had to go through that, Sage." We tenderly kiss and walk on as he says, "It's just life and it is different for everyone." When we are back at the canal the kids are waiting for us.

"Did you have fun?" I ask them.

"Yeah!" everyone yells as they climb off and jump down. They are laughing and talking about each horse and the wonderful feeling of riding. Sage and I take Lyra and Skywalker. They are the strongest and still seem full of energy. Sage lifts me up on Skywalker, then he hops up on Lyra and we ride off while the kids take the horses in their care to the barn.

We ride at a slow pace so we can talk and Sage asks what my plans are for the new year.

"I will be starting my third Earthship in the spring if the weather works for us. It will be built near Boise. The owners are well off, so it should be fun designing something bigger with interior gardens. I might also get a chance to go to some of the meetings at the capitol regarding the refugees' relocation. And I still have to keep up my studies, take classes and pass tests to keep my licenses up to date.

"Look, Sage, across the canal, I think that's the same gray wolf Camellia and I saw a couple of weeks ago," I bring Skywalker to a stop.

"I see it. Wish we had field glasses," he says, pulling back on the reins.

"Yes, I forgot them again. Isn't he beautiful, Sage?"

"And bold," he answers as the big wolf gazes at us with his golden eyes, standing about thirty feet away. Our horses are nervous, shuffling and whimpering, wanting to move away. As we gallop off, the wolf turns and walks away. We race to the barn and Sage wins. We laugh as he helps me down.

In the barn, Lyra and Skywalker whiny hello to their family, then we rub them down and brush them, fill their water pails, and give them feed.

Sage grabs me and gently pushes me toward the wall of the barn. As he presses against my body, his arms, one on each side of my shoulders, pins me down. I start to struggle until he kisses me hard and deep, then gentle and soft so I can kiss him back.

He whispers, "Laurel, I want you so much."

"Sage, I'm also infatuated with you, but I don't see where this is going."

"Don't say that, this feeling I have for you is not infatuation, I know what that's like. There can be a future for us." He holds me and tenderly kisses me again and again. We both jump when we hear a scraping sound outside of the barn.

"Hello, is someone out there?" Sage yells, and waits for a response.

He calls out again, nothing. He is careful, not knowing if it is the wolf, Kazan or the boys. He pulls out the gun he has concealed in the back of his pants and checks it. He gently pushes me aside, unlocks the door and slowly opens it. I hand him a flashlight and he waves it back and forth near and far. Nothing. He looks at the ground with the light and sees paw prints, but we will have to compare them with Kazan's prints. As we lock up the barn, we check on the chicken coop and the goats; they seem fine. Then I remember to tell Sage that Camellia and I also saw a large female black bear near the canal, but further away from our house. We even have pictures of it.

"The wolf and bear may be hungry and coming in closer for food," he says.

"I think you're right. The forest fires two years ago killed a lot of animals, destroying food they depend on."

"I should go home," Sage says, "But check the prints against Kazan's and tell folks around you spotted a wolf. They are dangerous."

We walk back to the house and he keeps his gun out until we are at the door, then he conceals the gun again.

Inside the greenhouse, the air is rich with the aroma of mulch, and the fruit trees are doing well. Sage kisses me goodnight, then we walk into the family room where mom and dad are curled up together in an oversized recliner reading, and the kids are playing a hologram board game on the table. Grams is knitting in another chair while listening to the kids, she has a smile on her face. The kids are having so much fun, giggling and talking about the game.

Everyone looks up with a smile on their faces as we enter the room.

"You might not have noticed how much you've been missed," dad says. Everyone laughs. "Eventually, you will come up with a good story about where you have been." Dad is smiling.

"You don't have to wait for the story—we have it," I say. "We were riding along and spotted a huge gray wolf with gold eyes who looked at us for some time. The horses were eager to run away with us, so we let them. Later, at the barn while cleaning up, feeding the horses and spending time on a few kisses, we heard scraping against the door of the barn. Sage yelled out in case it was one of you. No answer, so we looked around with a flashlight. We found nothing amiss except for some paw prints."

"Sage, Laurel is a great story-teller." Dad says.

"Yes, Laurel's right, Daddy," Camellia says. "We saw a wolf not more than forty feet from us, the same day we saw a big black bear. We have pictures."

"You were gone when we took the pictures and we never showed them to you," I reply.

"Well, that makes your story more believable," Dad says, chuckling. "Now, we have some dangerous work to do. Catching wolves and moving them farther north calls for some smart people, and I know who to call to help us with this problem. In the meantime, no one is to be outside alone without backup after sunset."

"Good advice, sir," Sage said, as Grams gives Dara some cookies for the family in a paper bag. Dad shakes their hands and Mom praises their manners and maturity.

"You are always welcome," Mom says.

I hug them, thank them for coming and walk them to the door.

I ask Dara, "What day is your mom free from her job at Idaho Potato?"

"She is off on Saturday and Sundays."

"Thank you. Goodnight."

They leave, and I wait until I hear the car pull away.

One morning, I walk to the kitchen in my flannel robe to get some coffee. Grams, always an early riser because of the habits of farm life, has made coffee. I give her a smile, my silent thanks, and walk to the greenhouse to look outside. The day is chilly with clouds. I take a sip of my coffee and then ask Jo about the weather forecast as I open my tablet.

"No sunshine today. Overcast and fifty-four degrees, dropping to forty-six degrees tonight."

"Where are the refugees, Jo?"

"Most are on trains or ships traveling to their destinations."

"When they get there, how will they be accommodated?"

"Countries are finding shelter for them in vacant warehouses, homeless shelters and church basements. They are getting mattresses and bedding from charities and clothes and baby supplies from private donors. It is the largest challenge most countries have ever faced. The Europeans have already been through a similar crisis when thousands of refugees left war-torn countries in the Middle East in the years 2015 and 2016."

"How did that work out, Jo?"

"Sweden had an open-door policy and received many more people than they had anticipated, but they handled everything in a very humane way. It hasn't worked very well. There was a terrible backlash. Greece and Germany ended up taking more than they wanted and they have had problems with groups who were against taking them. They couldn't employ so many people. Canada's conservative government originally would take 10,000 over four years, but they delayed by making them jump through a lot of hoops to prove themselves. Some refugees have left Germany. Overall, they tried, but so many couldn't find employment. These countries were inundated and couldn't handle the vast numbers of immigrants or the waves that never seemed to end. But the Europeans tried for a long time, finally turning them back."

"I want it to work for us because we can help each other," I say more to myself.

"Yes," Jo answers. I swallow the rest of my coffee and go back for a second cup. Dad is up and has already been outside.

"What did you find out about the paw print?" I ask dad when he enters the kitchen.

"It is not the print of a domestic dog; it resembles that of a wolf. I guess we will use you and your sister as bait and catch these guys before they eat all our animals. Grams told me a couple of chickens are missing, more likely eaten."

"Oh, no," I realized he was joking about using us for bait. "What should we do with the chickens until they're caught?"

"Your Grandpa Campbell once told me it was better to lose a chicken than a goat and it costs less. We could set some traps, but we don't know how many wolves are in this pack."

"Dad, traps are painful, maybe we could put out a bag of dog food for them and they would fill themselves up with that," I suggested.

"That's an idea, that may not work. We can try. I'm calling the parks department now," Dad said.

Dad leaves and I pour a second cup of coffee and walk back to my bedroom to get dressed. Camellia is just getting dressed to go to work at the hospital. "Camellia, do you want to use the bathroom first? I can wait."

"Yes, please, sis. I overslept this morning."

I lie back on my bed and look at the climate news on my tablet. An article about Central America gets my attention. After I read the article, I think about what I have been reading for several years about Central America. I find what happened to this nation strange, because it was always hard for climatologists to see how tens of millions of its people could survive for long in such marginal lands. They have often had food shortages due to a lack of water to grow anything, leaving hundreds of thousands dependent on food and water aid for several months at a time. We thought these Americans would be among the first to leave their lands. The immigrants would leave behind ghost towns, dusty ruins in lands that could no longer support them. How ironic that the land was destroyed by water?

I think about luck and fate. Why is it some people have to suffer so much over and over and others seem to be blessed? What a strange existence we have, and we know nothing about the big questions. Camellia interrupts my deep thinking by throwing a clean towel at me.

"What are you doing, sis...daydreaming?"

"Thinking."

"About Sage?"

"No. I was thinking about Central American refugees, after reading an article in the news today on my tablet."

"I'll have to take a look at it during lunch, if it's interesting," she says as she dries her dark hair.

"I think it is."

I turn on the shower, put on my shower cap, and step into the flowing water. After a while, I turn it off and lather up, then turn the water back on for a rinse. I feel better. I get dressed and text Sage.

> Hi Sage, Mom said Saturday or Sunday would be fine for your parents to come over for dinner at 6:00. Let me know which day is best for you and warn them that this casual invitation doesn't mean we plan to ever marry.
> Love,
> Laurel

CHAPTER 13

THE ANIMAL SHELTER

"Unstable weather produces killer heat waves and massive floods"

–James Hansen

I call the local food bank to see how they are doing. I want to know if they are getting enough food for all those in need and what the numbers of people needing help are compared with those of the past year. The manager tells me the food bank is in crisis because so many people are out of work and donations are down. I ask how we can help. They are considering doing a food drive, but can't afford to run many ads online. I tell them I will bring some fresh organic food and help them with ads online. They will give me an ad package.

Gram is working in the kitchen, filling a bowl to soak some beans.

"Do you know where Mom is?"

"She's in the office tutoring the boys."

"Has Dad taken off for Boise?"

"Yes, he left."

"Thanks, Grams." I go back to my room. Camellia has left. I put on my gardening clothes so I can harvest some vegetables to take to the food bank. I open the flap to the first greenhouse and look at what is left. I feel disappointed that I haven't thought ahead about the food bank and planted more.

I get down on my knees and start with the leeks, onions, Russet potatoes, winter squash, kale, collard greens and spinach. I get up, go to the corner near the door, and get the cart. I pull it along as I pick up the produce in piles on the ground. I look back. I have left us about a third, but we still have the latest planting in the second greenhouse. I sort the veggies and put them in paper bags. I will add some goat cheese. I shake off my clothes and leave the bags piled up on the bench in the garage and go inside. Kazan meets me at the door, wanting out. I pet him and hug him and open the door. He will be all right during the day.

I change clothes and comb my hair and call for a car to take two people to the area food bank and animal shelter in Rigby. The driverless car arrives twenty minutes later. I am able to get all the bags in the car because I ask for a car for two. After I drop off the bags at the food bank, I do something I hate. I go to the animal shelter to see what is going on, despite knowing how sad it will make me feel. The office is empty, but I can hear the background noise of animals. As I wait, I send Grams a message, remembering I had left without telling anyone. I am so absentminded. Finally, a young, dark-haired woman comes in the room and says hello. I tell her I came in to see how they are doing, if they are able to take care of the animals coming in.

She thanks me for asking. "We aren't getting too many strays now," she says. "The fires we had killed some feral animals and I think many are dying from the lack of food and or water, except some who have learned how to live in the cities and eat from garbage cans."

"Are most of your animals healthy?"

"Yes, we give them a thorough checkup except for MRIs or CAT scans. They are so expensive. They get all their shots and are spayed or neutered."

"Show me around."

"Glad to. Just follow me." She shows me the cats. They make me feel so terribly sad and powerless.

"I can take two cats that you think will get along with each other, maybe a male and a female."

"I'll show you," she says as we walk through a door.

She shows me a beautiful older shorthair Siamese.

"How old is the Siamese?"

"Chia is a very gentle, well-mannered female, age four. She knows her name."

"Is she trained to use a box?"

"Our cats are all litter-trained."

"I would like to give her a home. We have a dog, part shepherd and chow, but he is very gentle and was a stray."

"I'll have Jackie get her ready for you. Let me show you a nice male. His name is Tiger and he is very energetic and loves people. He is my favorite, but I think it's time he has a home. She held him out for me and he came right to me. He was so adorable and I knew we were meant for one-another.

I watch him for some time and then leave to look at other cats. I spend over an hour and want to take them all, and I cry when I leave with Chia and two-year-old Tiger. I love his personality. I give her a donation, tuck their papers into my bag and carry two boxes into the car. I ask the car to stop at Pet Co, where I pick up some cat supplies.

The car stops in front of my house and I am almost afraid to get out because I didn't ask for permission to add two cats to our crew. Why do I always do stuff without asking? I am afraid they will say no. I carry them into the greenhouse and think, *oh no, they will think the greenhouse is their bathroom.* I take them to the laundry room and set up their litter boxes—Chia's box in the bathroom near the toilet and Tiger's in the laundry room. The plan is to leave each cat in the room with their litter so they will get used to the location of their boxes. After spending time with each cat, I put food and water with them and leave to break the news.

It is almost dinnertime and I help Grams and mom get dinner on the table. Grams made navy bean and potato stew, it smells so good and I am starving because I forgot about lunch. Mom made a green salad. I set the table and put condiments out with a pitcher of iced tea. Then Mom buzzes everyone to come to dinner.

I sit, then Prairie comes, bringing his cushion to raise him up on his chair. Rain comes in, sweating, I look at him and ask, "Have you been running?"

"Yes, I was racing Kazan. He won."

"I bet you're hungry."

Camellia comes in looking tired. She plops down and says, "I'm hungry, I didn't have much for lunch today."

Kazan comes and waits at the table. I tell Rain he wants a treat for winning the race

"Let's not start that. No animals get fed at the table," Mom says, giving me a stern look.

"Mom, it's a joke," I say.

"Rain, did you teach Kazan to race?" Sis raises her head off the table as she asks him.

"It wasn't hard to teach him—he likes to run," Rain says.

Everyone is now sitting down. "I have news," I say. "First, I found out the food bank is in trouble, a lot more folks need food and there are few donations. So, I harvested about two-thirds of the food in greenhouse one, added some goat cheese, bagged up everything and delivered it to the store today. I talked them into doing a food drive that I'll help with."

"Sounds like you've been busy," Camellia says.

"You don't know the half of it yet. I went to the animal shelter to see how they were making out, most feral animals have died due to the fires, so they haven't been getting as many strays as they used to. I gave them a donation and brought home a couple of four-legged creatures who really need a home and are easy to care for." That gets everyone's attention.

"Chia is a four-year-old Siamese with a lovely personality and no claws. She is getting used to her litter box in the back-hall bathroom. Tiger is a two-year-old orange Tabby, a live wire who you will love, he's in the laundry room getting used to his litter box."

Mom says to Grams, "Surprised?"

Grams smiles and says, "No, this is her nature."

"You should have asked me, Laurel. It's my house also." Mom isn't happy.

"You are right, Mom. I can't help myself, I'm sorry." I start to leave the table and I hear, "I just hope they don't gang up on Kazan and kill him." Camellia forgets her mouth is full of stew.

"That's a pleasant site," Mom says, as the food runs down her chin while Rain and Prairie are laughing.

"Just one thing," Mom yells. "Remember you are responsible for them."

After they eat dinner and clean up, I take the kids to meet Chia, she is a soft, shorthaired light tan with black-tipped ears and face and beautiful blue-green eyes. Everyone holds her and she doesn't mind. Then they meet Tiger. He talks to everyone and climbs over all of us, purring like an engine. I am right, we all love him, but Camellia is most attracted to Chia.

Saturday is chilly, in the low forties, but the sun is shining, a pleasant day for going for a horse ride. I think about Dad, he is returning today, before he takes off again for a couple of days.

I start the day as usual with coffee, then make an appointment for a haircut and check the news feeds on my tablet. This winter's huge El Niño could be the event of the century, bringing higher, warmer seas, huge storms over the West Coast, tornadoes and high winds to the west, and major flooding in the deep south and on the East Coast. There is dire news for birds now that spring comes three weeks earlier. The birds arrive at breeding grounds to find that plant resources are already gone. Wind gusts of more than ninety miles per hour are reported at the Gila Bend Air Force Artillery field in Arizona. There are also methane outbreaks over large areas of Northern Europe after a five-degree warming of the shallow waters. I close my tablet and get ready for bed.

Another morning, another cup of coffee. I check on the animals and lead the horses to their corral so they can expend some energy. I let the goats and chickens out, then I go back inside and let Chia and Tiger out of their rooms, clean their litter boxes and freshen food and water. Tiger climbs up on my shoulder and watches me. As I open drawers looking for some nail clippers, he has to investigate every drawer. I try to clip his nails, but he thinks I'm playing with him, so I have to wrap him tight in a towel to get the job done. I let him go and he runs away.

I am feeling hungry, so I head in for breakfast. Mom, Grams and Camellia sit at the dining table eating eggs and toast. I say good morning, put some rustic bread in the toaster, and get the honey and goat cheese ready. I pour another cup of coffee and sit across from Mom.

"Camellia, you don't have to work today, do you?"

"No." She looks up at me from the table. "I feel like a nap later on."

"I set the cats free for a while so they can explore."

"You should have introduced them to Kazan first, he doesn't know they belong here now."

"You're right; I never thought about it. Mom, what's up with you and Grams? You're quiet."

"Tell your daughters, Senna."

"It may be nothing, Mom. I don't want to worry them when we don't know anything.'

Camellia and I are now so scared we are frozen. All the color has drained from sis's face and I'm quite sure mine is the same.

"I found a lump in my breast." Her expression seems normal.

"How long have you had the lump and how large is it?" I ask while

Camellia gets up and kisses her.

"I just noticed it when it started throbbing. It's about the size of a quarter." She is numb to the situation.

Camellia pulls at Mom, "Let me see it, I'm a nurse." With her arm around Mom, they walk to the bathroom.

"Have you seen the lump, Grams?" I ask.

"It's hard to see on the surface. You have to feel for it, and it's deep"

"Did Mom mention when she last had a mammogram?"

"She thinks maybe five years." Gram's eyes fill with tears and she grabs her hankie and dabs at her blue eyes.

"Breast cancer is curable today, Grams. They shoot the lump with a manipulated virus to destroy the lump and build up her immune system to kill any other cancer that might be in her body. Try not to worry; she will be fine."

But I feel very sad for Mom that she has to go through the process. I also feel terrible about surprising Mom with the cats, no wonder she was in a bad mood. She will feel better when Dad gets home.

Camellia and Mom come back. Sis hugs her and asks if she wants a warm-up on her coffee. She says no, she wants to get dressed. I give her a hug and say, "You will be fine, Mom."

Camellia and I sit back down. I wonder why I am so hungry, then remember I forgot to eat. The toast is still in the toaster. I flick it down again, wait a few moments, pop it up and take it to the table.

"What do you think?" I ask Camellia as I spread butter, honey and cheese on my toast.

"It is large but she should be okay. I will find a good doctor Monday, make an appointment and go with her."

"Thank you, sis."

"Oh no, Kazan!" I see Camellia's face and turn around. Kazan has Tiger in his mouth. I gently remove him from his mouth and hold him, trying to show Kazan that he is mine. Tiger just wants to run but I hold onto him and pet him and then pet Kazan. I let Kazan lick my hand as Tiger watches, then I let Kazan lick Tiger's paw. Tiger hisses and Kazan barks, then leaves us. I let Tiger go. Camellia is watching the whole thing. "Do you think they will get along, Laurel?

"Yes, they will."

"Are you still dating Cannon?" I ask as I get up and clear off the table.

"We haven't had another date, we are both too busy and tired after work, but we sometimes have lunch together." She grabs her cup and places it in the sink. "See you later," she says as she walks down the hall.

I guess Grams left when I was dealing with Tiger. I wash the dishes, clean up the table and kitchen and then go to my room to dress.

Dad's taxi stops in front while I am adding some strawberry plants to the greenhouse garden. I greet Dad at the front door and give him a hug.

"I'm wondering if everything is okay here at home," Dad asks. To be truthful, I have to tell him not everything is. He pulls a little away from me, holding my two hands and trying to look in my eyes. "I believe what you're talking about is serious," he says, letting my hands drop.

"When you talk to Mom, then you can ask her more. How was your trip?

"Eventually I'll tell you all about the trip. Now I'll go talk to your mother."

I finish planting the strawberries and clean up the boxes, then carry them to the trash in the garage. Rain is filling Kazan's kibble bowl and water bowl.

"Where have you been this morning?" I ask. "I missed you at breakfast."

"Kazan and I were looking for the wolves and we found some of their prints near the goat pellets we put out. We thought we could find their den, but we lost their tracks."

"Did you let anyone know you were going?"

"No, we were up early."

I look at him, "Rain what you did was dangerous. The wolves could have killed you and we wouldn't have even known what happened to you. Never, never leave the house without telling one of us."

"I had my gun with me."

"I'm sure you did, but being alone with one gun would not have saved you. A lesson for you is to study wolves on your tablet." I follow him into the kitchen, where he gets down his boxed cereal and a bowl. "Where is your brother? Did he follow you?"

"I didn't see him, he was still asleep when I left the house."

A knowing chill runs through my body as I run to his room and find it empty. I grab my tablet and ask Jo to find Prairie with the code of his implant. She says, "He is 2.4 miles from home. This is the location map."

The map shows our house, the cottage, the canal and a blue dot in the canal. That blue dot is Prairie, and he isn't moving.

CHAPTER 14
PRAIRIE

"Bone dry conditions, powerful winds, the death of a million trees."

– Park Williams

"Please send someone! Help me!" I yell after hitting the call button on my tablet.

"Grams, I'm going after Prairie. He's in the canal. I'm taking a horse, but I need help."

In the barn, I throw a saddle over a blanket on Cassiopeia and grab a length of rope. I use the step-up in the barn to mount her then tap her flanks with the end of the reins. She gallops through the barn entrance. We race to the side of the canal along the edge. I think how lucky we are that the canal is dry in the winter. I let Cassiopeia worry about getting too close to the steep edge while I concentrate on spotting my brother. It is in the fifties and cloudy and I am without a jacket. The nearby landscape is totally barren with a few weeds and grass growing among the rocks along the bank and the trail on the other side of the canal. Up ahead I see a few buzzards circling overhead, above something in the canal, and know it must be Prairie. I am almost there when I hear Dad's truck behind me. I see my brother laying propped up near the rocky bottom of the canal bank. I tie the end of the rope to the horn on my saddle and use the rope to lower myself over the six-foot drop-off. I reach him and call his name several times. I feel his pulse…it's strong and he's breathing, but he doesn't answer, and I check him all over. There is a pool of blood under the back of his head, and his bike is banged up and laying about three feet from his body. Dad used another rope to get into the canal with me. I look at him through my tears. "Dad, he's breathing and his pulse is strong. Should we try to lift him?" Dad's face is drained.

"I don't know if we should—you know what they say."

"Dad, should I call an ambulance?"

"A person may make things worse by lifting him," he says, as if he is talking to himself.

"Dad, I think we should try, it will take too long to get an ambulance here. It's faster if we take him ourselves."

Dad bends over him and calls him, then carefully lifts him as I look at Prairie's face…nothing. I grab the rope tied to my saddle and climb up, then lower the end of the rope to dad. He makes a two-part sling with his rope, one under the legs and the other loop under his arms, and with the rope he lifts his son's body up toward me. With the rope, I pull him up onto the ground.

The whole family has now made it to the bank to help with Prairie. I am so focused on my brother that I'm not listening. Dad gets behind the wheel of the truck and Camellia checks Prairie out and says it is fine to put him in the truck. I slide my little brother inside and Dad puts his son's legs on his lap. Camellia pulls his eyelids up and checks his eyes, then his heartbeat and tells Dad to go.

I hold Mom, telling her he is okay, just knocked out. We ride the horses back to the barn and call for a car to take five visitors to the hospital in town.

Rain's eyes are swollen and red, he blames himself. I put my arms around him and say, "Don't feel bad, honey, Prairie's accident isn't your fault." I am talking to both of us. Being the oldest, it has been drummed into me that I should look out for them. I have failed.

"I shouldn't have been looking for wolves."

"Rain, that was a bad idea, but had nothing to do with Prairie's accident. Even if he was following you, you didn't know he was following you. He was too far away for you to hear him crash, and you couldn't have kept it from happening."

"Why do I feel so guilty then?"

"Because you see yourself as someone you're not." *Like me.* "The real Rain is not aware of everything that's happening. The real Rain can't be everyone's protector." *Neither can I.* "The real Rain isn't a superhero. He is a smart, kind and loving boy. A very unique one-of-a-kind boy who is loved by everyone in his family."

Rain gives me a big hug and I let him cry on my shoulder while tears run down my face. Then I give him my hanky to wipe his face first and he feels better, he even smiles.

The taxi pulls up in front of the Earthship and we all pile in the driverless car and go to the hospital. Mom pays by pressing her palm against a metal plate near the glove compartment. The plate reads her palm like a signature and finds the credit account used for the car company. When we get out at the hospital, the car takes off for its next customer. We walk up the steps and through the swinging door of Rigby General Hospital, a pale, red brick, six-story building.

As soon as we see Dad, we all talk at once, so eager to know how Prairie is. Dad holds up his hands saying according to the doctors, eventually Prairie will be okay. He hit his head against one or more rocks when he fell and has a concussion. The X-ray didn't show any damage to his skull, but he is still out.

"Dad, when do they think he will regain consciousness?" I ask.

"There are drugs they can try to bring him around, but they have side effects. It would be best if he came around on his own."

"Did they try a large noise or cold water—something shocking?"

"Not that I'm aware of."

"If he is to wake up on his own, let's take him home where he is surrounded by tender loving care, Dad."

"How would we feed him, Laurel?" I feel a sharp pain in my chest; I need to help him. "Please let me see him, Dad. I want to try and wake him."

"I know how you feel, go try." I walk through the door to a small room as Camellia walks past me. He looks so little in the big mechanical hospital bed with a clear bag dripping a solution into his arm. Mom stands by holding his hand, weeping. His face has some bandages on one side where the buzzards bit and scratches from the gravel. I stand on the other side near his head and hold his hand.

I bend to kiss his forehead and whisper in his ear, "Where are you, Prairie? Come home." I repeat this over and over, he doesn't stir.

I hug Mom and leave for the gift shop to ask for a small paper bag. I take it back to his room, and Rain follows me. We are three in his room and I don't care about rules. I blow up the bag like a balloon and then I pop it as hard as I can. BANG! Prairie's eyelids flutter. We all forget we are in a hospital and yell, "Prairie, COME HOME!" His lids flutter again. Doctors and nurses come into the room yelling at us to be quiet. I yell, "Prairie!" and he comes to the surface. Dad, hearing all the noise, comes in and is so happy he is hugging mom first and then everyone because he knows his little boy will live. The doctor talks mom and dad into letting him rest overnight. I am afraid he will go deeper and want him to come home. I lose the argument.

Dad insists we all get some rest, but Mom won't leave him. At home, I hear Dad drive off again. I help Grams and Camellia make dinner and when Dad returns, Prairie's blue bent-up bike is in the back of the truck. I am getting the horses in from the corral and see him drive up to the old barn. After I shut the door of the horse barn, I walk over to talk to Dad. He is lifting the bike out of the truck and placing it in the barn.

"Did you get a chance to talk to mom about the lump in her breast?"

"Yes, we talked, it's very difficult for most people to realize that there is nothing we can do, but the doctors can."

"You're talking about free will, aren't you?"

"It doesn't exist. Life is difficult enough; why make it harder? Stand still and see for yourself that we can't change anything until we are meant too."

"I don't believe we have free will, but we still try, Dad."

"We all forget, daughter, that we are just actors on a stage." He smiles and sighs.

He puts his arm around me as we walk to the house.

At the dinner table, we are missing mom and Prairie. Those two empty seats make us feel empty, and I feel a loss of appetite. As we sit, Dad is talking about his earlier meeting with legislators and he shares.

"Some people like to talk and talk and never say anything, and others are against every plan except their own, so it's hard to get people to come together even on issues of life and death. A lot of time seems wasted, but maybe it's needed to get anywhere. The refugees are coming and we agree it's best for now to let them settle in one area. Using endowment land has been agreed upon. Due to the climate, the housing is very important and needs to be started now. Materials must resist fire, water and high winds, and the area must be off the grid and self-supporting."

"Did anyone mention the use of shipping containers underground? They are cheap, strong, and can be insulated and stacked," I say.

"Why don't you write up a proposal and include sketches for a city? I'll see that they get it."

I ask if I should cancel dinner with Sage's family tomorrow.

"Laurel, dinner with Sage's family is a great way to lighten things up, and that may be a good thing to do right now."

I go find Grams in the kitchen to see how she feels about having them over, when I ask, she says, "It would cheer everyone up." Camellia and I will help with everything. I find sis and apologize because I forgot to suggest that she invite Cannon.

"It's okay. I'll invite him another time."

"Would you mind helping Grams and me with dinner?"

"I'm happy to help. I'm going to check on Prairie in the morning, and if he isn't better, the doc is in for a fight with me." Camellia replies.

"I will go with you, sis."

"Good, I can use your help in bringing Prairie home. Oh, I just noticed Chia is on your bed."

"Yes, Chia has chosen my bed as her bed, but I like her company."

Later, I text Mom and ask about Prairie and if she wants to come home for a while, I will sit with him, she says he is the same and she wants to stay with him.

After I get ready for bed, I start thinking about the refugees and how to build a safe place for them. First, I need to know what the land will be like where they'll live. I text Dad and he tells me where to go to get the information and maps.

"Jo, can you find the least expensive place to buy thousands of shipping containers and what their average size is?" Jo says, "I will get started."

The following day Jo tells me that shipping containers on average are from twenty to forty feet long and steel construction is priced at two to five thousand dollars. Some are even 96 wide by 240 long by 102 high. These containers might be ideal because they are fire- and insect-resistant and can be insulated and stacked on top of each other or bridged between two containers. If one was stacked on top of another, one could be underground and insulated on the outside, giving a person a very safe place in case of violent storms or fires.

I'm feeling excited about the project of using containers for safe, permanent structures to build a whole town for the refugees, and that evening, with Tiger sitting on my chest, I fall asleep thinking about ways to design a town.

Early in the morning Camellia and I leave for the hospital in a taxi with a bag of clean, warm clothes for mom. The day is in the forties and overcast.

Prairie is moved from Emergency to an observation room and mom is awake. She says she slept beside him all night and he is still out.

"I think I'll take a shower while you girls are here," mom says.

"We will try again to wake him."

Mom carries her things in to the bathroom. I tickle his feet without results, then Camellia pays attention to his face and calls his name again his eyelids flutter like they did yesterday.

I look at Prairie and say, "If you hear my voice squeeze my hand." No response.

Camellia says, "They can't tell what's going on in his brain."

"I'm sure they have looked at that and I plan to talk to the doctor."

"Maybe we need a neurologist." Camellia remarks. "But today is Sunday, you can forget finding anything out until tomorrow."

"Do you think we should try putting him in the tub and filling it with cold water? I ask. "I keep thinking it might work."

"Let's wait until we talk to the doctor."

I ask Mom if she learned anything from the doctor, "Nothing new. He believes Prairie is just healing and will wake up when he's ready."

"Well, I think we need a second opinion from a neurologist, Mom. Last night I read several medical sites dedicated to information on concussions and nothing was said about a problem waking up after a concussion."

"I just feel so helpless, Laurel." I hold her and again talk about getting another doctor.

"I should have looked up this doctor," Mom says. "We don't even know if he has experience with a case like this. What do you think, Camellia?"

"We need to know more about how his brain has been affected."

I sit on the bed and hold my little brother and talk to him. "Come home, we miss you. Please try to wake up," I kiss his warm cheek.

"Mom, you may not have remembered that Sage's parents are coming over for dinner tonight. I was going to cancel, but both Dad and Grams thought I should go through with it because having them over might distract us and cheer us up."

"There is nothing we can do to help Prairie today," Mom whispers. "Your dad is right, and it's the last chance you have before Sage leaves."

"Can you come home this afternoon, Mom?"

"Yes, I'll come and then return in the evening. I need to pick up a few things from home."

"Why don't you go get breakfast, Mom?"

"I don't want to eat alone in the cafeteria. They will bring me breakfast. I just need to order something."

"We are going to leave, do you want to come with us, get away for a while?"

"No, I'll wait until later in the day, I'm fine."

Back home, the family is busy doing chores and getting ready for company. Dad drives his truck to the hospital to be with his wife and son.

Rain keeps his eye on the weather and keeps me informed, tonight will be even colder, and light snow is possible. We get the greenhouses and animals ready for the cold. Meteorologists talk about rain again along the Pacific Coast through the next couple of weeks. The West Coast is facing gale force winds, rain, and temperatures in the mid-thirties.

CHAPTER 15
PREMONITION

"Our failure to take action leaves our decedents a planet too hot to live on."

–James Hansen

Dad returns from the hospital with Mom. When asked, he says, "no change." Grams, Camellia and I are making dinner. Mom and Dad leave to get ready, and Rain takes on the chores with the animals. When everything is ready and in the warming oven, Camellia and I leave the kitchen to get dressed.

The doorbell rings at 6:00 p.m., and at the elevator I quickly get Sage's family in the house because the wind is cold in the elevator shaft. The family removes their shoes, boots, and hats, and Camellia meets us and helps me get everyone's coats hung up in the coat closet. We hug, shake hands or kiss cheeks to greet the family. Sage looks incredible and I feel like grabbing and kissing him. Lily wears a beautiful emerald green tunic over her winter white body suit. Dara wears her hair up. Her long neck and coloring is perfect for her soft peach cashmere turtleneck sweater and wool pants. Jay wears a thick blue sweater over his body suit. Ash, in a dark blue woolen jump suit, seems full of energy as he takes off looking for Rain. Tiger has climbed up on my shoulder; he is curious listening to all the noise. Everyone except Lily laughs at Tiger's antics.

In the family room, we sit, and Grams comes in and meets everyone. Then Kazan, Rain and Ash come in and Tiger climbs down and runs from Kazan. We are talking about the refugees when Mom and Dad join us. We move into the dining room and get settled. Sage saves me a seat next to him. Camellia and I place food on the table and Grams fills our glasses with flavored iced tea. Then we all sit down and fill our plates with fried rice, roasted marinated vegetables, and a green salad.

I ask dad to share with us what decisions were made in Boise regarding the refugees.

"You probably already know many refugees are arriving on the West Coast in the morning, it's just the beginning. The refugees will travel by buses and trains to the States, where they will live. They will be temporarily housed in anything available that is safe and clean. Sooner or later, permanent dwellings will be built for them on endowment land like ours in southeastern Idaho. The refugees eventually can rent to own the property. We will create jobs for those who are willing to work."

A few questions are asked. Sage asks where Prairie is, and that changes the conversation.

Dad tells our company what happened to Prairie. The news stuns everyone and reminds us that life is very fragile. The kids want to visit him, and I ask them to call us first, because only a few at a time are allowed in his room. Everyone looks sad until the food arrives, then expressions change and everyone seems to enjoy the food. Grams serves a dessert of chocolate pudding with strawberries and whipped cream.

"Who would like decaf coffee or tea?" Grams ask.

Dad is deep in conversation with Jay about construction. Mom and Lily are talking about what is going on in Rigby, and Dara and Camellia are discussing fashion. Sage grabs and squeezes my hand. I look in his eyes for the first time since we sat down. We each smile before I get up, pick up the coffeepot and pour our coffee and cream. Dad is now asking Jay about the art of plastering and Mom and Lily talk about Idaho Falls. Rain and Ash have already asked to be excused and Sage and I go off to the greenhouse hall, where he presses against me, pushing me against the wall, and we kiss for some time.

"I am going to miss you so much Laurel," Sage whispers as he hugs me.

"I know just how you feel, it will be harder this time. I'm getting more attached to you, sweetheart." The word seems to melt him and his kisses are so tender.

Then we hear voices coming toward us. Jay and Lily want to get home before the weather gets worse and we say goodnight as Sage and his family leave. After everyone has left, we clean up the kitchen and we argue over who will spend the night with Prairie at the hospital. I want to go, but Dad says no, he plans to go. He leaves an hour later.

I get into my warmest coat and boots and check on the animals. The horses need oats. I cover the goat barn with more insulation, lock up the chickens and head back to the house, where I feed the cats and Kazan and go to my bedroom.

Camellia is sleeping, so I change clothes in the dark and crawl in my twin bed. I have so much on my mind: Sage, his family, Prairie, Mother, the climate and my new shipping crate city project. I usually try to avoid bringing new people into my life, as fewer responsibilities helps me manage better. I'm feeling so eager to bring

Prairie home. I believe he will recover sooner in his own room. I will try to talk to Dad about it tomorrow and about another doctor. I forgot to check out his doctor on the net. I hope Camellia can get an appointment for mom with a great oncologist. I need to make plans to visit my Earthships; two are almost completed and a third just started taking shape.

Then before I drift away on my thoughts, I write in my diary the scary dreams I've been having about shooting people. That is a terrible experience for someone who is against hurting even an animal. Then last night as I slept, I had a premonition. I stood watching as a car blow up in a brown and gray background and I wept because my sister wasn't with me. I walked down a dirt road in the heat looking for her. Next I was standing in front of an old two-story farmhouse that needed paint. I remember the name on the mailbox was Ruth. I knocked on the screen door but no one answered. I looked down and noticed I was standing in what looked like splattered blood. I tried to open the door— it was locked and so I walked on, crying over the loss of Camellia, when I reached the highway. I wiped my wet face on my shirttail; it was covered with the blood on my face. That startled me and I woke.

Thinking about the vision, I lie there knowing something bad is going to happen sometime soon, and I am scared.

Another morning, and I wake with Rain at the foot of my bed with his shadow, Kazan.

"Laurel, I just heard that scientists found that the sinking of Central America was caused by climate change. The earthquake and tsunami alone didn't cause the worst damage. Do you want to read it or for me to tell you?"

"Tell me."

"Central America's foundation was limestone with lots of holes like a sponge for the bottom layer. But the top layers had been filled in with sand, soil and salt, and as flooding worsened because of higher sea levels, the acidic water ate away at the limestone and emptied the holes, bringing water to the surface and weakening the foundation until one strong earthquake destroyed the landmass."

"Thank you, Rain. You were right when you said you believed higher oceans were the cause, you are so smart."

His face gets a little red from embarrassment. Kazan wants me to talk to him, so he puts his paws on my bed making Tiger jump down and run away.

"Hi, Kazan, how are you, boy?" I say as I fluff his fur. He wags the stump he has for a tail and gets down from my bed, so I guess he is content with the attention.

"I'll let you know if any more reports come out," Rain says as he turns to leave.

"Thank you."

I want to just lay in bed, but with so much to do today, I can't. I get up and take a shower to see if it will wake me up. It helps. In my robe, I head to the kitchen for coffee. Mom and Grams are up drinking coffee and studying their tablets, and Camellia has already gone to the hospital.

"Any news on Prairie?"

"A neurologist is coming in today to check everything and they will get some pictures of his spine and brain," Mom says.

"Why did they wait so long for this, mom?"

"I'm told this is not unusual with a concussion."

"So, they just made an assumption without checking everything? That makes me angry," I feel the tears stinging. "I should have done more, asked more questions. Asked for a second opinion right away," I mumble to myself.

"We feel the same way, Laurel. Blaming ourselves won't help Prairie," Grams says.

"You need to calm down," Mom scolds. "You're just making matters worse. Laurel, you are like a dog with a bone."

"I know, but I'm going to ask Camellia and see what she has to say." I walk back to my room and text her on my tablet, then I get dressed for going outside. As I pass the dining room mom yells, "Don't you want some breakfast?"

"After chores," I answer.

I am going to leave through the front until I see the weather. The wind is shaking the tree limbs, I open the back door and find out it is in the thirties and I pass through the garage side door.

The horses will need to run for a while so I get them in their corral. I feed the chickens, gather the eggs, then cover up the hen house with straw. I feed the goats but leave the milking for Grams. The fruit trees are covered with insulated tarps, and the greenhouses are holding up to the wind. I go back to the horse barn and put out feed and clean water. I clean up the horse manure by shoveling it up and placing it in a wheelbarrow to remove later. That takes me an hour, so I put the horses back in the barn. At least they got to run around for a little while then I make it back to the house with the wind pulling me toward the back of the property. Some of the gusts are very strong.

In the house, again, I make myself some breakfast and another cup of coffee. Rain comes in with Kazan, who lays on the floor. I ask him if he had breakfast.

"No—not yet."

"Would you like some Swiss oatmeal with strawberries? That's what I'm making, a cup of hot chocolate while you wait?"

"Sure, that would be nice, thank you. You might not know this, but the refugees are stranded at some bus and train stations because of the weather. It's very cold and wet on the Pacific side of the country due to Darwin, one of the most powerful hurricanes to ever cross Mexico City from the Gulf of Mexico."

"That sounds terrible, Rain. Do the refugees have shelter and warm clothes? Can you find out where the ones are that are traveling to the Northwest?"

"I'll see what I can find out."

I set a cup of hot cocoa in front of him, and my tablet buzzes. I have a text from Camellia, she was able to get Mom an appointment with a highly skilled oncologist for Wednesday. That is great, I tell her. The neurologist, Dr. Brandon, one of the best in Idaho, is flying in at 10:00 a.m. to see Prairie, we should know a lot more tomorrow.

An Earthship is a very quiet house. I can't even hear the wind blowing. Rain and I eat and work on our tablets. I am trying to figure out when to make reservations for my trips to visit my construction sites.

"Jo, can you please plan a trip for me with regard to the weather? I need to go to Twin Falls, Nampa, and Boise within the next week if possible."

"Yes, Laurel, I'll get back to you."

Tiger jumps on my lap. He wants to be higher than the dog. I keep a bottle of water on the table with a spray nozzle in case he tries to get on the table. But he seems content on my lap.

"It doesn't look like the weather will get better for a week," Rain says. "The refugees for the Northwest are stuck in Portland. They had to be moved to a large, covered auditorium because of flooding. They will be sleeping on the floor tonight, but they have been given blankets, food, and warm drinks. I thought the number moving was ten thousand, but it's one hundred thousand. They are rushing everything because of future weather forecasts, Laurel."

"Wow, that's a lot of people to move," I say.

Dad comes home from the hospital for lunch and says, "They had Prairie out of his room taking pictures of his brain." Then Dad just stands in the kitchen and starts to cry because he feels so helpless. I hug him thinking I know how he feels, but I don't. Then I make him some lunch, telling him what Rain told me about the refugees and what I have found out about the size and cost of shipping containers. I tell him about stacking them so one would be underground.

"I would tell you to buy some blocks and start designing a grouping that could be repeated over and over again," Dad offers. "Something that people could understand better than a flat drawing on paper. Remember, some people are set in old ways of doing things and you might be wasting your time."

"To me it seems the fastest, cheapest and safest way, and people have been living in shipping containers for years, Dad. We'll have to look at all other costs of delivery and making them livable. I know, I'll have Jo work on it for me."

Grams comes in and says good afternoon, then asks dad about Prairie. They talk a while, then he asks about Mom and where she is. Grams says she is tutoring Rain. Dad leaves the kitchen. "How is Mom, Grams?" I ask.

"She is more upset over her young son than her own health."

"Of course, she would be. I'm concerned that the stress she is going through will affect her health."

Grams lowers her head when she whispers, "I know."

I put my arm around her and she kisses me on the cheek. "We just have to keep reminding ourselves it's not real," she says. "Life is just a dream. It still hurts like hell!" I am surprised her belief matches Dad's.

I wash the dishes and clean up and Grams starts something for dinner. As I walk back to the bedroom, Chia gets up and starts rubbing against me. I check my tablet to see if I have any new messages while I stroke Chia, and that reminds me to clean the litter boxes.

After the cleaning, I lie down on my bed and fall asleep with Chia's head on my neck. Over an hour later I awake with Chia on my chest and Tiger tucked into my waist. I get up and they run off. I look at my tablet. Camellia left me a message saying the MRI showed some swelling of the occipital lobe, which is the visual processing center of the brain. They did not find any nerve damage. The plan of treatment is to wake him up starting with a mild stimulus.

I text back:

Let us know when you are going to try and wake him so his parents can be there.

While I wait, I take a shower, cover myself in lotion, and start getting into warm clothes when Mom knocks on my door. She tells me the doctor is going to wake Prairie as soon as she and Dad get there, so they are leaving. I ask her to text me as soon as they wake him so I can say hi.

"I have a dinner date with Sage. He's leaving in the morning."

"We will let you know, honey." I kiss Mom and she leaves.

After I dress I find Grams with Rain in the family room.

"Here you are."

"We are going to watch a 3D movie. Do you want to join us?" Gram asks.

"Not tonight, Grams. Sage is leaving in the morning and will be gone for a year, so I am spending my evening with him."

"Be careful. It's going to be icy tonight."

"I'm glad you two will be home where it's safe. Be sure and lock up after me."

"We will," Grams says.

CHAPTER 16
ICE STORM

"Removing a mountain top to get coal is barbaric."

–James Hansen

Sage looks like a photo of a young Christian Bale in the old movie called *The Dark Knight* and smells like a woodsy aftershave when he arrives at my front door. I take him to the family room to say hello to Grams and Rain. Sage is dressed in a pair of vintage blue jeans and dark brown leather boots with a squared-off tapered toe. A heavy V-neck sweater in swirling hues of brown and navy covers an amber-colored cotton turtleneck shirt.

In the family room, we say goodnight to Grams and Rain. My brother doesn't even turn from the screen as they watch the action of brilliant colored dragons in flight.

I pull down my warmest coat with a down hood and cover my aqua body suit and vest of fake fur. I put on my winter white fur-topped boots. After I am dressed, Sage and I take a picture of each other smiling. We each carry our tablets in our shoulder bags.

The cold air in the elevator shaft takes my breath away. I feel warm in my outerwear, but in the car the cold air hits my face as Sage starts the engine. Then he turns the car around in the driveway and we start for Idaho Falls, a bigger city. The roads are already getting slippery so Sage drives around thirty miles an hour. We find our way to one of the nicer hotels in the Falls near the river that runs through the town and park as close as we can to the first level in the parking garage.

The post-modern, six-story steel and glass building is nice and warm inside, and a virtual roaring fire is burning in the bar off the lobby. This room with warm colors and a cozy atmosphere is vacant. We find a small booth near the warmth of the gas fireplace, take off our gloves, and just sit across from one another holding hands and looking at each other. I look in his warm gray-green eyes a couple of times, but can't read his emotions. We talk about our lives and the goals we have been working on, then a waitress stops by our table and asks if she can get us anything. Sage orders some warm Italian liqueur, and I ask if we can later have dinner served to us in this room. She says yes and leaves to get our drinks.

"Why are we sitting so far from one another?" Sage asks. "I want you close to me, Laurel."

I scoot over to his side of the booth and he puts an arm around my waist and kisses me on the cheek. Then as we wait, we gently kiss on the lips. Between the kisses and the liqueur, I feel like I am floating on a pool of honey. Then a buzz on my tablet brings me back to the room. I open my bag and ask Jo to accept the call. "It's your mother."

"Prairie is awake. The stimulant worked."

"Oh, Mom, that is great news! I'm so happy for all of us and especially Prairie. When can he go home?"

"The neurologist wants to run a few tests tomorrow, but he should be able to come home the day after, honey."

"Can I say hello to him?"

"Yes, here he is,"

"Prairie, you're back!"

"Yes, Laurel. I'm happy to be back, I missed all of you so much."

"Well, where were you?"

"I don't know its name, but the music was nice and so were the people. I'll tell you about it later…got to go now."

"Okay, honey, I sure do love you."

"I know…bye."

The waitress brings our menus, and I am still stunned as I open mine.

Sage asks me why I wanted to know where Prairie was? I explain how he told me he really missed us while he was gone. He couldn't miss us if he was just unconscious.

"It must have been a dream," Sage thinks aloud.

"I might believe it was a dream if he hadn't heard the music. The Mystics, Plato and many others who've have had out-of-body experiences talk about the inner music."

"That is interesting. Have you heard the music, Laurel?"

"Yes, I have, and I know I wasn't dreaming, but I didn't meet any people. The sound of the music is different in each dimension, they say. So, if you are a Mystic you will know where the person has been by the description of the music."

"I'll have to do some reading about Mystics," he says, looking at me as though he he is truly interested in exploring the music of the spheres.

"It's an interesting subject. Oh, I'm just so happy that my little brother is well." The tears come and Sage hands me his hanky.

"It's wonderful, sweetheart. Now that he is revived, I will feel at peace returning to Libya."

"I'm feeling so hungry, what should we eat? Have you eaten at this place before?"

"With Mom and Dad one time, I think it was Dad's birthday dinner. Let's see, for you, they have great salads and pizza. That's what I had and I don't know how good anything else is. The stuffed pasta should be good, and here is an eggplant stuffing with cheese."

The young waitress returns. "Would you like me to take your orders now?"

"Yes," I say, "the mushroom stuffed pasta with the Palermo sauce and garden salad with raspberry vinaigrette. Earl Gray tea, hot, please."

"Your order please, sir?"

"I'll have the eggplant dish, shrimp, and garden salad with an olive vinaigrette dressing, and red wine."

"Would you like some more liqueur?"

Sage looks at me. "Yes, please, it's so good." The waitress walks away.

"I'm so happy to be alone with you, Laurel. You know I'm in love with you."

I look at the warmth in his eyes, his tender expression, and I know he believes he loves me. "We have a very strong attraction for one another, but I don't think love happens so fast," I answer.

"I know it's more than that. I love you and hate to leave you for another year. But soon I'll be free, my sweet girl."

"Yes, you will be."

We hug as best we can with the way we are sitting. I get up, take off my coat and go to the bathroom. When I get back, Sage has taken off his coat. We put the coats on the booth across from us and sit close to the fire and each other, our legs and hands touching as we sip our liqueur. Then the waitress brings our salads. They are fresh and crisp. I ask Sage what his plans are after he is free of the Marines.

"I have two years to earn my masters, and it will be paid for." He fills his fork. "I will take most courses online and stay near you, if you allow, so I can at least see you on weekends." After eating some salad, he says, "Or we can live together between both places, your home and mine."

"Honey, I won't ever just live together with a man, even one as wonderful as you are. We'll see how we feel about each other over the year ahead." I finish my salad and put down the fork. The waitress arrives with the main course and warns, "Be careful, the plates are hot." She turns and leaves.

"Sorry, I shouldn't have said that," Sage says.

"It's okay. I know how a lot of people feel about living together. I'm just so spoiled with parents who are madly in love with each other after all these years. They believed in commitment and never lived together before marriage. I want their kind of life for myself because I've seen what the gifts of a love and life like that can bring."

"I want you to have that life also, with or without me, Laurel."

"Thank you. That's the nicest thing you have ever said to me." I put down my wine glass and start on my mushroom-stuffed pasta.

"This is very good, Sage." I pass my fork to him with a fat stuffed pasta dripping in red sauce. He takes a bite.

"You're right, very good. Want to taste my eggplant?"

"Yes, I would," I admit, and he gives me a bite. "It's delicious, awesome," I say. "Let's share—we have so much."

"Sharing is a good idea."

We talk about the subjects of our studies while we eat. Then we talk about our families. When we finish, we are stuffed. I want to check the weather before leaving. I get out my tablet.

"Jo, I need a local weather report."

"There is a warning in Rigby to stay off the roads because of ice, and many roads in Idaho Falls are closed. The temperature has dropped to twenty bellow. There have already been several wrecks on the highway between Rigby and Idaho Falls. Also, there is a problem with pipes and water mains breaking and flooding, then freezing."

"Thanks, Jo."

We look at each other and I say, "It looks like we aren't traveling tonight, and I need to call my family." Sage calls his family while I call mine.

"Hi, Dad, how is everything, did you make it home from the hospital?... Oh, you didn't make it home.... You guys are staying at the hospital overnight... Where is Camellia? Thank God she made it home. I hope the animals will be okay. We will have to stay here at the hotel tonight, Dad.... Okay, I'll see you tomorrow."

Sage asks, "What happened, honey?" As he closes his tablet.

"Mom and Dad are stuck at the hospital."

"My mom said she can't make it home, but she'll be okay, they have cots at the factory. Jack is home with Ash and Dara, so that's good."

The waitress comes and clears our table. We wait for her to bring the bill. Sage is still looking at his tablet, then looks up at me with a serious expression when he says, "This is the worst ice storm to ever hit the Pacific Northwest and Northwestern states, and the immigrants are caught up in this mess." His tender thoughts for the immigrants make me feel even more comfortable with my deep affection for him.

The waitress comes with tears on her face. She hands Sage the ticket.

"Are you all right?" I ask.

"No, not really. My mom was in an accident tonight and I can't get to the hospital because of the roads."

I touch her arm and say, "I'm so sorry you have to go through this."

Sage pays her and offers her his sympathies, and we go to the front desk and ask for a room. The cheapest one they have available with a double bed is $128 a night. Not even a queen bed.

"How much is a room with a queen bed?" I ask.

"One forty," the man says.

"I will take it."

He takes my thumb print and gives us key cards and a map of the hotel.

"You should have let me pay," Sage complains.

"Why?" I reply, "You bought dinner, I have a job." We walk around until we find a little store with toothpaste, brushes, combs, and a shower cap. Sage leads the way to our room and unlocks the door. This typical hotel room is a little musty, but we can't open the windows. I want to talk to Grams but it is so late—I don't want to wake her. I call Camellia; she won't be able to work tomorrow.

"Sorry I woke you, Sis. I was just so worried about you guys. Is everything okay at the house? The animals? The water may be cold, but the house is warm. I don't know why unless it just takes a long time to heat water that cold...I'm so glad you moved the chickens into the cellar. Goodnight, Sis."

Sage is getting our room warmed up with the heater. Then he turns on the water in the bathroom and lets it run a long time, but it is freezing.

We watch the weather on the screen and see lines of trucks pulled off the roads. Several vehicle accidents are scattered over the highways, frozen pools of water spilling from bursting pipes and stiff bird's dead on the sidewalks. We get in bed at around midnight. We are in our underwear. I leave my socks on because my feet are always cold and the sheets are cold inside the bed.

"How about I hold you until the bed warms up?"

"That sounds great." My teeth are chattering.

With my back against his chest, he curls his body around mine. I move my hair away from his face and he's kissing me on the neck. After warming up, I want to talk about sex with Sage, but at first the words do not leave my mouth. I've never talked about the subject except with Camellia, and she didn't know more than I did. I don't know how to begin, then when he starts caressing me, I just blurt it out.

"Sage, I've never had sex and don't know much about sexual relationships."

"That doesn't surprise me, sweetheart, you're very young. I haven't had much experience, but I have read books about the sex, read a lot of books on female anatomy, and listened to guys talk. I probably understand the female anatomy better than most women. But we can explore each other and find out what feels comfortable."

My need to kiss him is so overwhelming that I turn around. My lips find his and the feeling is blissful. We explore each other's bodies, kissing one another's sensitive areas, it feels so good I float in the afterglow, thinking how lucky I am to have him for my first boyfriend, a man who cares enough for me and my age and is wise enough to make love with me without intercourse. He doesn't need protection tonight. I have intercourse to look forward to, if we become man and wife. I am happy that we gave each other this gift of loving before parting for another year.

The next day Sage and I leave Idaho Falls for Rigby by traveling very slowly over icy roads. He enters the house so he can say goodbye to everyone and welcome Prairie back. Then we enjoy a long goodbye kiss. Sage leaves me, and that is the first time I realize that I might love him. Suddenly I want to cry, his leaving makes me feel very bad, and as the day's pass, I realize it is what they call love sickness. My appetite is gone and I mope around for days.

During the month after Sage returns to Libya, I spend a lot of spare time with my little brother out of concern and as a distraction. Prairie tells me about the in-between world he visited while he was in the hospital healing. He woke up in a great light with soft music, so he didn't know how he got there. The people communicated by sending pictures to each other's minds, that's how he made friends with some children who showed him around. By his description, it sounds like he was in a place like the beautiful wild areas that were once a part of our world, except more vivid. He saw mountains, lakes, rivers and trees, plus many different kinds of flowering plants and colors unlike any colors on earth. He saw no animals. The people were very friendly and kind, treating him like a royal guest. The buildings were mostly made of sunbaked reddish clay. The food was never cooked and consisted mainly of fruits and nuts and green and purple veggies.

When I ask what they talked about. He says, "We talked about our worlds, they ask about mine." He wanted to know where the music came from and they looked surprised that he didn't know that the music was a part of everything, because every living thing has its own vibration. They also told him he was only visiting and would return to his family.

Dad soon comes back home and works with the state to get the immigrants settled temporarily in vacant warehouses, church basements, and any place that has running water, bathrooms and electricity. Pamphlets are being sent out to middle-class homeowners explaining the situation with the Central American people and their needs. The pamphlet asks those people in the community that have an extra bedroom and bath to please consider letting a family use it for up to six months.

I give Dad my proposal including landscape layouts and using the shipping crates for homes. Dad is also going to interview families who are willing to live in our cottage and work the farm with us for a home and food.

The lump in mom's breast is cancer. Her oncologist is treating her with an engineered virus and the tumor is shrinking. Next week she will stay at Idaho Falls Memorial Hospital for three or more days for treatment to build up her immune system.

The freezing weather lasts through February, then comes the sheets of rain along with dark overcast days, and flooding again. El Niño is acting as predicted and we spend most of our days inside when we can, undercover. Camellia has to make trips to the hospital and vet clinic where she works part-time. I have to travel to Twin Falls to check on an Earthship project once a week. The contractors are working on the interior. They are able to get the roof completed before the weather changes for the worse.

We have to go outside to feed the animals. The horses become restless with a need to run. Rain and Prairie need distractions and the animals are a help. Dad drives Rain to Idaho Falls to pick up Ash so they can spend a few days together. Sometimes Dara returns with them to spend a day with Camellia. I try to keep Sage updated and a part of our lives with texts and face time on my tablet, but just seeing his face now makes me feel weak in the knees.

Living with all the mud from the heavy rains is a problem for the animals and us. Dad decides we need some covered walkways. That would be a new project for warmer, sunnier days.

For most people, food is now harder to come by and the food pantry is out of many of the things people need, like powdered milk and canned beans, veggies and bread. Most grocery stores. Most of the time, they only have enough food on hand to stock the shelves every three days before another delivery, and they are sold out after one day with many empty shelves. Trucks are slower to deliver their goods to the stores due to the weather, and the stores are only open three days a week when they have stock to sell.

Online sales have delivery problems also. The most common drugs the pharmacies carry are sold out most of the time because when they do receive an order, one person will buy or steal half a dozen packages to be safe. A new law limits purchases of only two of the same items now. Over-the-counter and prescription drugs like those for people with diabetes have been very difficult to keep on hand, and patients have died. People start gathering in huge numbers in Washington and state capitols, trying to get Congress to act. Something has to be done to save the lives of so many people. It may not get better until the weather improves without legal enforcement.

I called my Aunt Essie and Aunt Edna to see how they are doing. They have plenty of food in their basements. Mom has planned to take food to her poor relatives nearby. She calls Meadow and ask what she needs. Then she tells her about the cancer and that Forester will bring them some food.

Dad is worried about Mom, the lack of food and medical supplies for the people and making sure his family has what they need. He knew this would happen, and planned for the disaster. I can tell he is upset about everything that is going on now, because he is quick to lose his temper, knowing he could lose everything we have stored underground and is constantly trying to improve our surveillance and defense systems. Whenever he pulls out the scrolls of paper with the specs for the electrical or plumbing designs of our property, Tiger comes running and will jump on the table to play with the string that ties the scrolls and lays on the sheets of paper. It's funny to watch. Each time Dad gently removes him, Tiger returns. Dad is very patient but finally says, "One could do without a cat. Tiger, you are a pest!" Tiger just sits and looks at dad and then jumps at him, rubbing his fur against dad's hand. Dad can't help picking him up and scratching him under his chin. Tiger loves Dad and maybe he senses his worries.

Dad is aware of the extremists around us, like the groups of neo-Nazis who live in the woods not far from our town, and the white nationalists living in the wilds of the panhandle and the Third Wave near the Canadian border.

We are talking one afternoon and he asks, "How is Sage doing? You never talk about him, I wish we had some young men like him around to help protect us."

"Well, I haven't felt much like talking about him because we are both unhappy. His outfit was sent to the borders with Libya and I'm worried about him. He isn't feeling prepared for his new assignment of defending the border."

"Why did they send him to that hell hole?"

"To protect the border near our embassy." Dad just looks at me and shakes his head, then says, "Don't fill your mind with anything negative and you will both feel happier. He will be okay."

I interrupt Dad and ask, "What ever happened to the gray wolves we saw near the canal?"

"Oh, I forgot to tell you. They have been moved far north of us."

"I'm glad to hear that, and hope they will find food this winter."

"Their chances of survival will be better farther north than here."

"Would you like me to lock up Tiger so you can work, dad?"

"Don't lock him up too quickly. I don't want him to blame me."

"Okay, I'll play with him for a while, Dad."

Tiger climbs up on my shoulder and we go looking for Prairie. He is in the greenhouse front hall playing on the floor with his robotic wildlife.

"Can Tiger play with you for a while?" The rain has stopped and I want to check on the horses.

"Sure, Laurel." I put him down and he pounces on a green lizard. It smells wrong so he takes off after a big spider. We laugh and I leave them playing together.

The rain has stopped and I want to take the horses to the corral. We have a coat rack and boot shelf in the laundry near the garage door and I pass Grams, stop, and ask if she wants to go for a ride or walk with me.

"Let me get my boots and jacket on." She smiles as she looks at me and adds, "I'd love to go for a ride," I help her with the boots. The horses whinny as we open the barn door and let them out of their stalls and lead all but two into the corral. Then I help Grams get up on Cassiopeia and I get on Skywalker and we ride along the canal bank and let the horses run for a while. We then pull on the reins to slow them down. We talk as they prance.

"How have you been feeling, Grams?"

"Great now that Prairie is with us, I'll feel even better when Senna gets back from the hospital."

"She is going to be cured, Grams. I talked to her this morning and she feels fine, she just wants to come home. Grams, did you get a chance to talk to her doctor yesterday?"

"Yes. He wants to keep her in the hospital for a couple more days, he originally said three days but it will be five days. The virus wasn't strong enough so they have increased the dosage. The doctor said, 'This is not unusual. Every patient is unique and it can take a while to find the perfect dose for each person.' She still has to go through immune therapy, so she could be in the hospital a little longer."

Cassiopeia blows air from her nostrils, a warning. Up ahead of us are three men on horses. Skywalker is nervously prancing. We stop and I lift my field glasses to get a better look. I don't like what

I see and don't want to lead them back to our house. "Let's turn back and cross over the canal at the next intersection and move toward town. Jo, can you hear me? Let Dad know what's happening and what we are doing."

"I will, Laurel."

We increase our speed to a medium gallop and then we come to the intersection, a bridge over the canal. I stop and turn, looking back through the glasses. "They're getting closer."

CHAPTER 17
RAIN

"Super El Niños are serious and present a sound theoretical basis for much stronger and more dangerous weather events."

–James Hansen

We gallop down Maple Street, then cross over Tenth and then down Elm. Grams is a good rider. This area looks like a ghost town, the vegetation is overgrown, dead and the windows on many storefronts are boarded up. There are only two vehicles parked on the street, a red Ford truck and a white van. We ride several miles through the outskirts of town toward the vet clinic because we know Camellia is working today. Behind the clinic there is a rail under a couple of deciduous trees. It's a great spot for animals in the spring and summer, but now everything is bare except for a few patches of grass. We tie up our horses and knock on the back door.

Opening the door, Camellia is surprised to see us and asks, "What are you doing here?"

"We're hiding, let us inside," I say.

"From who?"

After she locks the door we tell her about the three men with shotguns. "The men may have gone to the house. Oh, call Dad," she says.

"We had Jo contact Dad to let him know what was happening so he had some warning."

"Jo, did you give dad my message?"

"Yes, Laurel."

"What is happening at the house, Jo? Contact all AIs and let me know."

The waiting room has an old faded blue sofa and a couple of chairs. I look out the windows, open the door, and look up and down the street. Nothing.

"Any information, Jo?"

"Just a minute."

We wait in silence…my anxiety is increasing.

"Laurel, I have contacted all AIs except Rain's and Forester's personal assistants. They are not responding. I am tracking Rain's implant and he's traveling north on Highway 85. Prairie is in the safe room and his assistant is responding, but has little information. His father told him he needed to wait in the room until he came for him."

"Jo, call Wyatt at the Rigby Sheriff station and Uncle Lesley about the situation. Ask them to meet us at the house. Continue tracking Rain, and send a drone after him."

Camellia sits behind Grams on Cassiopeia, and I lead with Skywalker toward home knowing danger might be waiting for us. We ride like the wind. When we arrive at the bridge over the canal, we stop. I grab the glasses hanging around my neck and glass the homestead for any movement. Nothing, so we slowly approach the back of the property, lined with naked trees. Kazan is barking. I remove the gun from the belt at my back and make sure Camellia and Grams have their guns loaded and ready then we follow the bark, which is coming from the old barn. I dismount and lead Skywalker to the corral.

I ask Grams and Camellia to stay back behind the barn and cover me. I leave Kazan in the barn. I don't want him to get hurt. First I search the cottage…empty. I walk around the Earthship to the rear garage door. It's locked, but I have a key. Inside, the truck is gone and there are several muddy shoe prints left on the concrete, one set smaller than the others. My emotions get the best of me and the tears come, warm and salty. I know some of the prints are Rain's. I look at my watch. We left the vet clinic at 12:30.

"Jo, keep tracking Rain's implant, how far can he go and still be tracked?"

"As long as Rain is above ground, satellites can track him."

"Can you send me two drones, one to watch for any movement on our property and one to check the interior of the house for movement? I will leave the door open to the garage and house, you know where I am?"

"Yes, I can read your implant."

The birdlike drone flies into the garage, and I buzz Camellia on her tablet. "Move into the back door of the garage!" I yell at her.

The wide garage door stands open for the Sheriff, and I enter the elevator and push the hold button to keep it from closing so the drone can enter. My gun is in my hand, and the drone flies overhead. The password is pressing my thumb against a plate opening the elevator door and the door to the safe room. I rush in to the safe room and Prairie jumps up from the cot, his face is stained with dirt and tears. I grab him and hold his small body.

I whisper, "what happened?"

"Dad hid me in here when he got your message about some men coming toward the house."

"Where is Rain and Dad, honey?"

"Dad tried to talk Rain in to staying with me, but he said no, 'I have an implant and can be tracked, let's see what they want.' Dad didn't like the idea, he said it was too dangerous. Rain said, 'I know, that's why I won't leave you.'" That's all Prairie can tell me, he is so shaken up.

"Stay here Prairie while I check out the house, I'll be right back." Grams is now behind me and I ask her to stay in the safe room with him.

Camellia has her gun as we prowl the house looking for Dad. The kitchen is a mess with drawers pulled out and pans, dishtowels, and other things thrown on the floor. We hear a car pull up and we hide in the pantry, where bags of flour and pasta cover the floor.

"Hello, is anyone home?" a voice yells through the garages open door. I peek out the hall window and see a patrol car in the driveway.

"We are here!" I yell, taking the elevator up and going through the open side door into the garage.

"Are you alone?" I say to the Sheriff.

"No, my partner is checking the grounds."

"Are you safe?" he questions.

"Not all of us," I tell the officer.

"The drones have completed their search," Jo reports.

"Where is dad, Jo?"

"He has no implant—I can't pick him up."

I explain everything that has happened to Wyatt, the Sheriff. He is tall and slender, dressed like a cowboy, removing his curled-up hat as he talks to me.

"Wyatt, please go after my kidnaped brother Rain," I ask him. "He has an implant that you can follow. Talk to my assistant." I hand him my tablet. Wyatt listens as Jo explains Rain's implant and how to receive his signal and the capabilities of the drones she sent. "Go after him now, please! Dad might be with him. I will soon follow you." I implore him.

"Jo, please order me a car."

Wyatt takes off following Rain's signal. Camellia leaves for the barn to get Kazan. I go to the safe room to get Prairie, and he hugs me again. He is so scared that he's trembling. I take him to the bathroom and wash his face. Grams is in the kitchen cleaning up the mess on the floor. "The thieves took most of our food," she says. I tell her to look in the hall pantry. If that's cleaned out, go to the hidden storage room.

I hear Camellia yelling on my tablet as I approach the garage and run to her. I meet her outside the barn. Kazan is still barking.

"Laurel, I found Dad in the barn with Kazan!" she screams. "He's been shot! I called an ambulance." We run back to the barn, Dad is conscious, his shirt covered in blood.

"It's his shoulder—he's lost a lot of blood," Camellia says as she keeps pressure on the wound with her hand and checks his medical wristband. It tells her his blood pressure is too high, he is dehydrated, and he's losing too much blood.

Dad keeps repeating, "Go after Rain! They have Rain!"

"Dad, its Laurel. The sheriffs have gone after Rain, we will find him, don't worry."

The siren of the ambulance can be heard and Camellia runs off to show them the way to the barn and tells them to take dad to Idaho Falls where his wife is. I take my sister's place, putting pressure on dad's wound. I tell him everything will be okay, that he will heal and Rain will be fine. As I hide my fear from dad and Kazan whimpers.

The knock at the open door is Uncle Lesley. We tell him all that has happened. The men in the ambulance approach the barn with a pallet.

"Have you found Rain's tablet?" Lesley asks.

"Jo, my AI couldn't pick up a trace of Zak."

"Give me your tablet, Laurel, I want to try something. If it's here we might pick up something." He sends a signal that all tablets in the area can pick up even if they've been turned off. He then takes count of the computers he reaches and the number is six—his own and five others—so that means one more is here somewhere, either dad's or Rain's.

Jo tells me my car is waiting. Lesley hands me back my tablet. "I am going after Rain," I yell while running to the waiting car. Lesley yells for me to wait and reaches my car as I get in the front seat.

"Jo, is Rain still traveling?"

"Yes, he's traveling north."

"I'm coming with you," Uncle Lesley says.

"No, you have a family that's depending on you. I have the information on my tablet to stay in touch with Sheriff Wyatt and his men who are following Rain. I just want to be there for him when he is found. Mom is in the Idaho Falls hospital and Dad has been shot and is leaving for the same hospital. Dad's losing blood, go see them, please."

I start programing the computer in the driverless to take me north on 85. My car takes off and I open up maps in my tablet. I look at my watch; it is 3:40. Rain has been gone at least three hours.

"Jo, let me know if anything changes regarding Rain's movements." *Why would the men who stole our food and shot dad kidnap Rain?* I call Camellia and tell her I've gone after Rain and ask her to take care of Prairie and Grams, and to lock up everything. I have the map on my lap and can see a red dot representing the truck—our truck that holds Rain. The car the cops were in is represented with a blue dot. There is a lot of distance between the red and blue dots.

With my tablet, I call Wyatt and ask why he hasn't called for backup from police at a town closer to the truck.

"We are trying to do this in a way that will keep your brother safe," he says.

Later I call Lesley to find out the condition of Mom and Dad.

"Your dad is in stable condition," Lesley says. "Senna is with him. She wants to talk to you."

"Hi, sweetheart."

"Oh, Mom, it's so good to hear your voice. How is the autoimmune therapy going?"

"I have been sick to my stomach off and on, but the blood tests show improvement in my white cells."

"I'm so glad to hear that, how is Dad doing?"

"He is getting a blood transfusion and is asleep. He will survive."

My tears are flowing and it feels like I have a rock in my throat.

"Try not to worry, I'll bring Rain home."

"Be careful. We need you and love you so much."

"It breaks my heart to see you go through this mess. Give Dad my love." At that moment, it feels so good to hear mom mention she loves me.

I am feeling so tired and hungry. I look in my shoulder bag and find a nutrition bar and a bottle with a little water left in it. After I've finished consuming them, I push a button and my seat becomes a recliner. Then I take a pain pill for my headache. Looking at my tablet again, the time is 4:23 p.m. and I will try taking a nap.

I wake from a frightening dream; I am falling. Now the car stops.

"Jo, what is going on?"

"The kidnappers have stopped at a house north of Butte, Montana. The police have called for backup from the local police and are waiting."

"Why have we stopped?"

"The car stopped at this station to get charged up. It will take off when powered. I have reprogramed the car for the house in Butte. The address is 208 Willow Brook Lane, Butte Montana."

I push a lever down and open the door to use the ladies' room in the station. After a few minutes, I get back in the car with a couple of bottles of water and some snacks from the vending machine. I ask Jo if she released a drone earlier from home. "Yes, and the drone was a good choice because it has cameras aboard and can travel faster than we can," she informs.

"Show me what the drone is looking at, please." A picture emerges on my tablet. I can see a simple brown brick house, the windows are covered with shutters, a faint light is able to get through. Dad's empty truck is parked in the driveway. Later, by simply swiping from right to left in front of the screen, I can flip through all the pictures and even see the police car parked a block away.

I watch as a couple of unmarked black cars and a black van arrive and park around the corner. My car is now charged and takes off.

I text Wyatt and ask if they are waiting for the people in the house to go to sleep. He tells me the problem is they don't know where Rain is in the house. I tell him about the drone waiting outside of the house. My AI can communicate with it and send it inside to take pictures as it finds Rain's location, "you just have to get the door open for the drone. It's small—about the size of a hummingbird. If you can get the door opened, you don't need to wait for me because we can use my tablet to instruct the drone. I won't be there for three and a half hours," I tell Wyatt.

"We need to wait until they are asleep anyway," Wyatt says.

As my car speeds, along, I call home, "Camellia, how are all of you?"

"We are fine, but worried," she says. "I'm so glad you called."

"I wanted to wait until I had something to report, the police are waiting outside a house in Butte, Montana, where Rain is being held. We will get him in a couple of hours."

"How? Isn't it dangerous, he could be killed."

"We have a plan to keep him safe, but yes, it's always dangerous when the police try to extract someone from these types of men. I will tell you about it when we have him. Is Prairie asleep?"

"Yes, but it took a long time and several funny stories. He is so scared. A couple of Lesley's army buddies are staying with us for a few days to look out for us and help Lesley sleep tonight. They are nice guys."

"That's great. Lesley is so good to us. Did you find the missing tablet?"

"We found Rain's, they must have dad's."

"Say hi to Grams and Prairie for me when he wakes. I'll talk to you in a couple of hours."

The car is moving at sixty-five miles an hour and according to the map I am 230 miles away. It will be 10:00 p.m. before I arrive. I just hope they will be asleep.

"You have a message from Sage."

"I'll take it, Jo."

We are closed down in our tents because of another powerful sandstorm. This morning it's so dark outside that you can't see your own hand.

Do the storms last very long?

Usually four to six hours, time to clean our weapons, polish boots and study. Sand gets in everything. We started wearing masks to filter the air we breathe after scientists warned the dust particles are small enough to get in our lungs.

How often do you have the sandstorms?

At least one storm a month, sometimes more depending on the season.

Dad never told us how awful the storms are in Libya. The heat and sandstorms we had in Arizona became so intense we had to leave

Our body suits do a good job of protecting us from the weather.

I hear those suits even recycle your body fluids.

Yes, they do a great job of keeping us hydrated, Laurel. Due to our incredible technology, we can survive in these deserts of 130 degrees and still defend our outposts. What are you up to?

I'm in a car on my way to Butte Montana where Rain is a hostage. It's a long story and I will have to tell you all about it later. I will text you when we have Rain.

Be careful, please call as soon as you can, I will be worried, Laurel.

"Sorry to interrupt Laurel but something is going on at the Mulberry house," Jo warns.

Sage, I'm getting an important message from Jo. Sorry, sweetheart, I have to go. Talk later.

I'm looking at the drone pictures as it circles around the house every ten minutes unless it notices some movement. Someone came out of the house. It's a long-haired man smoking a cigarette. If he walks around the corner and down the block, he will see the black van. I try to notify Wyatt so they can move the van. No time! Now someone is getting out of the back of the van and hiding in the shrubs near the house. The man with the cigarette turns the corner and stops, drops the butt and removes a gun from his back. He crouches down and moves toward the van. Now at the side, he tries to peer through the window; it's too dark inside. He continues around the van until he gets in front of the big windows. He notices the van has no state inspection sticker on the window, and he moves around to the side again and tries to open the door.

The policeman in the bushes jumps out and grabs the man with a wire around his neck, shutting off his windpipe, and he falls to the ground. A second policeman climbs out of the back of the van and helps the first move the kidnapper into the van. With a quarter moon, it's quite dark. The drone uses a special camera for shots at night. Wyatt texts me:

We had to take him, he became suspicious. One down!

I will be at the house in an hour. I realize that Sage is probably worried due to the way I cut him off. I didn't want him to know what is going down because he would worry, but now he will worry even more if I don't call him back.

"Jo, how is the drone doing?"

"It is still making rounds and has enough energy to complete the assignment." I look at a few more pictures and see no one.

"Jo, please try to get Sage"

The car has slowed to fifty because we are in a forest, where there is danger of an animal crossing the road. I check the program for the car and everything looks fine.

"I have Sage on voice for you."

"Thank you, Jo."

"Hi, honey. Sorry I had to cut you off like that."

"Laurel, what's going on. Where are you?"

"I'm in Montana near Butte, on my way to get Rain. He was kidnapped and I might have to cut you off again because I'm in an ongoing situation with the police, the kidnappers, drones and my driverless car. Let me start at the beginning...

When I finish my story, Sage replies, "You have more going on than I have encountered since I arrived in Libya."

I tell him I will call back later. I am fifteen minutes away from Rain and very nervous. I park behind the van, two blocks away. I call Wyatt.

"Hi, I just arrived."

"We have the keys to the doors. We will send the drone through the kitchen door. Let me speak with your AI."

"Jo, Deputy Wyatt would like information on the drone."

The kitchen is at the back, a block from the van. The drone lands on top of the van and Jo communicates with it, giving instructions to start in the southeast corner. "Take pictures of each room and its occupant. After each room has been photographed, fly back and out through the same door and land on the van."

I am trembling, so worried that my mouth is dry. As I look at each picture the drone takes, I grab my bottle of water and drink. I see the kitchen with food covering every counter. The family room has a dark unshaven man sleeping on his back on the sofa. The bathroom is empty. In a small bedroom, Rain is sitting handcuffed, his arms chained to the metal headboard of a twin bed. He has bruises on his face and dried blood from cuts on his arms. He seems asleep. Across the hall is a large bedroom where two men sleep on twin beds. The drone is coming back down the hall and lands outside on the van.

Wyatt texts me:

We are going in now with three armed men and knockout drugs. Rain will be secured first.

I have to get my mind on something else after I watch the SWAT team leave the van. Jo asks. "Do you want the drone to go back to Rain so you will know what happens?"

"Yes, but I'll watch when it's over."

I call Camellia, not thinking about the time.

"Hello…"

"Hi, it's me."

"Thank God—I've been so worried."

"Well, it isn't over, but we are with Rain. The drone I sent took pictures of him in a house we are parked near. The kidnappers are asleep and the SWAT team has just entered the house. I couldn't watch; it's too nerve-racking. But they are securing Rain first. We will get him, honey. You should let everyone know. How is Dad?"

"The bullet entered through his chest just below his shoulder. He is lucky it didn't hit a bone or lung—he just lost a lot of blood. But he will be fine as soon as he knows Rain is okay. Thank God, Laurel."

"I do, Camellia. See you soon."

"Laurel, you'd better see this," Jo says.

I look at the picture on my tablet and it shows the kidnapper who was asleep on the living room sofa up and walking to the bathroom. I notify Wyatt that the man on the sofa is awake now. Both the front and back doors can be seen from the living room. Wyatt notifies his men.

When the kidnapper returns to the living room, he notices the back door is open. He must remember the kidnapper who went out to smoke. He shuts the door, sits down and appears to be thinking. Suddenly, he gets up and looks in at Rain then walks down the hall and checks out the second bedroom and the two men sleeping. He returns to the back door and opens it and steps outside looking for the other gang member. That's when he is taken out with the wire around the throat cutting off his air supply. He is put in the van by two officers. Having Jo work with Wyatt and the drone is working better than expected, because one kidnapper left the house to look for the other.

Jo says, "Rain is next." The officer is slowly taking his cuffs off and sliding his arms out of the chains. Rain tries to stand up but nearly falls over. I start watching the pictures from the drone as the officer picks him up and carries him to my car. I get out and open the back door. Rain is put on the backseat. The officer says, "He is dehydrated, but seems okay. Follow the black car behind the van. It will take you to the nearest hospital to have him checked out."

"Okay, thank you. What about the two men asleep in the back bedroom?"

"We have them now, it was easy to get them as they slept."

Jo, brings the drone back to the car. I slide into the backseat, hug and kiss Rain and hand him a bottle of water and some snacks. He is stunned. The drone flies into the car and lands on top of the backseat.

Then I get back in the front seat, lock the doors, and switch the car from manual to automatic. We take off following the black car through the hills.

Jo has Sage online.

"Sage, we have Rain. He is in the back seat as I'm following a car to the hospital. They tell me he seems fine, just dehydrated, but that is just a quick determination. I am fine, it's just so nerve- racking and frightening. Everyone did a great job and we had some luck. I am just so happy to have my brother back."

"Wow! You did it, Rain is free and you are safe. I am so happy for you! Rain might need some psychological help after going through something so devastating."

"You are right, this could mess his mind up. I'm also worried about physical damage. I can see a small hospital up ahead, talk later, bye."

We follow the black car through the trees into a small city and a white three-story hospital. We pull up into the Emergency parking lot. Wyatt is parked near me in the black car. He gets out and grabs a wheelchair near the front door. I notice that Rain drank all the water. Wyatt and I help him out of the car and into the wheelchair. I follow as Wyatt pushes him into the hospital. A middle-aged blonde nurse with a charming smile greets us. Her name tag says "Linda."

"I need my brother checked out. Rain is the victim of a kidnapping."

Wyatt shows her his badge and talks to her. "We don't know what they did to him. He's in some state of shock and hasn't said a word since we were able to free him."

"Let's have a look at him," Linda says as I help her get him on a gurney. Rain's eyes are open and I keep talking to him as the nurse wheels him down the sanitized hall into a draped cubical. I stand back and watch as she checks his vitals and then puts a needle in his wrist, creating a port to run fluids through. She gets a bag and hangs it on a stand, starting a drip into his vein. "He should feel better after this. He is very dehydrated," she says. She looks in his mouth and tells him to stick out his tongue, which he does. Then she checks his ears and cleans up the dried blood on his arm and the cuts and bruises on his face.

"Were you hurt?" I ask. He looks at me as though I am a stranger and I cry. He looks away. I signal for the nurse to go with me, and we leave my brother on the gurney. We walk into another empty room, and I ask the nurse to get us a doctor.

"Why won't my brother talk to me?"

"We have no idea what he has been through," she says. "There are a number of reasons he won't talk to you."

"I need to get him home to Rigby, Idaho. Can he travel when he is fed and hydrated?"

"Let us check him out a little more deeply," she replies.

CHAPTER 18
HEALING

"It is true we started too late, the planet has changed and will change even more. The economy that powers it can't be turned off quick enough to prevent hideous damage."

– Bill Mc Kibben

A Doctor Taylor comes into the hospital room and talks with the nurse. Rain lays on a gurney and I sit in an uncomfortable chair. I am so tired and sad, and just want to take my brother home. I feel so worthless being unable to help him, knowing he has been through a terrible ordeal. The love I've been holding in my heart for him is waiting to be released, so I just let the tears flow from depths I never knew I had. I sit for a couple of hours.

The doctor says, "I think it's best if your brother spends the night here. We will get you a room with an extra bed so you can stay with him all night. You don't look well enough to drive far tonight. Let's see how he feels in the morning." It is settled; we will spend the night.

The nurse moves Rain and me to a small room on the third floor with a door. The nurse undresses him and cleans him up with a tub bath. She puts his clothes in a plastic bag. "I'll wash these so he has clean clothes tomorrow," Linda says, then gives him some pills to take and leaves. Before I climb in bed, I kiss my brother and tell him everything will be all right.

I can't sleep. I hear Rain moan several times off and on during the night, and watch him kicking in his dreams. I doze off momentarily and wake up to an antiseptic odor. Nurse June, a slender young woman with curly blonde hair, is now on duty. I read her name tag as she looks at me.

"How is my brother?"

"We are giving him an antibiotic for an infection."

"How did he get that?"

"From some untreated abrasions that became infected."

"Has he eaten anything?"

"Not much," the nurse replies.

"Has a doctor been called in for him?"

"Doctor Taylor, an internist, saw him last night."

"What did he think?"

"You can talk to him after breakfast. He will come by."

I get up and go to the bathroom to take a shower and get ready for the day. I then watch Rain and ask him if he is hurting. He shakes his head.

"Why won't you talk to me? Are you mad at me?" Again, his head moves from side to side and he looks away.

Breakfast arrives and I am famished. I remove the brown plastic top of my tray. Scrambled eggs, toast, jelly and coffee. I help Rain sit up and place a pillow behind his back and his tray on his lap. I butter his toast and dilute his juice a little, the way he likes it. I move my chair closer to him and start eating. He also picks up his fork and starts on his eggs. I spread some jam on our toast and he takes a few bites. I talk to him about the family and how everyone is feeling and doing. Then I talk about the bad men now in jail. I see tears form in the corner of his eyes and roll down his cheeks.

"Did the men hurt you, Rain?" He nods.

"I did my best to get to you—you know that, don't you?"

He says, "Yes." It is soft, almost a whisper.

We finish our breakfast. "Do you want to go home with me today, honey?"

"Yes," he says. I move his tray and kiss him on the forehead.

"I love you so much, Rain."

Doctor Taylor walks in, says hello, and checks out my brother.

"Are you ready to go home?"

"Yes," is his faint reply.

"The nurse will bring your clothes and you are free to go with your sister." He asks me for my parents' phone number so he can instruct them. After I gave him Dad's number, he asks to talk to me. We leave the room and walk into the hall. The young-looking doctor has a serious expression on his face when he tells me he is recommending to my parents that Rain be treated for trauma after all that he has been through. He hands me a paper with his letterhead and below that is the name of a Doctor Alexander in Idaho Falls with his address and phone number.

Then Dr. Taylor said, "In cases of rape it is most important to start professional assistance as soon as possible to prevent even more complications for the patient."

"Oh, my God, doctor! He was raped?" I exclaimed.

"Unfortunately, that is the case." He replied. "I will also give your parents this information, but I want you to stress the seriousness of the issue."

I am so shocked I can only thank him. In the room, I am crying and sick at heart and to my stomach.

Nurse June comes in and removes the needles, tubes, tape, and bags of fluid from Rain's body. She is a talker. Rain picks up his clean clothes and walks to the bathroom.

The nurse, almost whispering, tells me. "Did the doctor tell you your brother was raped by at least one of those men?" Linda noticed that his underwear was bloody, and she bagged them as evidence for the police. She examined his rectum, took swabs as he slept, and put some healing salve inside. That's why we gave him an antibiotic and tested his blood for any disease. Wyatt picked up the underwear and the swabs this morning so they could be sent to the lab and tested. He brought Rain new underwear from Wallco."

"Thank you so much, June. Doctor Taylor did tell me." Then I break down. I feel a sharp pain in my chest, then I feel like I am going to throw up. I gag, and the tears come with great force that I feel weak. All the while, June is hugging me until I have to sit down again and just sob and sob for all my brother had to endure. When I am spent, I say, "Wyatt is a good guy." I grab her hand and squeeze. "You did tell Rain that you knew what happened."

"Yes, she replied. Boys his age are very shy about being molested, but he needs to come to grip with it because it has to come up in the trial. Your brother is suffering a great deal, and those men should stay in jail a long time for what they did to him."

Deputy Wyatt returns. I tell him I keep thinking about Dad's tablet—we need to get it back. I ask Rain if he knows where the bad men put Dad's tablet. With the word "Dad," his eyes sparkle with tears. "Rain, honey, Dad is okay and he loves you so much. Tell me if you can."

He doesn't answer, so I look at Wyatt. "Remember, the bad guys have the tablet and must have had him open it. I bet they can do a lot of damage with the information on the tablet. Please find it. Can we also get our food and truck back?"

"We will bring you any unopened food in your truck and look for the tablet when we go back to the house," he replies. He puts his hand on my shoulder, a gesture of sympathy for all I am feeling. "If we don't find it, we will get the information from the men."

"Thank you, Wyatt, for all your help."

"Sure, that's my job, we'll be in touch." He turns and leaves.

After lunch, Rain and I are on the road heading home. The car is set again on automatic so I don't have to drive. I am sending texts to everyone, letting them know that I am bringing my brother home.

I contact Sage and let him know as Rain sleeps in the passenger seat. I tell him what the doctor told me and we talk about everything. Then I let him know how important he is in my life and I miss him.

"I work at keeping very busy with all the duty I can get so I won't be thinking about you all the time. Now it will be harder not to."

"Don't put yourself in any danger because of me, please. I am sorry, but know how you feel because it hurts when I start missing you. I just have so much to do during the day that I don't think about you a lot. But the nights are when I imagine holding you in my arms and remember everything. In the morning, the first thing I do is miss your presence in my bed."

"Yes, sweetheart, the nights are both the worst and the best. I miss you so much. I just hope and pray that things continue to be relatively calm around the embassy so I can come home soon."

"Me, too. Goodnight. Sweet dreams, Sage."

Dad is coming home from the hospital later in the day. But Mom is still being treated. I ask Rain if he wants to tell me what happened. Not yet; it's too painful. He will take his time. After a while my brother falls asleep again. I feel like I understand what it must be like for Rain when you first realize how small and unprotected you are in this world of negative forces and that God, if he exists, doesn't always save his children from terrible things. Once I was in a swimming pool with other kids. I was fearless by nature until I got in over my head, realizing I could not touch the bottom with my feet. I swam toward the edge of the pool when a couple of older kids held me down, pushing me under the water. I fought and fought so hard to get them off me without success. Then I just stopped and played dead. Almost out of air, I couldn't hold my breath any longer. When they left, I rose to the surface. I never enjoyed a pool again.

I ask Jo to reach dad.

"Laurel, I could tell you that you are one of the bravest people I know, but that might make you do something even crazier," he says. "Thank you for getting your brother back."

"Dad, I have already done things crazier than this. I just rode in the car. Jo, the police, Wyatt and the drones did everything. I was never in danger. How are you feeling, Dad?"

"They patched me up at the hospital and I'm fine, just stiff in the shoulder."

"How is mother feeling?"

"Upset because she wants to come home. She misses her home and everyone so much. She won't let them keep her much longer. I expect her to break out any day."

"I can imagine how she feels, and it must be terrible for her. I'll take Rain to see her before we come home."

"You should. We are all so eager to have him home."

"How is he?"

"To be honest, not very good, Daddy. They hurt him and I think he is ashamed that he let you down." I can't stop the quivering vibration in my voice. I am crying.

"He never let me down. He wanted to protect me, and I would have done the same. He was being a man, and I feel so bad because he is just a boy. Time will heal both of us. Don't you worry, my dear daughter. It's my fault because I had everything up but not running. I didn't expect to be hit during daylight. But now we know and will always be ready. I know it will only get worse as food becomes scarce. I found a nice family to live in the cottage and help us. They are refugees from Central America and they speak English. You will like them."

"That is good news. We need to start planting again as soon as I get home, see you soon, Daddy." The car stopped at a charging station and I bought us some water and snacks. Rain went to the bathroom and moved to the back seat where he could stretch out.

I turn around after a while. Rain is still sleeping. The vista outside is rolling hills with black tree stumps, and I can tell we are near Idaho. Rain wakes up and looks around.

"We are almost home, but I want to stop and see Mom at the hospital in Idaho Falls. Is that okay with you?"

"Yes."

When we arrive at the hospital in Idaho Falls, we park in the covered parking lot. It is a nice clear day but on the cool side. Rain is without a jacket. We enter the double doors and go to the reception desk and wait for the lady to get off the phone. It is a large room in warm colors of brick and wheat-colored drywall and walnut exposed wood beams and trim.

"Yes, can I help you?" the lady asks us.

"Yes, can I have the room number for Senna?"

"Let me see," she says as she looks at the large computer screen. "Senna is in room 330."

When we reach Mom's room, she opens the door and a huge smile lights up her beautiful face. She hugs Rain and kisses his cheek and just holds onto him. He hugs her and tells her she smells good and he has missed her fragrance so much. Their eyes shine with tears. Then she pulls me into her hug also and kisses me. "Oh, it's so good to see you both," Mom says. "I have been going crazy, feeling so lonely, like a big dark hole inside me. Come sit down and tell me what's going on."

Rain doesn't talk much but he seems less sad. We stay and have dinner with Mom. He may never want to talk to her about the terrible things they did to him; it would hurt her too much. She must never know. I feel so bad about walking away from her, but I can't take her home until she is released.

When we arrive at the Earthship and park in front, we unload the car and Rain carries the stuff inside. I program the car to go back to its lot, and it takes off.

At our Earthship, the doors to the elevator open and we inhale the earth and sweet aroma of fruit and berries in the greenhouse entry. Rain and I slip out of our shoes and place them in the coat closet. We walk on the earthen floor of the family room, where all the voices and barks are coming from. Rain is soon engulfed in family and a happy barking dog. The cats are hiding. I too am sucked into the happy reunion of kisses, hugs, laughter and tears. I can only think of what Mom is missing in her lonely hospital room. At that moment, I know I will bring her home no matter what the doctor says because she could not get better without all this love.

That night I ask my dad to let me bring mom home and explain why. He agrees with me. I sleep with Prairie and hold him in my arms after making up some goat stories for him. It feels good to be in the same room with my brothers. I realize again how very fragile humans are and how easy it is to lose all that we love.

In the morning, Rain wakes us. We give up on any more sleep once Kazan starts whimpering to go outside. Rain is in his robe and goes out with him.

Dad yells, "Remember, we are on lockdown." That means our defenses are operating and we have to stay in the inner fence.

During breakfast Rain asks me what's going on with the immigrants.

"They are here and more are coming into the country at about 100,000 a month. There are many angry people resisting, mostly because of food and medical shortages. But states have no authority when it comes to migrants. The Supreme Court has repeatedly reaffirmed that the Constitution vests the federal government, not the states, with power over immigration, naturalization and deportation. No state can add or take away from the force and effect of such a treaty of statute. It is the historic policy of the United States to respond to the urgent needs of people subject to persecution or in need of protection from the loss of life in their homelands. That is why the president is within his right to tell the states they must take and make a home for the Central American migrants. President Anderson is asking that every state with a population less than 150,000 take some migrants because it is the humane thing to do and America was built by the hard work of immigrants from all over the world."

"How is it working out?" Rain asks.

"There are always those mean-spirited, selfish people who don't like to share or don't trust anyone who is not of their own tribe. Dad said Idaho is planning on taking 50,000 migrants. Montana, Wyoming, Utah, North Dakota, Minnesota and Wisconsin will have to take their share, but they are still working on the plans."

In the kitchen, Grams is making coffee. I say good morning and hold her in a warm embrace. She kisses me and thanks me for bringing Rain home. I tell her I will also bring mom home.

"We can nurse her at home," I say. Grams gives me another hug. Dad comes in and sees me with Grams and says, "Did you tell her?"

"Yes, Dad, I told her."

"Good, because I can't stand it anymore!"

Camellia enters the kitchen and we tell her. She is more worried about our decision. I tell her a person needs to feel a lot of love to heal.

"What medical school did you go to, Laurel?" she asks.

"Love International, sis. I'm sure we can pour bags of fluid in her arm."

"It's more complicated than that," she replies.

"Camellia, if it doesn't work we will all have to move in with her because she can never get well feeling lonely and miserable all the time."

Camellia smiles and gives me her famous wink and I know she was just giving me a hard time.

We make a pile of blue corn cakes and scrambled eggs with real maple syrup and goat yogurt. We have our family back except for mom. After breakfast, Dad calls the hospital and asks mom's nurse to have her doctor call him.

After the chores are done, I ask Rain to help me plant in the greenhouses. It is a cool, sunny day in March. My brother adds wheelbarrows full of mulch to the soil in each greenhouse. Then he picks up a hand tiller and tills the mulch into the soil and makes the soil into rows.

Kazan follows me when I run to the cellar to get some seeds that were started in peat moss. On my knees, I crawl along, popping plugs in the soil. Then I daydream about Rain falling in love someday and a new life for him as I push seed after seed into the ground. Before I realize it, it is time for lunch. I have finished planting one greenhouse.

Later that day before dinner, Rain and I talk a lot. He is talking again. He and Dad had a long, private talk the night he came home, and it helped Rain feel a lot better about himself. Kazan follows us into the house and sits next to Rain's chair at the table while we eat. Camellia is at work, but Dad, Grams, Prairie and I eat together. Chia waits on Camellia's chair, and Tiger lies under Prairie's chair. Dad says he will bring Mom home this afternoon.

We all yell, "hurrah!" Dad asks us to stick to the house because the Vargas family will come by to look at the cottage.

"Show them around, but turn off the armaments before you let them in, okay?" Dad says.

After lunch, Dad calls for a car. He misses his truck. I call Wyatt and leave a message for him to call me. I help Grams clean up and ask if the outlaws took the food in the pantry.

Grams says yes while picking up empty bags.

"We are so lucky that dad and mom saw this coming a long time ago," I say.

"Yes, we are. It will be nice to have fresh food from the greenhouses again." She hands me a bowl with a request. "Please pick the strawberries growing in the greenhouse hall. Thank you. I just haven't had time to get to them."

I should have brought a bowl for avocados as well. Wow, I need to make some strawberry shortcake for dessert. I pick strawberries until my tablet buzzes.

"Laurel, you have a call from Wyatt."

"Thank you, Jo."

"Hi, Wyatt, what's happening with our tablet and truck?"

"Do you want the good or bad news first?"

"Bad first."

"It turns out the devils belong to a gang called the Revolutionaries for Change, a hawkish group. This radical-right violence continues to plague the U.S. Increasingly, extremists are on the move. They don't like immigrants moving in. You may not have seen the last of them, Laurel. We believe this attack on your family has more to do with your father's position on the migrants than it does with food."

"I'm not surprised, Wyatt."

"The good news is we have your truck, food, and father's tablet."

"That is wonderful news. When will we get them?"

"I'll bring them over late today if someone can drive me back to the office."

"Sure, I'll drive you back."

"See you later, then."

"Thanks, Wyatt."

Next, the doorbell rings. It is also an alarm reminding me to turn off the armaments. I go to the hall closet and tell the AI running the house to shut down armaments except the one for the back fence along our property line. I leave the house from the elevator with my gun hidden in the back of my pants.

CHAPTER 19
THE VARGASES

"El Niño's long lasting return would set the spark for one of the most destructive conflagration's the world has ever seen."

–James Hansen

At the front gate is a small dark man standing beside a black car. As I walk toward him I can tell he is Mr. Vargas. Dad described him to me. When I reach him, he says, *"Hola!"*

"Hello, you must be Mr. Vargas. Bring your family and follow me."

He introduces me to his wife, Alta, daughter, Gabriela, and three sons, Jorge, Luis, and Sabato. They are a very attractive family. I take them to the cottage first and show them the new lifetime roof called Propanel, a corrugated metal with a baked-on enamel surface that reflects sun light. They wait while I unlock the front door. It is freshly painted and has all new fixtures. They seem happy with everything. Then I show them the greenhouses, fruit orchard, goats, chickens, and horses. Last is the Earthship. They are very surprised by the look and design. We enter the front door elevator, descend to the first floor and the doors open. I introduced them to Grams, Rain, Prairie and the animals. Grams pours us some iced tea and puts a platter of cookies on the table. We ask them many questions about their lives and trip to America. I am saddened by all they have endured. They lost a young daughter, who drowned with the sinking of their home and land. The shocking vision in my mind robs my lungs of air for a few minutes as I hug the mother. We walked back to the Earthship after they approved of the cottage.

Dad and Mom walk in the elevator door. I introduce my parents to the Vargases and Mom and Dad sit with us. Dad tells them Mom has been in the hospital and that we just found my brother, who was taken by kidnappers. They stay for dinner and meet Wyatt when he comes by and Camellia when she comes home from work. Mr. Vargas and his family agree to our arrangement with them. My AI, Jo, writes up our online agreement of a rent-free house and food from the garden, eggs, and goat milk in payment for two hundred hours a month of work from the family in the greenhouses, with the animals, and on the land and help in securing the property and families. I print the papers on my copier. Mr. Vargas signs the papers. They could move in now and start April 1. There will be a four-month trial period when either family can back out. After four months, they will be expected to stay for a year. We will continue with yearly leases with a two-month notice if they want to leave.

I drive Wyatt, who brought our truck, back to his office and thank him, he is such a fine person.

Mom is so happy to be home, sleeping in her own bed, enjoying her family and eating Grams' wonderful, healthy dishes. Prairie has missed her so much that he insists on sleeping with her at nap time and won't let her out of his sight during the day. Rain checks on her every few hours, and Camellia takes over her infusions and shots. Plus, she reports to mom's oncologist.

On July first, we all agree the Vargas family is working out perfectly for us and they seem to enjoy their life here. They are going to stay with us!

It hasn't rained in six months. The canal is dry and we are conserving water. We are very worried about all fires burning across many western states and California. We already have a forest fire burning in the panhandle. The Vargas boys are all strong and hardworking. Jorge, aged eighteen, and his brother Luis, aged sixteen, are helping their dad, Ernesto, and my dad clear the land of leaves, dead grass and weeds as a protection from fires. Ernesto drives the tractor to till the land, and they take turns raking up the weeds and leaves that are already dry, easy fuel for fires.

Camellia nurses my mother back to health, but now Mom needs to put on some weight. Dad is totally healed from his gunshot wound, and Rain, well, we don't know if he has totally overcome his terrible ordeal. Rain is seeing Dr. Alexander twice a month for the trauma inflicted on him. He still wears his scars from a demoralizing and painful experience and is seeking a more spiritual life with the Mormons. In my youth, I studied the Bible and went to seminary, and now he is enrolled in seminary. The difference between us is that I was a hard nut to crack. I asked too many questions that couldn't be answered and looked for everything to be backed by my own experience. Rain relies more on faith and trust in God. He is more like his dad: self-disciplined, honest and expecting the best from God even if it feels like the worst.

I work part-time at my business of building Earthships and have finished the one in Twin Falls. The owners are very happy with their new home and they plan on advertising for me. So far, every job has come to me through word of mouth. I have two new homes to build, one is in Pocatello, sixty miles away. The second one will be built in Idaho City about thirty-six miles northeast of Boise and about 280 miles from home. But over time I have found an honest, reliable crew who are artisans. They love the work and believe in the cause of saving more humans and animals. I suggest to most of my clients that there is safety in numbers, and some are following our example of adding extended family or immigrants to their homesteads for more protection. We keep in touch with each other on our Earthship United blog. My dad is available for those who need help in defending their property.

The three men from the Revolutionaries for Change gang who kidnapped Rain are found guilty of taking a child across state lines and holding him against his will while beating and raping him. They plead guilty without a trial and receive thirty-five years each. With good behavior, they will be out in fifteen. For shooting Dad, one man receives an extra five years on his sentence. They will be locked up for a long time, but we will still watch out for other members of the gang.

The drought is very bad in the Midwest and Northwest. The wells have dried up in many towns and cities, and water has to be trucked in at $5.00 a gallon. This leaves little for food and basics for most people. The Mormons always save for bad times, and they have set up a network to help the elderly with water and food at no charge. Dad and Rain are helping with that a couple of days a week.

We are back to growing food for the food bank, and our farmers' market is open and running. That is a big help to our community.

On my birthday the family gives me a big birthday party, but I surprise everyone because I bring most of the gifts. From the animal shelter, I bring Gabriela Vargas a gray and white tabby kitten and young Sabato a golden retriever female puppy. Sabato names her Carmel, like her color. I give pregnant goats to Luis and Jorge, and I give Alta Vargas a rooster and two chickens. Ernesto receives an American Saddle Pinto colt in chestnut and black with white markings similar to an Appaloosa. I have all the animals delivered at the same time, and everyone is delighted, especially me.

Grams makes me a fabulous chocolate and strawberry birthday cake, and I get new riding boots and some clothes. I am so eager to speak to Sage. I know he will be waiting for my call, but I have to wait until after my party. Camellia gives me a gold locket for Sage's picture and a big birthday hug. I ask her what happened to her and Cannon.

"I guess we just didn't have time for one another, and he thinks I'm too young for him. He is dating an older girl now."

"I'm sorry."

"Oh, I only felt bad until the Vargas family moved in with all their good-looking boys. But I'll just fool around until I graduate. I think Rain has a big crush on Gabriela."

"Really? I never noticed."

"Laurel, you are not one to notice the little things in life unless it has to do with animals."

"What a terrible thing to say about your sister…even if it's true." We both have a good laugh.

Grams gives me a big hug and a beautiful locket that belonged to her grandmother, who came across the plains on a covered wagon and lived to be ninety-three. The picture in the gold locket is of a boy she loved but had to leave in Inverness, Scotland. I thank her and say, "I hope to treasure it the way you have and give it to my daughter."

"I know you will," she answers.

Dad's gift is a small and unusual revolver that holds twelve shots and has my name engraved on it. He says he found it in an antique showroom and had it engraved. He tried it out and was amazed at how accurate it is. He was told it is a custom job.

"Thank you, Dad. I love it."

He continues, "I have been wanting to tell you that the migrant resettlement community liked your ideas on using shipping containers for housing the migrants. They put a section together, one shipping crate stacked on top of another the same size and bolted them together, creating a two-story house with one story underground. They will be finished outside with insulated painted panels, inside with more insulated drywall, painted, given modern fixtures and metal roofs to catch water with solar cells on the south-facing wall. The migrants will love the houses."

"Well, I am pleased that it worked out, Dad, and hope they used all fireproof material."

"I checked. They did."

Rain smiles at dad when he kisses him on the forehead. It is hard to keep your hands off Rain. He is so attractive with his dark brown wavy hair and beautiful eyes, a mix of blue brown, and green. He looks at me and says, "I'd like to hug you also."

We hug and he says, "I never thanked you for coming for me—I was so traumatized. I'm thanking you now."

"Nothing to it," I say, smiling at him. "You will always be my brother and I have your back, kiddo."

Rain adds, "I found some interesting stuff on my tablet today. We have to go back three million years to a time called the Pliocene for the three-degree rise in temperature that scientists say we will reach in my lifetime. "

"Yes, Rain, that's why scientists have a pretty good idea about what life will be like."

He continues, "Looking into the past can tell us what just might happen in the future, and we have deep-thinking computers that can look at all the data."

Then I add, "The data isn't perfect because the earth is more complex than the computers, but they tell us a lot that could happen."

Prairie comes over to take part and asks, "Why do you think more people aren't coming to Idaho?"

"Because they don't know where it is," I say. Everyone that can hear me laughs. "When we lived in Texas and Arizona, people would ask me where I was born, and when I said Idaho they would always say, 'Where is that?' Idaho is the best-kept secret. That's why we came back."

Prairie gives me a birthday hug, and I whisper, "I love you, little brother." He really smiles.

We are sitting outside on the covered sidewalks for some shade. As the Vargas family leaves with their animals, Dad says, "Just put them in with our animals for now. Later you can build them a home, but they might be happier with friends." They thank Dad and just take the dog and cat in the cottage. Chia and Tiger are playing in the paper bows and ribbons while we clean up the food and put away the chairs and folding tables. Rain puts the paper in the recycle bin, and we save the ribbons for reuse.

I notice Mom leaving early and I wonder if she is feeling ill. In the house, I see her in her room lying on her bed. I lie down by her and say, "I bet you are worn out from the party and everyone. I'm sorry you don't feel well, Mom. Can I get you anything?"

"No, honey, I just want to rest a little before dinner."

"I love you, Mom." I kiss her on the cheek.

"I know you do and I'm sorry I've neglected you, depended on you so much. I always had so much to do, and as the babies came the older ones got pushed to the back."

"I know, Mom. Someone has to be the oldest and there are some advantages. I'd better see if Grams needs help with dinner."

I walked away feeling like something was missing between us, but what? Was it because she didn't tell me she loved me? I know that actions are more important than words, yet I need her to say those words. I feel like crying when I see Grams, and she asks me what is wrong. I tell her about my conversation with Mom and how I felt walking away from her. "You have had a lot on your plate lately, and you have been very worried about your mother," Grams says. "Your feelings are natural. Those we feel most attached to are the ones we find hardest to communicate with because words are not adequate to convey feelings."

"I feel like she doesn't love me, Grams."

"You are wrong, sweetheart, and someday you will find out the truth."

At bedtime, I have Jo text Sage while I change into my pajamas and brush my teeth.

"I have a text from Sage," Jo says.

Good morning Sage.

Good evening Laurel. Did you enjoy your birthday party?

It was so much fun.

Sweetheart, I am looking forward to seeing you in your new birthday suit.

Sage, you just made me blush.

Good, you have a lovely body and I can imagine it growing even more beautiful with age.

Is your body going to grow more beautiful with age, Sage?

If I keep working out the way I have, when you see me again you'll be looking at Tom Cruise.

Sage, you are already more handsome than Tom Cruise was as a young man.

Laurel, I have some bad news for us and have put off telling you. I was supposed to be released at the end of two years. That isn't going to happen now because we are fighting a war against terrorists in Libya near our embassy. The Marines can keep me longer than two years now. I will still get my one-month leaves. I knew this was in my contract, but didn't believe they could legally keep me. I am stuck for now.

What can I say that will change anything? I am angry that they can get away with holding people against their will. Even if it was in the small print of a contract, if people can't read the small print it is still cheating. Did you read the small print, Sage?

I read it, just didn't think Libya would go to war after our help in reducing the risks. I am so sorry Laurel.

So am I. The last six months in Rigby have flown by for me, I have had so much to deal with, and now this news.

How is everyone?

Dad has healed. Rain is not his old self and may never be, but he is in therapy trying to deal with his experience. The bad men are behind bars, and mom's last test shows she is cancer-free. I just want normal peace and quiet for a few years.

You told me about the Vargases. How is that working, sweetheart?

They are great. We are so lucky to have them helping us.

They are lucky to have such a kind and loving family to work for.

Thank you, Sage. How is your family?

Mom still works at Idaho Potato Co. She just got a promotion. She has been with the company a long time. Now she manages sorting. Dara graduated and is still managing her farmers' market and trying to decide on a career. She likes working with her hands and brain and has found several online companies that help you find your best suited career. So, she is going to get some help.

Getting help is smart and she is a very smart young lady.

You are right about that. And Mike, he was really affected by what happened to Rain and because of that he has taken an interest in forensic science. I think he wants to be a detective. Imagine that!

I can see him in that role, Sage. How is Jack?

Slowing down, he is worn out. I guess we'd better say goodbye, these long-distance texts rack up the charges.

I'll see you when you are home again on leave. Goodnight, sweetheart.

It is early in October, about the time Luis turns sixteen. He is strong and quick at getting work done. When he works with others, it's a competition for him. He likes everything neat and tidy. Luis has a dry, sarcastic wit. He knows how to keep us laughing.

The doorbell rings and I go to the front gate, where a dozen people stand under the roof of the gatehouse. They are haggard in their rags and masks, wearing dark glass goggles and towing wagons. The frailty of the youngest tears at my heart. I ask where they came from. One mother says, "On the other side of the railroad tracks about two miles down Second Street."

I ask, "Have you seen the food bank or the farmers' market on First Street near your home?"

She replies, "No, didn't know 'bout them, miss."

"We give free food at both. When you go, there is no charge for those who can't pay. In the future, please go to those places. Today if you will wait here, I will bring you some food and water. If you move from this place you could get seriously hurt because our property is armed for our protection. Do not move."

I walk back to the house, go in, lock the door, and buzz the Vargas home. "Hello, Gabriela, are the boys or your dad around?"

"Yes, Miss Laurel, please wait…"

"Jorge here, miss."

"Can you help me with something?" I ask.

"Yes, yes."

"There are twelve people standing at the front gate begging for food and water. Can you fill a few jugs with water, canned beans from cold storage and get four dozen eggs, goat milk, a few bags of flour and fresh vegetables—enough for twelve people for a few days—in a wheelbarrow or the truck and bring that to the people?"

"Yes, Laurel, I'll get some help to make it faster."

"Thank you, Jorge."

As I walk back to the gatehouse Kazan joins me. I keep my head and upper body covered with a paper-thin cotton shawl to protect my fair skin. The breeze feels like the air in a furnace. The people seem to be staying under the shade of the roof's overhang. Kazan sits in the shade and watches the people as I tell them my friends are fetching some food and water for them.

"In the future, you must go to the farmers' market or food bank for supplies," I say. "We are not set up here to help you."

An older man with graying long hair under a straw hat asks if I know of any work around here. I ask what his name is. He says it's Jack Graham. He repairs machinery of all kinds.

"Do any of you have tablets?" I ask. Three people raise their hands. "You need to help each other to survive. With your tablets, you can help other people find jobs by advertising over the net. It's important that everyone charge the same per hour no matter what your station in life has been. Work out a system paying each other with time rather than money like an hour for a haircut or teaching a child for three hours in exchange of mending and patching clothes for three hours. Create a Time Bank on a pad to keep track of every debt and payment. Can you do that?"

"Yes," some say.

Jorge, Luis and Rain come with two wheelbarrows filled with paper bags and jugs. They are teasing and laughing over who is the fastest. I ask families to stand together. Rain and Jorge give each family, depending on size, one or two jugs of water, a bag of flour, eggs, a jug of milk, and a bag of vegetables. Several people say they will be glad to work for the food. I tell them to tell that to the food bank and farmers' market. I watch the people leave and say a prayer for them. Jorge takes Rain and the wheelbarrows back, with Kazan at their heels and Luis and I walk back to the house. He understands my mood after seeing those poor people and takes it upon himself to distract my thoughts. I laugh all the way to the house, listening to his sarcastic jokes. After we part, I think about Gabriela, a lovely girl, hair streaked in blond and ginger like her brother, Luis. Some different genes slipped into their makeup, making them seem like they don't belong in their own family.

I must remind Gabriela to wear plenty of sunblock on her exposed skin. We don't want any more cancer at our house.

CHAPTER 20
THE LONG SUMMER

"A biologist has suggested the next century could be the age of loneliness."

– Edward O. Wilson

It's the hottest August, ever in Idaho's history. By the middle of the month it is 118 degrees. Crops in the fields are dying. Cattle and pigs are being slaughtered as fast as possible before they die. Many die before they can be slaughtered, leaving farmers with too many freezers of meat, some sold cheaply so families can survive, while others become destitute.

Another month without rain, and the price of water has gone up to $5.25 a gallon. People look and smell dirty in town and on the streets. We still have water in our cisterns, but we don't use much to stay clean. There are a lot of us, and we drink a lot of water and drip water for the vegetables and fruit. Camellia comes home from work crying most afternoons because she sees children dying of dehydration and starvation. Being unprepared is the worst ignorance going on in Rigby. We want to help, but we are already doing the best we can to help supply the food bank and farmers' markets with our organic produce.

We are aware that any animals or people left in the Southwest are dead or dying. They have already had a seven-year drought, but now the aquifers, lakes, and rivers have all dried up in the 120 degrees, without any rain for eight months. The topsoil is blowing away day after day.

Down near the Gulf of Mexico, conditions are better. They have rain off and on, but it will be a downpour and water runs off the soil in many places, taking the nutrients with the water back to the sea. The ocean is swollen with all the heat and added water, and it keeps flooding the lowlands. People are learning to live their lives on boats and eat what they can catch from the acidic sea. Those who can afford using portable desalinization machines have drinking water for their families and some water to sell.

The Pacific Coast is holding on with occasional rain and desalinization plants, but low-lying areas have been lost to the sea. South of San Diego a large drifting slum the size of a small city has come together, boat tied to boat. This bizarre world is made up of nightclubs and huge rubber containers of marijuana farms strung together on rafts under tents and watered with portable desalination equipment. There are restaurants, bars, massage parlors, and assorted businesses that have managed to survive. The good news for California is that another deeper aquifer was discovered a few years ago, under the mountains.

The Atlantic coastal cities and towns are a foot under water most of the time. The people who can are leaving the cold, damp, foggy shores for Colorado, Nevada, Nebraska and Kentucky, gambling on how they will live. If they get some rain from time to time and learn how to protect themselves from forest fires, they may survive.

Spring and fall are growing shorter by four weeks now. My diary tells the story of days passing and the climate changing for the worse. It is October and feels like August. I have made several trips to Pocatello and Idaho City to check on the Earthships we are building. I have enjoyed watching as the craftsmen and women work, but I see the added difficulties due to the heat. I have just returned from Sun Valley, usually a beautiful cool place in the summer months, but on the day I was there it was over 110 degrees. Still, I contracted my sixth Earthship. The hotter it gets, the greater the demands for Earthships. I am excited because every house is a new design with interesting challenges to overcome due to location and desires of the clients.

When I was in Pocatello, I took some time out to visit the new town of immigrants near Bancroft. They named their new town Rica. It is comprised of five hubs each like a wheel in design, in the center room for a large community center with the homes like the spokes of the wheel and the remainder of homes served as the rim of the wheel design. I was very happy with the results because it was laid out around a community and playground center. They had even added an indoor play and school area. I talked to some of the residents to ask questions. I wanted to know how the citizens thought the complex could be improved. They gave me fresh ideas that could be added, like a craft center for pottery making, gardening and a place for 3D machines. A party room would be great for them. They are all about families, celebrating birthdays and births, and inviting many friends and relatives. I told them I would try to get a few extra buildings set up for them for the community area that was vacant.

I learned that the citizens of Rica were given the jobs of building the interiors of their homes and painting everything. They also did all the landscaping. They now raise their own food by gardening and raising chickens. They barter with one another for survival, and many have jobs in surrounding towns. They also told me that almost everyone in the area had treated them very well. That made me very happy, feeling so much joy in having a part to play in this community. I was eager to tell Dad.

By the middle of October, the fire in the panhandle had finally burned itself out, taking many houses up in smoke with it. People moved and adapted to other places. Some moved into tents, mobile homes, old shipping containers, mines or caves, gathering wood and anything they could burn for winter.

Two of my Earthships are almost complete, and the third in Idaho City is ready for the roof. I just received a signed contract for the fourth to be built in Sun City. I won't get any more orders until next spring because we don't want to build in the winter. But it is time for me to check on the jobs again, so I will leave in the morning. I ordered the driverless car yesterday. Camellia will go with me because she is ready to take her finals in Boise for her veterinary license. Grams plans a special dinner because we will be gone for almost a week. It still hasn't rained and even all the water we have saved is now getting low, so Grams will only give us one plate for everything. She painted our names on our cups so we can use them several times before washing them. And we are back to washing underwear only and wearing clothes until they start to stink before washing. Sheets are left on beds for months.

Mom is very involved in creating plants that can survive in Idaho and help its people survive. She has created a lab in part of the greenhouse hall because the light is best there. In the meantime, Dad is building her a small glassed-in laboratory.

Grams says, "Laurel, are you daydreaming again?"

"Yes, Grams, I'm thinking about the water problems, among other things. But it will rain soon now and everyone will be okay."

"Could you mash the potatoes for us?"

"Yes, with buttermilk or butter?"

"Use some yogurt and salt, dear."

As I whip the potatoes, I think about Sage and feel the heartache, wondering what he is doing. The mushroom gravy is almost ready. In the oven are roasted beets, onions, carrots, and broccoli.

On the counter is a fresh-baked Washington apple pie for dessert. Rain has gone to the underground to bring up some vanilla ice cream. Prairie can't keep his blue eyes off the pie as he plays with Tiger. Dad sits at the table reading his tablet. He looks up at me and says, "I'm wondering if you girls will remember to take your guns on your trip."

"We will not forget our guns after what we have been through," I reply. "I'm never without mine now."

"Good. I hope Camellia is as determined."

"I will remind her, Dad."

After a delicious dinner and dessert, Camellia and I take over cleaning the kitchen. Then after finishing in the kitchen, we go to our room to pack for the trip. Rain comes running into our room, acting excited.

"Guess what?" he says.

"What?" we both yell.

"It is starting to rain."

"Wow, that's great!" I reply.

"Your prayers have finally been answered," Camellia says to Rain, teasing him over his newly acquired taste for all things Mormon.

"How do you know I pray for rain?" he says to her.

"I can hear you. With *your* name, you should be able to conjure up rain."

"Now I know you're just making fun of me, Camellia." She grabs him and hugs him.

"You're so cute I can't help teasing you."

"Laurel, make her stop."

"Stop picking on Rain."

"Can't a girl have any fun?"

"Not at his expense."

"Rain, what is the weather going to be like the next four days?"

He opens the tablet he has in a sling over his shoulder. "The forecast is rain every day and temps of thirty-five to fifty-five degrees."

"Well, I guess we can repack," Camellia says.

"Thank you, Rain, for being our favorite weatherman."

Before I go to bed, I talk to Dad about the vision I had about the blown-up car and the loss of Camellia and about my worries of leaving them. He says, "We will be fine. We are much better off with the extra help we have now. The men and boys are all good shots, and we are always armed. I am more than ready for an attack now. So please enjoy your trip and don't worry about us. But you two be very careful—Camellia will be with you. One of us is always awake, watching the live pictures on the monitors from our drones."

I give him a kiss and remember to ask him to ask for five very large shipping containers for the immigrants in Rica. Then I go to bed.

In the morning, after breakfast, Prairie and Mom are waiting for a goodbye kiss. It's 7 a.m. and we are leaving as most of the family is still sleeping.

CHAPTER 21
TERRORIZED

"The Hadley Center's team discovered that carbon cycle positive feedback loops could tip the planet into a run-away global warming cycle."

– Mark Lynas

Camellia and I are on our way to Boise, Idaho, in a driverless Honda. The weather is overcast and it's sprinkling, and the temperature is sixty-three degrees. She is asking what Sage and I will do after he completes his military assignment. "We will decide when he gets home," I say. "I already told him we won't live together."

"What did he think about that?"

"I don't know, but it didn't seem to bother him. He just said we would figure it out when he is free."

"Does he know you won't leave your home and family?" she asks.

"No, we haven't talked about it. I could never leave my brothers or you. My brothers are too young; they still need me. Mom gets caught up in things the way I do and isn't able to give them enough of herself, and I can help out by making up the difference. I guess I'm too young to leave home. I would miss all of you too much."

"Would he want to live with our family?"

"I doubt it. I wouldn't want to live with his family."

"I imagine I would feel like you do. It is strange, the way we feel when so many girls are eager to leave and set up a life with the men they love."

"Maybe I don't love Sage enough. It may just be infatuation. Time will tell. What about you? Anyone new in your life?"

"I like Jorge and I think he likes me. I find him very attractive."

"Well, he is."

"It's fun just thinking about an affair with him."

"I think it's the uncertain times we are living through that makes our lives different. We don't want to leave our families in times like this."

"Have you spent any time just taking to Jorge?"

"Yes, about his life and dreams."

"Look, Camellia, it's raining much harder. It seems to be getting colder also."

"Let's turn the heat on low," she says, and I adjust the heat.

"Tell me about Jorge's life."

"He was really into playing soccer, his team was one of the best in middle school, like our high school. He was popular with lots of friends, then after he lost his little sister he lost the ability to dream of a future. He still feels the loss and hasn't been able to take anything except his family seriously. He and his family have really been through something terrible—they have lost so much."

"Jorge is smart. Sabato told me he was at the top in his school, so he should do well in America." I said.

"Have you talked to Dara lately?"

"You know, I haven't and I like her. I've just been so busy. Sage mentioned that she didn't quite know what she should focus on as a career."

"Yeah, it was easy for us—we grew up knowing. But for some it's difficult."

Pocatello never seems to change. When we get to the Earthship, the car stops and parks in the driveway. It is still raining. We get out with our umbrellas and I ring the doorbell in the gatehouse. Over the speaker, Valery says, "Come up to the house, Laurel."

Camellia and I walk about two blocks on a paved path. The arched black gate is open, and after we pass through it closes automatically behind us. I open the ornate glass door and step out of the elevator into the glass atrium. Camellia says, "Wow, this is beautiful!" The area is filled with tropical plants, and a few birds fly among the trees. We close our umbrellas and stand them near the door.

I introduce Camellia to Valery, a small, slender woman with short red hair. She invites us into the great room with limestone floors and a fireplace trimmed in clay terracotta. We sit at a glass-top table and drink coffee as Valery tells Camellia about the house and how they love the ambiance—the design and materials. She asks me about our horses because they want to buy some fine animals. Due to our experience, I recommend an underground shelter for horses. She says that they are pleased with everything and will be happy to do some online advertising for me with pictures of the house. I thank her for her help in advertising for me and suggest we do a visual reality walk-through of the house for an online network. We take the tour and visit for an hour before we leave.

We get back in the car, and I program it for Sun Valley. Camellia can't stop talking about the Earthship we just left with its interior gardens, wildlife, pets and indoor swimming pool. We find a charge station to charge the car battery. It will take fifteen minutes, time to freshen up and get some water. It has stopped raining.

The Earthship being built in Sun Valley at 5,000 square feet is the largest house I have ever designed and built. It is ready for the roof, and with the rains coming we need to get it on the house. Camellia and I stop at a nice little restaurant for some lunch. We order fresh organic salads and grilled cheese sandwiches on whole grain bread. We sit in a leather booth and talk about Valery's house.

After a couple of hours, we are in the mountains, headed to Sun Valley. New trees are coming to life. The last fire left everything bare. That was two years ago, and the last time I was up here everything was quite brown, but now the green leaves are coming back. The car parks in front of the gatehouse and we get out to climb twelve steps. At the top of a ridge we can look down into the hole in the ground. The light gray blocks of the unfinished Earthship stand out against the insulation, rock, and soil. But in front of us is the elevator that takes us down to the first floor of the house. A crew is working on the insulation and interior walls. Camellia says, "Wow, this is the first totally underground Earthship I've seen and it's huge."

"Yes," I say. "It's the first one I have designed and it is quite different. The roof, the latest-cutting edge, material is being poured into custom triangular sections made of a new glass material that changes color with the exterior light, and solar cells are incorporated into the material. When it's finished all you will see is the entrance for the elevator, which will contain a large mechanical room and coat closet. There are three glass pyramids of various sizes with gutters to catch water and move it into underground cisterns."

"You mean it will just look like a hill topped with three colored glass pyramids?"

"Yes, it will, Camellia."

I spent some time checking the work and talking to installers and craftsmen. I asked the manager when the roof would be shipped and he said in a couple of days. He had been calling the factory every day to put some heat under them. Everything was looking good. I told him and he gave me a big smile, which made him look like the cartoon character Bob the Builder with his steel hat on.

We leave for Boise. We still have a long drive ahead of us, but we can nap in the car. Camellia is a little nervous about taking her final tests to be a licensed vet. She is studying her books again.

"Hey, sister, you will pass easily. Stop dwelling on it. You are very smart and always pass tests."

"But I have never had to pass one like this, remembering everything about every domestic animal's body."

"Animals' bodies are all about the same inside, so leave it to fate now and be happy with whatever happens. Humans have little if any control over their lives."

"I know you believe that, Laurel, but I'm not sure I do."

"Then you haven't read the most up-to-date books by scientists who study the brain. Most say we are wired at birth and early on, already knowing everything in our script at a deeper level. We are just actors who already know our lines."

"When we get back home you can give me a list of those books."

"Right now, I'm going to take a nap, Camellia.... Jo, nap time. Wake me if I'm needed."

"Will do."

We lie back in our reclining seats. We both fall asleep for a couple of hours, then Jo wakes me as does the car, warning me we need to power up. Jo and the car know where all the stations are located on our trip, and the car stops at the next station. I get out. Camellia is still sleeping. I plug the car in and walk around in the building, which is full of food and beverage machines. I buy a couple bottles of water, swiping my card in a slot in the machine. I go to the bathroom, and before leaving, I buy us a chocolate-covered ice cream cone. I get back in the car and push a button, and we take off. Camellia wakes up and I hand her a bottle of water and the cone.

"Oh thanks, I am feeling a little hungry."

"We will be in Boise very soon now and we can have a good dinner after I check on the last house."

The owners are home at the Boise house, and Beverly and Joe Wilson, in their fifties, invite us in. They invite us to take the tour. The house is at ground level with soil and plants covering three sides, making it look like it is tucked in a hill. The inside of the house is like ours, only larger with two more bedrooms. They also have soil floors in the main rooms and love their choice. They moved in a month ago, when it was very hot and really enjoyed the coolness of the house. We have a pleasant visit and they are happy with the house. So am I. They wish Camellia good luck on her finals before we drive off.

"I am really proud of you, big sister," she says. "It seems everyone is happy with your versions of Earthships."

"Thank you. I just hope the houses keep the families safe."

The sun is setting when we reach our hotel in the city. We carry in our bags and have them taken to our room, then leave for a great restaurant a couple of blocks away.

The Blue Falls is popular so we might have to wait for a table. We walk in and give a name to the head waiter. He says ten minutes. There are two android guards with clubs. We take seats at the bar and order flavored tea.

After sitting at the bar for almost ten minutes, the waiter says, "Two men at the table across from the aisle would like to buy you a drink."

"No thanks," I say. Camellia shakes her head. "We don't drink alcohol," she says. I look over at the guys and write a big "thanks but no thanks" on a napkin and ask the waiter to deliver my note. That doesn't stop these guys. The tall, dark, well-groomed leader comes up behind me and says, "I didn't think offering you a drink would be taken as an insult, miss."

"I'm not treating the offer as an insult, sir."

"Can I buy you a soft drink then?"

"No, we were just waiting for a table and it looks like our waiter has one for us." The waiter is motioning to us. "Thank you, sir, but we are going to go eat."

Camellia stands up and we walk toward the crowded dining room, and the man follows us. After we sit the man asks if he and his friend can join us. Camellia uses her charm when she speaks. "Could we take a raincheck? We have traveled far and I have an awful headache. I hate to turn you down—you're so handsome—but I need to get to my room and sleep as soon as possible."

I add, "It's been a long day for us and we just want to eat and sleep, so please excuse us, sir."

"My name is Paul. Maybe another time, okay?"

"Thank you, Paul," I say as he turns and leaves. He scares me, and I tell Camellia I don't think we have seen the last of these guys.

Another waiter comes to our table with the menus. I find a pen and paper tablet in my bag and write a note to the head waiter. Then I look at the menu. When the waiter returns, I ask him to send my note over the head waiter. We give him our orders and he leaves. After a few moments, the head waiter stops by. I tell him I am worried about the two men at the bar, one of whom has approached us and is quite insistent that we spend time with him. I give the waiter my note to keep in case we continue to have trouble with them.

"Don't talk to them or treat them any differently," I say. "I don't want to further upset them. Just keep an eye on them when they leave.

The head waiter says, "I will let the guards know. They will keep an eye on them, miss."

"Thank you, sir."

He leaves, and our waiter brings the food: fresh salads, pasta with greens, cheese, mushrooms, and artichoke hearts.

We both like the meal, and as we eat, we get into a conversation about Mom's health and our futures at the ranch. Later, we pay our bill and head for the room. Paul and the second man are not at the bar. I pass the head waiter and ask about the men. "They left the building about fifteen minutes ago," he says.

On the third floor in our hotel room, Camellia and I are in bed and my gun is under my pillow. The door is locked and a chair is slid under the door handle. I keep the light in the bathroom on and the door partly shut. I lie there for several hours listening before falling asleep.

Camellia has to be at the College of Veterinary Medicine at nine o'clock, so our alarm goes off at seven and we quickly shower, dress, and leave the hotel. I ask Camellia to stand back as I unlock the car door and look under the car for anything that shouldn't be there. I lift the hood and do the same. After I check out the car, we both get in and I say my passcode and we back up. I look at the ground where the car was parked all night and something about it doesn't look right.

"Camellia, get out!" I shout.

I get out and look at the ground. It is wet, as if the car was slowly leaking all night. We return to the hotel and sit in the lobby while I order another car, claiming trouble with the car I had. In ten minutes, we have another car and are on our way.

I drop Camellia off at the college after we pull into a drive-thru and get a couple smoothies and coffee for breakfast. Camellia hasn't said much because she knows I can only focus on one thing at a time and can tell I didn't trust the two men from last night. I follow Camellia into her room for the test and watch her sit down at a table. I look around the room. Everything seems normal so I leave to do some shopping. I am back at the college in a couple of hours. I park in the parking garage and take the elevator to the fifth floor. Peeking in the room where I left Camellia, I find her with her head down and hands typing. I sit waiting, and at twelve she sees me and we meet in the lobby.

As we walk toward the elevator, I put my arm around her and say, "Well, how did it go?"

"I think I passed," she says. "I remembered more than I thought I would."

I push the down button. "Of course, you passed the test, little sister." We both laugh.

"Do you think those men are gone?" she asks.

"I don't know, but we should still be cautious. They could have followed us. Before we leave I need to check out the car again."

"What could they do to the car?"

"Things that could leave us stranded, tell them where we live, or kill us."

"Kill us? Why would they want to do that?"

"If they know who we are, or our father who is helping bring immigrants into the state. If they are against immigrants, they may want to hurt Dad by hurting us."

After checking the car out the best I can, we drive off and head home. We stop for lunch before we leave Boise, and again notice armed androids at the restaurant. At Mountain Home, we decide to go back the same way, but our route is very remote for many miles in places along the way. We pass through the Fort Hall Indian Reservation and the Saw tooth Forest.

After riding for a couple hours, I try to call Sage, but without luck. After another couple of hours, Jo says, "I have Sage on voice."

"Thank you, Jo…. Hello! Can you hear me, Sage?... No, it's not the best connection. Okay, try calling me back……….That's a little better. How is it for you…. Camellia and I are returning home from Boise, where she took her finals to get her license…. Yes, she will soon be the best vet around."

Sage wants to say hi. I pass her the tablet, "Give me a few years to be the best, Sage," she says. "Someday I want my own business, after I've worked for someone else long enough to gain some knowledge on how to run a business…. We are all looking forward to your return, Sage…. Thank you."

I take my tablet. "What have you been up to?… Oh no, that's terrible news, Sage…. Just a minute…. Camellia, the embassy in Libya was attacked yesterday…. Who attacked you?… Algerian terrorists? Why?... How are you? I'm so glad you didn't get hurt, honey. What's going to happen?… Sorry, I forget it's all classified.… We are all fine.… Mom seems okay…. Yes, Rain is better. How is your family?… Yes, that is a worry…. Love you too…. Bye, Sage."

"What is he worried about?" Camellia asks.

"Jack doesn't sound like he's feeling well when Sage talks to him."

"I wonder why. You think it's because he had to retire?"

"Retirement can have a devastating effect on some people."

We see the Twin Falls sign, and as we pass it I look in the rear-view mirror and see a black Toyota with tinted windows and make a mental note to keep checking it out. Camellia says she is going to take a nap and lowers the back of her seat. I want to stay awake for a while. I don't want to stop to find out if we are being followed until I am in a place with plenty of people. Fifty miles passes and I find a small store and station with people, so I stop with the black Toyota still in my mirror. Camellia wakes up and wants to get out and walk. I lock the car with my thumb print. I keep an eye on our car and the occupants of the Toyota while Camellia goes to the ladies' room.

Armed android guards are everywhere there is food and people. Food has become very expensive and worth stealing and reselling. When Camellia comes back, I ask her to watch while I go to the ladies' room. Turning the corner, I see Paul from the hotel and turn and walk toward the women's restroom. When I come out I go to the soft drink section and pick up some bottled water. I pay the robot for the water and look for Camellia. I look inside the store. I ask the guards if they saw her leave. They didn't. I think I must be going crazy.

I run outside and the black Toyota is gone. I run back in the store and ask the androids for help. They search the place. She is not inside. They call the police and alert them to block the highway going toward Idaho Falls and Boise looking for a black Toyota. The kidnapped girl has an implant, and I have Jo give them Camellia's number and passcode. Then I get in the rented car to follow the Toyota and take off.

An explosion is all I remember, and everything went black and I was gone.

CHAPTER 22
RECOVERY

"Two additional degrees would be a disaster."

–James Hansen

My mouth feels so dry as I wake at dawn. I reach for a large, clear pitcher of water. I have to turn on my side to reach the water. My side hurts, and when I grab the water I spill it in my bed. Surprised by the weight, I try again. I try to sit up to drink but it's so hard and I think I've become so weak, as I put the straw in my mouth and drink. The water both hurts and refreshes my mouth and throat.

Hurting all over, I wake again, in a white room where everything is blurry. It feels like I have been hit by a truck, but I can't remember an accident. Why am I here? Where is here? Everything is—the light turns into shapes when I come to again…people are looking down at me. Who are they? I find my voice but something's in my throat. I try, "W..he rrr…mm…I?"

A tall, thin shape comes toward me.... "Laurel, can you hear me?"

"Who...who... rr...oo...?"

"I'm Doctor Tanner. You were in an accident. Your car blew up. Your car doors were unlocked and the explosion threw you out of the car."

I point to the tube in my throat over and over and try to get them to take it out so I can talk, then I pass out.

A soft light is coming through the bottom of the window blinds, and I can see that I am in a hospital bed. I'm in a hospital! I throw back the covers to see what's wrong with me. My legs and hips are in lightweight casts. I can't move my legs. Oh no! An eruption is starting in my chest. I can feel the scream that wants to come that turns into uncontrolled sobbing. When I'm spent, I lie back and try to remember what happened, then I recall the vision I had months ago. This must be it...my last memory...my last memory...driving... Camellia.... Where is Camellia? I search my bed, finding the call button for the nurse. I have to find out about Camellia. A nurse enters the room in pants and shirt, the shirt filled with cartoon characters.

"Laurel...you hungry?" she asks.

"How long have I been here? Where is my sister? What happened?"

"There was an accident. You have been in this hospital 8 days. Your leg, hips, and some ribs were broken, and one piece of rib punctured your lung and a shard of glass punctured your throat. Your sister Camellia is fine now and has been visiting you every day. Your surgeon, Doctor Carter, is in Boise but is still active in your case. Your family also wants to speak with him. They had you moved from Boise to Rigby General five days ago, we will set up an appointment with him on Face-on. You need to ask him these questions about what has happened to you." She hands me a list of questions.

"Breakfast now?" she asks. At first I can't think. I have so many more questions.

"What would you like for breakfast?" She hands me a menu but I don't need to look at it. "Coffee with cream and sugar. Whole wheat toast and jelly and scrambled eggs, please. Where is my tablet?"

"I hear it didn't survive the crash. But your sister left you a backup." The nurse opens a drawer in the nightstand and pulls out a new tablet and hands it to me. I'm so glad I have a backup for Jo at home.

I text Camellia, asking her to come see me and tell me what happened. I text dad and tell him I am going to live, come see me. Then I text Sage and leave him a message.

Sorry, I've been unconscious for about ten days, but the nurse tells me I will be okay. I don't know if I will dance again. I guess a car blew up with me inside and the explosion blew me out of the car. I have to work with this new tablet until I can get my backup of Jo downloaded. I hope you haven't given up on me and started dating someone else. I still love you.

My breakfast arrives and I am so famished I eat like a truck driver. Then I fall asleep with food in my mouth. Camellia wakes me, telling me to chew and swallow first, then hands me a glass of water with a straw. I followed her instructions, but the cold eggs make me gag.

"Camellia, no small talk!"

"Can't I even ask how you're feeling?"

"You don't want to know! Start at the beginning," I ask.

The story is strange, more like a dream from the past that I vaguely recollect. Now we are at the station and I go to the ladies' room. Camellia walks to the ice cream freezer, bends over, feels a sharp stab in her arm, and looks up at Paul from the black

Toyota. As she becomes paralyzed Paul walks her out of the store, joking about her having too much to drink and I'm sure the dumb Androids just gazed. She is awake in the backseat of the Toyota. The doors are locked and her shoulder bag with the tablet is gone. She can't move and pretends she is knocked out but can feel her gun held in a belt at the curve near her waist on her back.

Her wrists are taped together and she starts moving her fingers undoing the plastic tape binding her wrists behind her back with her long nails as the car moves. She has let herself fall to one side on the seat in case the two men in the front seat look back at her. They are arguing about a roadblock ahead. She uses the noise to remove the sticky tape as they turn around and go down a dirt road. The car bounces around on the bumpy road and Camellia struggles getting her arm to reach back behind her and removes the gun from its holster, pushing it under her side, and waits for the numbness to leave her body as she loosely wraps the tape back around her wrists.

For about fifteen minutes she listens to the jerks in the front seat argue about what to do next. They decide to hide out in a farmhouse, one that looks deserted. The guy named Paul in the passenger seat reaches back and shakes her. She lets out a groan. He says to Frank, "How much of that stuff did you give her? She's still out."

"I don't know," he answers. Then the Paul calls someone on a cell phone.

"Yes, we have her and the other one is dead…. Yeah, we blew her up, but listen, we ran into a roadblock and had to leave the highway. Now we have to kill some time until it blows over…. What are you saying? … What?… I don't believe the media. She couldn't have lived through that explosion. If she is alive, you can get to her in the hospital."

Camellia feels sick when she hears the news that I might be dead or they could kill me. She is terrified but knows she has to act as soon as they get to their destination. When the car slows down and stops at a farmhouse, Frank says, "Stay in the car and watch her while I check out the house." As he leaves the car, the Paul in the passenger seat looks back at her. Satisfied, he turns around. Camellia knows that if she shoots him, Frank would hear the gun go off and come after her knowing she has a gun. Camellia falls forward at the waist, covering up the gun in her hands. She has to be able to surprise both of them and take them out one after the other. She waits, removing the tape again, and it is hard because her hands are stiff and she really has to pee.

When Frank returns after scouting out the house, he spouts, "An old lady lives in it. Her name is on the mailbox and I didn't see anyone else. This will be easy."

He starts the car and pulls up the long gravel driveway as Camellia keeps down. Then abruptly, she raises her partially numb right arm and shoots Frank in the back of the head, then immediately shoots the Paul through the seat in his chest as she watches the windshield spray with flesh and blood.

The car slams into the garage door. Shaking, Camellia reaches over the seat to unlock the doors when the passenger grabs her wrist. She shoots him in the head with the gun she had moved to her left hand and unlocks the doors. Camellia's face, hair, and hands are covered in blood. A lady meets her at the front door, afraid. Watching her through the screen door, Camellia says. "I just shot the men who kidnapped me. Call the police, and please let me use your bathroom."

"You are something else, sis! Wow, I can't see you doing that."

"It seems like a nightmare to me," she says. "I was shaking so bad in that lady Ruth's bathroom I threw up. I threw up again when I saw all the blood and flesh on me in the mirror. I had to ask Ruth for rags just to clean myself."

"Did it take long for the cops to get there?"

"I was so sick and busy getting clean, I only know that the car that smashed into the garage door was still running when they came. The ambulance arrived. After the police questioned me, the men in the ambulance grabbed me before I passed out and it felt so good to lay down. I was trembling and dehydrated, they said. I told them over and over again you must be found. The killers could be after you.... They have two guards outside your door. But Jorge doesn't trust anyone, so he and his brothers are here a lot."

"I wish I could hug you, sis," I say. I cry, thinking about all she has endured.

She moves the chair next to my bed and holds my hand and we just look at each other and I am making eye contact. The nurse comes back to check me and make me drink eight ounces of water. Then the orderly picks up my tray.

"How is everyone at home?" I ask.

"They are fine. They visit, but you haven't been awake. They will soon be here, Laurel."

I nod off again, and when I wake Dad and Mom are sitting near me. Dad holds my hand. As I open my eyes, I look into Dad's eyes, then smile at Mom.

Mom stands up and kisses me on the cheek saying, "Glad you are finally awake." "Good morning, sunshine," Dad says and I somehow find that funny—it seems so out of place. He grabs my hand and lays his head on my pillow near my head and cries, then we both softly cry.

"Eventually you will blame me for all the tragedies our family has had to endure," Dad says, "and I'm sorry for not realizing how much or hard you could all be hurt through my political actions. Eventually I hope you will develop a deep understanding of the difficult events we now face, Laurel, and can find it in your heart to forgive me.

"I will be okay, Dad, and I don't blame you for anything. This was destined. I had a premonition about it happening but didn't understand what I saw. You may never understand my joy at knowing Camellia is not laying in this bed instead of me. I believe I was sent into this play to be a protector of my siblings, all of my family. I could be dead, but am happy that by some trick of fate I'm alive. I am so proud of both you and Mom, for standing up and fighting for your beliefs, your work to inform the community and for being the best parents a child could have."

Rain and Prairie peek into my room and I motion for them to come in. They are so happy to see me and try to hug and kiss me, which is hard.

Dad keeps saying, "Careful, boys." Then I help Prairie up on the bed so he can lay by me.

"Did you see the people, Laurel?" Prairie asks.

"Do you mean the people in the land of music?"

"Yeah, did you?"

"No, I guess you have to be innocent and a very special child to go there."

Then Rain sits near me and asks, "What happened to your legs? Do you know?"

"For all I know, Rain, I might have bionic legs now. I haven't talked to Doctor Carter yet. No one will tell me except him." Rain helps me sit up and I hug him. His expression is so serious and I know how worried he is about me.

Mom gets up to leave so Grams can come in. She says, "They didn't want too many people in the room." Dad stands and I ask if they had contacted Sage. Dad says he has been in constant contact with Sage. "He knows as much as we do. He is so in love with you, Laurel."

The nurse comes in and says, "Doctor Carter will visit you on Face-on at 2:00 p.m. today, so the family might want to stick around." Grams comes in as Mom and Dad leave. Rain moves over for her and sits in a chair. Grams kisses me on the forehead and asks how I am feeling.

"I'm feeling stiff, but okay, Grams."

"Did you eat anything?" she says, as she sits in the second chair.

"Yes, I was so hungry I can't believe how fast I ate. I guess glucose and water aren't very filling."

"Eight days is a long time to diet. You must be as light as a feather." Prairie laughs, still at my side.

"I wanted to lose a little weight, but not this way," I say.

"You weren't even chubby, Laurel. Why did you want to lose weight?" Rain asks.

"Some of my clothes were a little tight." They just laugh at me.

We spend an hour talking about the ranch, the weather and the animals. I tell Rain I am surprised his shadow, Kazan, didn't come with him, and he seriously replies that they don't allow dogs. I tell Grams my mouth is watering for her recipes. She tells me she doesn't think I will be here much longer.

Then nurse Beverly, the name I notice on her label, says, "It's time for Laurel's nap. Her parents and grandmother can come back for the conference call with her doctor." Everyone leaves me alone with my thoughts, and I go to sleep.

It seems I will be doing lots of physical therapy for the next two months at this hospital. During the Face-on conference with Doctor Carter, my surgeon tells me I was lucky that my body instinctively curled up in a ball as it was thrown out of the car by the explosion. I hit the ground on my left side, so my head and internal organs were protected. The damage occurred to my left side. The left femur, or thighbone, was cracked. The tip of the ilium of the pelvis was shattered, and both the tibia, or shinbone, and the fibula, which is the outer bone of the calf bone, were broken. The gluteus muscles that protect the hips and thighs were bruised. A piece of bone had to be surgically removed from the right thigh to repair the crushed ilium. Using the cells from my own bone made from the shattered tip of the ilium, a cement was used to repair everything and the bones will naturally heal.

"I have instructed Doctor Margolin to remove the cast on your right leg and hips so you can go home," Doctor Carter says. "The cast on your left leg will not be removed for another two weeks. You can use crutches to move around for the following month. Make an appointment to have the cast removed on the left leg and start physical therapy. I am in contact with Doctor Margolin. He will give you further instructions."

As the switch is turned off on the screen, my parents and I look at each other and cheer because we were expecting a far worse prognosis. They hug me and let the family waiting in the hall come inside, along with the Vargas family. Dad tells everyone the final conclusion and everyone claps. Everyone in the Vargas family is so happy and loving toward me.

"I just don't know what to do or say except thank you, I love all of you," I say. Camellia kisses me, as do Grams and the boys. Feeling so much love from everyone, all I can do is sob. They know my tears are not those of sorrow but of so much joy.

A few days after the cast on my right leg is removed, I go home in Dad's truck. He is so happy that we had taken our guns with us on our trip. He tells me the FBI is investigating the crime to find out who was behind the abduction and car bomb.

It is so good to finally be in my own home again, walking around, even if the crutches are hurting my arms, especially my underarms. I guess I will get used to the pain. I write in my diary.

> *This is my first day home on November 2. Sage will soon be home again and my mind constantly flies to him and the misery I feel missing him and knowing how much longer I must wait to have a life with him. Wanting him feels like an addicted smoker must feel longing for a cigarette.*

"So, glad both my girls are home," Mom says with hugs. "How was your trip? With so many distractions, we never asked about the best parts."

"It was fine starting out," I say. "We had a good time."

"Was the test hard, Camellia?"

"Yes, but I think I passed, Mom."

"Wonderful, sweetheart."

"Mom, I loved seeing some of the Earthships, and the owners are delighted with them," Camellia says.

"That sounds like such great advertising for you, Laurel."

"How have you been feeling, Mom?" I ask.

"Good, but I still tire easily so I guess I'm still on the mend."

"Talk about tired. I could go for a nap before dinner," I say.

"Go ahead. We can talk later, dear."

"Thanks, Mom." I hop to my room, lay down, and pass out.

When I wake, my bed is covered with cats, a dog and boys. I have the feeling of being missed. Like darts the questions come, along with Kazan's licks. Rain wants to know what the trip to see the Earthships was like. Did we see any animals? How did the Earthships turn out and who bought them? Prairie wants to tell me all that happened while we were gone. I look at my watch; I slept over an hour. I give the boys hugs as I listen and answer questions.

As I leave the bedroom, the parade follows me to the kitchen, where I kiss Grams and hug her. She is making dinner and Mom is helping stir the soup. Camellia is asleep on the sofa in the great room. Dad hugs me before he picks up the plates to set the table. He suggests hand washing before dinner, and the boys run to the bathroom. I wash in the kitchen and pick up the utensils and napkins. Grams turns off the oven and pulls a tray of baked vegetables out and places them in a bowl.

We wake Camellia. The food is on the table and the animals are under the chairs waiting for dropped tidbits.

I ask, "How are the horses?"

Dad says, "In great shape."

"What about the goats, Rain?"

"Jill the Mom goat is pregnant again," Rain says. "She stopped nursing Billy. So, we haven't had milk. When the new baby comes, we will have milk again and we can give Billy to Sabato who can use him as a stud. That way we will still be able to visit Billy."

"What about the hens, Prairie?"

"Lost two," he replies. "I saw the feathers. Something ate them when they were running around." A tear comes to his eye.

Dad says, "It's not your fault. It happens sometimes with chickens. We will get two more."

"Had any break-ins, Dad?"

"No one has been successful yet, but they have tried twice at night."

"Any ideas on who is trying?"

"No clear pictures yet. I'm betting on Revolutionaries for Change members, but it could be hungry people," Dad replies.

"So, what are we doing to catch them?"

"Bright lights to get better pictures, that go on when our drones sense movements in the yard," Rain answers.

"We had a little rain on our trip. Did you get any here, Dad?"

"Yes, we got a couple of inches."

"A person is having a birthday soon," Dad says. "What would she like for her birthday?"

Camellia comes to life. A dimpled smile brings the light to her face, and her dark eyes sparkle as she says, "Oh, I don't know, Daddy. Passing the test to be a vet is my present to myself."

"What's your favorite cake, little sister?" Grams asks.

"Coconut cream banana cake."

"If it's a nice day, we can party outside again," mom says. "If not, we have the great room."

"The eleventh of November is on Wednesday next week, and we need to invite the Vargases. Can I invite Dara and Mike?" Camellia pleads.

"Of course, you can, sweetheart," Mom says.

"When is my birthday, Mom?" Prairie asks.

"It was on August twenty-eighth, honey, remember…after Laurel's birthday."

"Oh, I forgot, Mom."

Rain runs out to feed animals. Camellia and I clean up the kitchen and talk about how long it has been since we have seen a movie. "Moving to Rigby brought us back to the past," I say. "Yes, about fifty years back," she answers. We both laugh, knowing we aren't missing much in the extremely depressing world we left behind.

It is a nice evening, calm and sixty-three degrees. Rain, Camellia and I with Prairie decide to go for a horseback ride. We let Mom and Dad know that we are going to a park north of us.

"Are you sure riding is a good idea, Laurel?" Mom asks.

"The doc said it is okay as long as I have help getting up. Rain and Camellia will help me on the step up."

"Take a drone to scout around you, be careful and get back before dark," Dad says.

The horses have just been fed, so they are in the barn. Camellia sees Jorge and invites him, and he accepts after asking his dad. He jumps up on Cordozar and we all take off. Prairie sits on Cassiopeia in front of me. He is still learning to ride and is getting good. Camellia is on Lyra and Rain chooses Dorado. Later Mom shows up on Skywalker. The horses are feeling very frisky, enjoying the weather and the run through the scrub. I give Prairie the reins and he smiles. We let the horses run for three miles.

We rest at the park while we enjoy the evergreen trees and the beautiful pink sunset. I am reminded of sleeping under the stars as a child when we camped out in the warmth of our sleeping bags, counting the falling stars until we fell asleep. The park is public land and we are stunned when we hear a gunshot near us and see the drone take off to get pictures. We immediately move the horses into the cover of the trees, and Prairie and I lie down as flat as possible on the back of the horse. Jorge comes over and I tell him I don't know if we should wait until dark to try and go back.

CHAPTER 23

SHOTS FIRED

"It could take decades for the ocean to rise several feet and you can't go back."

–James Hansen

"The moon will be half tonight," Jorge says. "That will help us be a target, but also help us see where we are going."

"The shot could also be someone mistaking a rider for a deer," I add.

"Or someone is ready to eat horseflesh," Jorge suggests.

Mom crawls over to us. "Let's hold the reins and crawl out between the trees," she says.

I can't do that, so Jorge places Prairie on his horse with him. He says, "Spread out and be quiet."

As we leave the trees, I lie flat on Cassiopeia and give her the freedom to return home. She seems to understand and moves in closer to the houses and other structures. Camellia moves around and ahead of me, walking with Lyra's reins. Jorge moves ahead and tells everyone, "We are too bunched up. Spread out."

I am shaky and feel weak. Soon we will be without cover. Cassiopeia takes off running. I have to get to Dad. I hear another shot and another rider behind me. My heart is beating like a hammer and I feel like I can't get enough air in my lungs, but I can't stop. Mom has mounted Skywalker and is near me on the run. Rain's horse is running; he and Mom are okay. We cut through someone's property to get to the road in front and near our house.

I lead Cassy to the gatehouse and ring the buzzer. "Dad, it's me. Someone is shooting at us."

"I'm coming," he answers. Camellia, riding with Rain on Dorado, slides down to the ground, crying.

"I had to leave Lyra behind," she says.

Prairie is crying. "Are you hurt?" I ask.

"No, I'm scared." Jorge wraps his arms around her.

"Are you all right, Camellia?" Jorge asks. She shakes her head, meaning no. Dad is suddenly holding Rain. We are waiting for Mom to show up on Skywalker. When she rides in, we ask at once, "Are you okay, Mom?"

"Yes, but Lyra was shot and we didn't dare try to bring her."

Then Camellia says, "I have to go back and see how bad it is."

"I'll go with you," Jorge says.

"Where is she?" Dad asks.

"On the property, we cut through—the house with the old gray barn."

"I'll get supplies and the truck, put these horses in the barn, and lock the door," Dad says. Then he helps get me down from Cassy and gives me my crutches. We enter the garage.

"I'm calling the police," I say. Mom waits with me in the gatehouse where I pull out my tablet and call the police and the vet hospital for an ambulance. In a few minutes, Dad, Jorge and Camellia leave in the truck with medical supplies and sheets from the house. The drone flies into the gatehouse and Rain turns it off. He removes the canister of audio and video snaps.

I can hear the sirens from the police as soon as I end my conversation with the captain—one of many assets of living in a small town. I feel so much better with Dad taking charge. He is always cool under pressure and master of all he surveys. I believe he will know just what's needed to be done for Lyra, and will keep everyone safe.

In the house, everyone gets ready for bed earlier than usual. We are spent. Even Prairie, who has become a night owl with a long-lasting battery, is very tired when I pull down the covers and get him settled for the night.

"Laurel, why do people want to hurt other people?" he asks.

"They think they are separate from others," I say. "They just don't realize that we are all one, connected by the light within us. We all have the same light from the same God, and when we hurt someone we are also hurting ourselves. Do you understand?"

"Yes, because sometimes I feel a part of everything."

"Yes, we are fortunate. Goodnight, sweetheart."

I lie on my bed waiting for everyone to return, and I spend my time sending the story of our evening to Sage. Grams makes us some hot Earl Grey tea with cream and takes it to the breakfast area. There we talk until we hear the elevator stop. A few minutes pass and everyone except Camellia has returned. We all sit at the table drinking warm tea.

Dad says, "When we got to Lyra, a truck was there to pick her up. We ran them off with the bright lights from our flashlights and a few shots over their heads. Jorge memorized their plate numbers for the police. Lyra was shot in the right flank. We called an ambulance to take her to the Vet Clinic, where Camellia is treating her. She will be fine if she doesn't get an infection. Camellia wanted to spend the night with her."

"Will she be all right alone in the building, Forester?" asks Grams.

"Yes, I think so, Rose," Dad says. "It's locked up tight. I don't think much could scare her after all she's been through lately. You can be sure they were after horse meat because they could have shot one of you. The sheriff will catch those guys, don't you worry, but when you put the horses in the corral send some of the drones out to watch the neighbors and keep an eye on the monitors. I will give the police the film and audio from the drone sent out."

Dad leaves early in the morning for a council meeting, but he leaves the truck. Jorge drives Rain and me to the clinic to check on Lyra and Camellia.

We park in front and ring the bell. Sleepy-eyed Camellia comes to the door. She slept on the sofa wrapped in a horse blanket. Rain and Jorge hug her. I bring Lyra an apple. We all love our animals. They are a part of our family, and Camellia especially loves the horses. We follow her to a back door that opens into an operating room. Lyra is standing in a cubical with a large patch of gauze on her hip. I serve her the apple slices. She eagerly chews them up, and we all rub her neck and head.

"Is she ready to go home, Camellia?" Jorge asks.

"I don't know why not. I can treat her at home. Bringing her here was for the operation to remove the bullet, now evidence for the sheriff."

"Do you mind riding her home, Rain?"

"I'll ride her home."

"Good, because you are the lightest person and less likely to hurt her." She locks up the clinic and leads Lyra out the back and around to the front. Jorge bends over and creates a loop with his hands, and Rain steps in and up on Lyra. She doesn't complain. Camellia and I get in the truck with Jorge and drive slowly in front of Rain.

The following day is beautiful for November, cool and sunny. We are all very busy. Mom is moving her stuff into the new glass laboratory Dad built her. There are a lot of plants to move. The horses are in the corral. Rain and Prairie are feeding animals and Camellia and the Vargas children are harvesting food from the greenhouses for the food bank, farmers' market and all of us. I've called a car to take me to the hospital for my first try at physical therapy.

In the afternoon, the sheriff comes by to let us know the boys that shot Lyra have been picked up and are being held in the county jail.

"How old are they?" I ask.

"The Baker brothers? One is nineteen the other seventeen."

"Did they say why?"

"They have a lawyer and aren't talking."

"Have all the deer left for higher altitudes?" I ask Wyatt,

"I can tell you I never see them anymore. Maybe we killed them all or maybe some got away. I hope they did."

"So, I guess next they will try to eat all the horses and mules," I say.

"Yeah, I reckon they'll be next in this new world."

"Can I visit those boys?"

"Yes, you can, Laurel. They will be there for a while."

Later in the day I ask Jorge to drive me to the jailhouse in Dad's truck.

I take a box of produce for the prisoners, I have no idea what they are eating. Jorge and I walk in and give the food to the desk sergeant and say, "Share this with the prisoners, please." We are taken to their cells next to one another. I introduce myself and Jorge to a boy named Will and one named Allen, the youngest.

The boys are tan with sandy hair and brown eyes and are sitting on bunks covered in a wool blanket and pillows in white cases. They won't look at us when I say we are Lyra's owners.

"Why do you boys shoot horses?" I wait…no answer. "Don't you like horses? You are lucky 'cause the horse you shot will live, but you could have killed a person and then you would be in prison for life, and that would be more terrible than you can imagine." I know they feel shame. I would call them the sandy boys because their skin and hair are the color of sand. They are dressed in faded blue jeans and cotton T-shirts. "You might as well talk to me now so you can get out sooner."

We wait, then I say, "I guess you boys never studied American history. If you had you would know how important a horse has always been in America and throughout many countries in the world. You could say horses have been man's greatest treasure. That is why in America we don't eat horses. I think it's important that you understand horses."

We leave after I've left a message for the sheriff to call me. I am forming a plan in my mind that might help everyone. Educate the boys about horses. On the way home Jorge, because of his age, thinks of better ways to reach these boys—more of a hands-on way by taking care of horses. I will ask him to help them. I know few people who can be around horses and not end up loving them.

Camellia's birthday on November eleventh is celebrated on a beautiful day. We cook roasted corn, potatoes, and Alta Vargas brings homemade tamales. Grams makes her favorite dessert and we all enjoy the delicious cake, but this one may be the last cake, unless we can trade for flour. Those invited and the family sit outside in the sunshine with the animals. Camellia bought gifts for the Vargas family and our family: a pair of green-cheeked parrots. They are beautiful and we are delighted to bring the song and color into the house. Camellia says they were trained to drop on white paper so they can fly freely in our house. They come with large metal cages and birdseed.

By the end of November, Lyra is healed and the boys who shot her have spent a month in jail studying the history and life of horses along with their online education. The Sandy boys are no longer entitled to own guns and are sent home after the family is fully investigated. The family is billed for the cost of the damage they caused. Then the boys spend a month taking care of our horses, feeding, watering, brushing them and cleaning the corral. Jorge teaches them how to do everything, including how to handle and ride them. Later the boys' father buys them each a horse to love and care for. They thank Jorge for his help and so does our family.

On November 28, 2034, the United States Congress passes a bill, signed by President Anderson, that will take effect on January 1, 2035, ending all subsidies for meat, fish, dairy products and grains to feed animals.

Tonight, I feel so happy to write this date in my diary because to me it is the most important date since modern humans appeared on planet Earth. I'm trying to remember the most important parts of the following message from our president:

> One of the causes of climate change is our demand for animal protein. Carbon-belching cattle has surpassed the transportation industry as the greatest source of greenhouse gas. Two acres of rainforest are cleared each minute to raise cattle or crops to feed them. Thirty-five thousand miles of America's nearly dried-up rivers are polluted with animal waste. It takes twelve times the water and five times more land to produce animal protein than equal amounts of plant protein.
>
> We, the federal government, have already stopped the import or export of animal protein. We have notified all our trading partners around the world. They need to feed

their own people as we will be feeding ours. We won't be shipping what we grow to other nations. Only countries with people the UN declares to be near starvation will be allowed to receive shipments of grains from America.

Today we add a tax of $5.00 per pound to go into effect on January 1, 2035, on the legal sale of animal protein now in slaughterhouses. Once these animals are gone, commercial slaughterhouses will be closed and illegal to operate. Heavy fines and prison sentences will be the fate of anyone caught illegally handling or selling animal protein. It is against state and federal law for individuals and/or businesses to advertise on the air, Internet, newspaper, mail or magazines the benefits incurred by the use of animal products. The $5.00 tax will be used to feed the poor and educate the public on the reasoning behind converting to plant proteins and the beneficial use of plant proteins in human diets. Humanity, in time, will understand how to make the change while creating a more humane and less polluted world. Family farms may legally use the byproducts of domestic animals for food and with the external fertilization and production of designer eggs in cell biology available and the choice of creating a male or female animal. The slaughter of male animals because they can't produce is not necessary. And family farms may sell unfertilized eggs and dairy products. Family farms may not enter the business of selling animal flesh for food.

Most of the wild animals and fish are either extinct or at the edge of extinction. As of November 28, 2034, the fine for killing a wild animal will be a prison sentence plus $1,000.00 for taking the life of the animal. We must prevent the final extinctions of the few wild animals that have managed to survive.

If the human race is to have a future, it will be one without the dependence on animal protein. People will die, and not from the lack of animal flesh. Everything that a human need for food can be found from fruits and vegetables, dairy products, nuts and seeds. The land and water available must be used to grow plant protein for a hungry nation and world at large. Everyone in Congress knew this bill would create terrible wars among the people and those in the meat-producing industry. Even more people will die from starvation if they cannot be fed. We are looking at the possibility of extinction and are trying to prevent the end of human life on Earth.

FROM THE AUTHOR

Hello dear reader. What did you think about the story of *Earthships* Book 1?

I hope I raised some interesting questions for you to ponder.

If you enjoyed this story, I ask that you please consider leaving a review on Amazon or Goodreads. Other than your purchase (for which I'm very grateful), it is the single best way to ensure that I keep more awesome climate fiction books coming your way.

Contact Information
Website: www.bonniejanehall.com
Email: bonniejanehall@gmail.com
Tumblr: www.coolartistdesigner.tumblr.com

Introducing Earthships Book 2
A Blue Sky: Will Earth's Children Remember?
Look for Earthships Book 2 during the Christmas holidays, 2017

MEET THE AUTHOR

I was born in Rigby, Idaho, the oldest of four children. I spent my spectacular childhood as an artist, storyteller, avid reader and adventurer. I grew up in two small ordinary houses, my grandparent's city farm and my parent's wonderland with orchards, flowers and vegetable gardens.

I married young and moved to Southern California and later to Arizona where I had two children and to Dallas where I had one child. Then I lived in southern Texas teaching migrant children and started my own interior design company. And, finally, I moved to Austin, Texas where I realized my passion for writing both fiction and non-fiction.

Like most people, I have experienced my share of traumas, but the tragic loss of several loved ones kindled a fire inside of me and suddenly words filled my head like sparks and I wanted to write about this unpredictable life. My passion is to write words that make people think deeply about their own lives and the kind of world they want to build.

I have spent twenty years studying climate change and reading books by well- known scientists and watching documentaries. I am stunned that with the most important subject of possible mass extinction of life on earth facing us, there have been so many silent voices during the past fifty years.

Bonnie Jane Hall

BIBLIOGRAPHY

1- *Lynas, Mark. Six Degrees,* National Geographic, 2008.
2- *McKibben, Bill. Eaarth,* Times Books, *2010.*
3- *Hansen, James. Storms of My Grandchildren,* Bloomsbury, *2009.*
4- *Scranton, Roy. Learning To Die in the Anthropocean,* City Light Books, *2015.*
5- *Hamilton, Clive. Earthmasters,* Yale University Press,*2013.*
6- *Wagner, Gernot and Weitzman, Martin L, Climate Shock.* Princeton University Press. *2015.*
7- *Martin, James. The Meaning of the 21st Century,* Riverhead Books, *2007.*
8- *Reynolds, Michael. Earth Ship,* Solar Survival Press,*1993.*

www.ingramcontent.com/pod-product-compliance
Lightning Source LLC
Chambersburg PA
CBHW070908180626
46817CB00003B/963

* 9 7 8 0 6 9 2 8 5 9 9 6 4 *